The Emperor's Body

ALSO BY PETER BROOKS

FICTION

World Elsewhere

NONFICTION

Henry James Goes to Paris

Troubling Confessions

Psychoanalysis and Storytelling

Body Work

Reading for the Plot

The Melodramatic Imagination

The Novel of Worldliness

The Emperor's Body

A NOVEL

PETER BROOKS

W. W. NORTON & COMPANY

New York   London

For information about permission to reproduce
selections from this book, write to Permissions,
W. W. Norton & Company, Inc.,
500 Fifth Avenue, New York, NY 10110

For information about special discounts for bulk
purchases, please contact W. W. Norton Special Sales at
specialsales@wwnorton.com or 800-233-4830

Manufacturing by RR Donnelley, Harrisonburg
Book design by Brooke Koven
Production manager: Julia Druskin

Library of Congress Cataloging-in-Publication Data

Brooks, Peter, 1938–
The emperor's body : a novel / by Peter Brooks. — 1st ed.
        p. cm.
ISBN 978-0-393-07958-6 (hardcover)
1. Napoleon I, Emperor of the French, 1769–1821—Death and
burial—Fiction. 2. Jarnac, Philippe-Ferdinand-Auguste de
Rohan-Chabot, comte de, 1815–1875—Fiction. 3. Stendhal,
1783–1842—Fiction. 4. Diplomats—France—Fiction.
5. Triangles (Interpersonal relations)—Fiction. 6. France—
Politics and government—19th century—Fiction. I. Title.
        PS3552.R659484E67 2011
        813'.54—dc22

                                        2010037727

W. W. Norton & Company, Inc.
500 Fifth Avenue, New York, N.Y. 10110
www.wwnorton.com

W. W. Norton & Company Ltd.
Castle House, 75/76 Wells Street, London W1T 3QT

1 2 3 4 5 6 7 8 9 0

In memory of Polly and Ernest Brooks
When to the sessions of sweet silent thought . . .

The Emperor's Body

Dawn had broken, a pale, cold, comfortless dawn. The lanterns burned still, with a fitful, sputtering light. The wind swept in rattling gusts from the south. The rain began again, glacial, penetrating. The workers were now two meters below ground level; they swung the pickaxes slower now, thudding them down into the walls of solid masonry. No one spoke, just from time to time a muttered curse in English as a pickax glanced sideways from its target, a brief exchange in French between Philippe and Las Cases. Then a pickax went through; a crack appeared in the masonry. By nine o'clock, two more, and the lantern held close gave a sideways glimpse of wood in the hollow beneath. The coffin itself? The redcoats of the 91st came to attention. Abbé Coquereau, who had gone to the tent to don his surplice, approached with the holy water.

The rain now redoubled in violence. The masonry soon was split and fragmented down the sides, revealing the large flat stone that sealed its center. Block and tackle were lowered, ropes made fast to the stone. Slowly it rose, tilting, at a dangerous angle, as if it might crash back on the workers below. A dozen pairs of hands reached to secure it, and topple it onto the wet dirt. The watchers pressed forward. Then, as if spontaneously, all hats—shakos, bicornes, kepis— were off; the knot of Frenchmen and the English soldiers alike stood bareheaded in the pounding rain.

There beneath them was the mahogany coffin. The wood was wet, and covered with a light mold here and there, but it appeared entirely intact. In the gleam of the lanterns you could see glints of silver, the heads of the screws holding down the lid. Coquereau moved to the head of the coffin, and began his prayers. Dr. Guillard appeared with a bucket of chloride, to disinfect the crypt. Philippe and Captain Alexander stepped forward, ready to descend into the excavation and fix the ropes to lift the coffin out.

The rain and wind covered the sound of the Abbé's prayers. Philippe turned back from the graveside and strode to the nearest tent, beckoning one of the deckhands to follow. He stood at one of the trestles set up to hold the coffin when it came out of the ground, and scribbled a note to be taken in all haste to his commander, Joinville, back on the frigate:

Tomb, 10 o'clock

My Lord,

I hasten to relate to you that after continuous labor, without interruption and with the greatest success since midnight, we have succeeded in lifting off the stone covering the crypt and that the coffin is in a state of perfect conservation.

I shall now proceed, in accordance with the orders of His Majesty's government, to the opening of the coffin and then its final sealing. I believe that by 2 o'clock at the latest we will be under way for Jamestown. Everything up till now has gone perfectly.

Chabot

Designs

SOMEWHERE DOWNSTAIRS a door keeps banging in the wind. It makes it hard to concentrate. But the wind is good. I've been watching for the signs of spring for weeks, hanging out of my third-storey window, summoning it from this long winter. The wind through the open window brings a smell of warming earth. Maybe if I left my desk now I would see buds on the apple trees.

But I have to stick to it. There are so many strands to pick up, to weave together, at the same time to keep separate. I suppose that's the way people are in the time allotted to them—strands that get in one another's way, each one trying to weave its own pattern, becoming twisted, fraying at the ends, snapping even. With no guarantee the picture ever will get woven into the fabric, that anyone will see the sense of it.

I don't know why I use this image in any case—I've never woven anything, I can't even abide needlepoint, I never could sit still and occupy my hands with any sort of knitting or crocheting. I am like my mother in that respect, if in no other. I suppose she would have lived a less anguished life if she could have found pleasure in woman's work. And I might have behaved more in keeping with everyone's expectations of me. Though that would have bored me to tears. I *was* bored, through and through, which has something to do with what happened, but not everything. In any event, I willed it to happen, at least the part that was at all within my control. But here's the difficult question: Could I have willed it to happen in any other way? I mean, what was it that determined my will, its direction so to speak, its aim? That's less clear. And it would be good to try to gain some greater clarity— just as it would be well to see how these strands should interweave, how persons and events that may appear wholly separate in fact have everything to do with one another.

It's at least clear that I am the only one who can at this point sort it all out, give it shape. In particular, show that what looks like separate stories really are one. No, they aren't one, not to the casual observer, and not in the history books. This is all true history, but only some of it makes its way into official history. The rest makes no difference, really, except to me.

These walls, the window held open with its long forged iron hook, the plain but graceful marble chimneypiece, the faded red Turkey carpet that lies between the divan and the ornate mahogany desk where I sit, in an old Louis XVI bergère I have made comfortable with three cushions (all this furniture inherited from Father), the corner library where the books are ranged two deep and sometimes a double row high on the shelf, the side table piled high with books and papers—everything I see in fact somehow is here in this space, in its relation to me, because of what happened. I live in a style you might call bourgeois bohemian, comfortable enough, I should think, for any creature seeking shelter, warmth, and calm, yet clearly not of a pomp and elegance acceptable to Louise, or even less grand acquaintances. More to the point, not quite the kind of place or life expected of me.

It is getting close to noon, and soon I shall have to close up my desk—locking it, as I always do, quite unreasonably since no one would think of touching its contents—and walk to the omnibus that will take me into Paris. Lunch with Louise d'Haussonville, still a friend despite my indiscretions, maybe in fact secretly envious of them. Still calls me *ma petite Amélie*. But before I go down into the streets of Passy, I want to at least get straight on the topic headings I need. The rubrics. Thus:

> *The Consul*
> *The Diplomat*
> *The Body, of course (if there)*
> *The Voyage Out*
> *The Island, and what happened there*
> *The Return—the Champs-Élysées and after*
> *Me in all this*

No wait. There is more, Daponte and all that. The rendezvous of the portrait, etc. It's all complicated. There are different demands depending on whose point of view you're taking. I need to rise to a level of grand, godlike omniscience. But that wouldn't quite do it, since the different perspectives are everything. It's only partly a matter of what happened. That's why I say it doesn't all fit in the history books. It's more how to look at what happened.

We are dealing with different minds, walled off from one another. The question is how to get from one to another, when in reality—in history—they couldn't, though I know that at certain moments, at least, they tried. Beyle wanted to write it all out, make himself the master of all the strands and all the minds, but in the end he couldn't. My own mind sometimes astonishes me by what it appears able to see, or to invent, to work out in any case, so things appear to take on meaning. This may be a delusion, I suppose. History may be that tale told by an idiot, for all its sound and fury ultimately signifying not a thing. And yet, consider that things might have turned out differently, that there is no necessity in what happened. Either you have to say it was sheer chance, or you have to believe that we do weave patterns in that fabric. Or rather: that we try to. The designs we produce are often ludicrously, or tragically, crude and formless versions of what we'd intended. Smudges of design really.

2

The Consul

H E SETTLED himself into the worn leather armchair, reflecting once again that it was the only comfortable piece of furniture in the whole of this bleak consulate, and began his inspection of the mail that had accumulated during his absence. The late afternoon sunlight slanted through the dirty windows onto the two stacks of paper. The one on the right was the official stuff, from the ministry, where he knew there would be renewed demands for an exact count of trading vessels—subdivided into sailing ships and steamships—entering and leaving the port, for statistics on the export of sulfur and pozzolana ash for making cement, and the import of French silk and codfish. Codfish: the irresoluble problem, since if the French cod was clearly of superior quality, the English seemed to deliver theirs fresher. Faster ships. A disgusting taste anyway, codfish, but in this country where fish was required of everyone at least once a week, an item of commerce worth letter upon letter from the ministry. The other pile might hold something more interesting, maybe a bank draft from his publisher. This he very much needed.

Dust danced in the rays of sunlight. He was getting nowhere. His eyes were tired, his back ached from the nine-hour coach ride from Rome. To be sure, if he put in more regular hours at this desk things would not pile up to such an extent. But to be condemned to an uninterrupted string of days in this godforsaken port would bring the black devils into his soul. Rome was all that made it bearable. And now that Countess Cini seemed to show some interest in him. Did she really? What had she meant, two nights ago, when they were leaving the palazzo on the way to the opera (Bellini's *Norma*), and he had kissed her hand and held it a moment, and her eyes had softened and she had said, *Ma, che tenerezza!* Nothing more. The rest of the evening she was gracious, but distant.

He rose from the chair and moved slowly to the window, stretching his back as he went. The tiled roofs of Civitavecchia lay below him, reddish brown, patched. Glimpses from between them into the narrow streets with their windows shuttered against the sunlight. An occasional figure—always in black, always a woman—shuffling in the streets. An air of poverty and affliction hung over it all. A sense of exile and melancholy. As he scanned the city walls, he noticed a straggling funeral procession on its way out to the Camposanto. A priest in his round black hat, a rumpled white bib over his black robe, leading a hearse drawn by an emaciated horse, with four old women in black straggling behind. Ashes to ashes. What a place to end his days.

His eyes moved over rooftops to the quays, the only place where the mournful town seemed to come alive. A steamboat newly arrived, he noticed, its smokestack still throwing up a spume of black vapor. He reached to his left and took the telescope from its stand. He brought it to bear on the stern of the steamboat. Yes, there it was, the tricolor flag of France. One of his ships.

The door behind him swung open with its usual grating sound, and he turned to see Tavernier's unpleasant foxlike face appear in the opening. A rush of annoyance overcame him: How many times had he told his wretched aide to knock before entering? Damnation. With his own absences, his chancellor was becoming more and more insubordinate, assuming the functions of consul himself. He prepared for expostulation, once again.

"Sir . . ." Tavernier began, with an expression of abject flattery in which he detected a trace of mockery.

"What is it? Why do you enter like this?"

"My humble excuses to His Majesty's Consul, but there is an express packet, just arrived by the *vapore* from Marseille. Marked urgent, you see."

Tavernier sidled deferentially into the room. His black suit and white shirt were as always impeccably clean, yet somehow his sallow face with its ratty whiskers and crooked obsequious half-smile made him look like a hired assassin, or a spy. Which he was: constantly reporting on his superior's absences to the ministry. Yet indispensable precisely because of those absences.

Tavernier held out the diplomatic pouch stamped *Roi des Français.* "I thought you should see it at once, sir."

"Yes. Thank you. You can go now."

He sensed that Tavernier had more to say, but he turned his back on him and seated himself at the desk with the pouch. To his satisfaction, he heard the door close.

He opened the pouch, and drew out the packet of papers. The top sheet was a letter from the Secretary of the Ministry of Foreign Affairs, Desages, writing on behalf of Prime Minister Thiers. As he scanned the page, he found himself sitting upright, his fatigue forgotten. In a moment he was on his feet, the Secretary's letter in hand, pacing the room.

Amazing. Desages' letter was dated 12 May 1840—just three days ago—and it announced that the government had obtained permission from Her Britannic Majesty's government to make an expedition to the island of Saint Helena, there to exhume the body of Napoleon and return it to France, so that it might henceforth lie in a suitable tomb in Paris. The return of the Emperor. As a dead body, of course, dead—let's see—nearly twenty years, having expired in a truly godforsaken spot at the end of the world.

Saint Helena. He'd seen the engravings of that island, rising like a rock from the ocean somewhere off the southern tip of Africa, and of Longwood House where the famous prisoner idled away his last years, constantly replaying in his mind the shifting tides of battle on the plain of Waterloo. Seen, too, the renderings of the cemetery with its sole tomb. And they would dig into that tomb. In a momentary hallucination, he saw a coffin uncovered by the gravediggers, then its lid unscrewed and turned back. A fearsome ghoul appeared, the Emperor with eyes glaring from the sockets of a skull from which the flesh hung in flaccid ribbons, under that famous hat cocked jauntily to one side. The ghoul rose from the coffin, brandishing a sword, thrusting aside the shroud. The mouth opened, as if to cry a battle command. But instead it vomited a flux of dark liquid.

He went to the washbasin in the corner and splashed water on his face. Decidedly, his imagination was becoming morbid.

He returned to the pages on his desk. There was a three-page minute of the correspondence between François Guizot, French Ambassador to the Court of Saint James, and Viscount Palmerston, the British Minister of Foreign Affairs—from which it appeared that the British after all these years offered no objection to returning the body of their illustrious captive to the French (after all the indignities they had made him suffer while alive and in captivity—why make trouble over a decomposed body?).

Then a summary of the session in the Assembly, and the motion of Monsieur Rémusat which led to the response by Monsieur Thiers for the government. All carefully staged, of course— Rémusat couldn't have made his motion without knowing Thiers and Guizot had prearranged everything. But his eye was caught by an interesting phrase in Rémusat's speech, where he referred to Napoleon as "the legitimate sovereign of our nation." Curious, that, when you recall that for the regimes that succeeded his, Napoleon was always the "usurper," the man who had grabbed the throne from the legitimate kings.*

Now memory came roiling through his mind. Milan, in the wake of the young Bonaparte's victories. The missions he had led in Germany, as agent in charge of supply for the Grand Army. Moscow in flames. That was, yes that was the farthest he had ever been, not only in distance from Paris, but in the testing of what he could do. That incredible night before the retreat began, when he joined a group of officers in their forage through the dark palaces of Moscow against the lurid backdrop of fire hanging on the horizon, approaching inexorably.

He had twice begun to write a book about Napoleon, his Napoleon, to recount his own experience of that glorious adventure, his own youth and the youth of the world, when anything was possible, when everyone he knew was in uniform and you had to set out for Brunswick or Vienna at a day's notice, when you were a piece of a great irresistible machine that was reorganizing all of Europe—when to will it in the name of Napoleon Bonaparte was to see it happen. But he had started those two unfinished books to judge, too. To pass judgment on the moment when Napoleon betrayed the Revolution, betrayed the principles of '89 and the spirit of the Jacobins. When he had himself made

---

* The reader will find a chronology of the shifting political regimes in the Appendix (see page 265).

Emperor, and created the court of Saint-Cloud, and started naming barons and counts of the Empire, and revived all the fustian and pomp of monarchy. A self-betrayal as well: Caught up in the life of court etiquette and its intrigues, surrounded by stupid toadies and counselors, he lost that incredible power of eagle vision, that capacity for instant decisions that led him triumphant through Marengo and Arcole and the Pyramids and Austerlitz. To the butchery of Eylau. To the madness of the Russian campaign, where an army of 400,000 men vanished in the snow. To Leipzig. To Waterloo.

Where were those manuscripts? He wanted to reread them. Now would be the moment to finish them, to publish his judgment on the Man of Destiny. His journals, too, from his years as commissioner, especially the journal from 1812, the Russian campaign, though he'd lost a volume during the retreat from Moscow. Wasn't the government taking a risk in bringing back this corpse? The Bonapartists were far from inactive. The foreign nephew, Louis-Napoléon, had attempted a putsch at Strasbourg. Did King Louis-Philippe and his ministers think they could rally the Bonapartists by this gesture? Was their grasp on power really strong enough to resist the wave of nostalgia for past glory that this corpse would bring with it? Did they understand the childishness of the French, who had never forgotten this fateful memory? What a folly, this expedition, what a magnificent folly. What would it lead to?

He was back in the chair now. He knew that the packet must also contain instructions on how he was to handle this news in his dealings with the Papal States—there would be tiresome conversations with the Ambassador in Rome, too—but his reverie was too all-consuming to deal with this now. He turned instead to the other stack of letters, the one on the left, turning them over with his fingertips, looking for that letter from Buloz that might contain a bank draft, royalties from his last novel. Not there, apparently. But a small, elegant envelope emerged from pile, one without any markings but his own name and address. He knew the hand, and his heart gave a momentary thump as he recognized it. He smiled at himself. Good, still capable of a thump of the heart at the possibility of an encounter with Giulia.

Giulia's message was discreet—as all her messages had become since her marriage to Martini—but perfectly clear: he was to meet her at the Albergo del Campo in Siena on the 24th, for what looked to be a four-day rendezvous.

Giulia Rinieri, now Martini. What of her? She was the ward of the Tuscan envoy to Paris. Beyle had flirted with her, in a distracted sort of way, for years. He admired her immense dark eyes under their arched brows, and her elegant figure, with its almost unbelievably narrow waist, and the fine feet shod with the finest Florentine slippers. But at age forty-seven—as he was in that miraculous year 1830—he ruled himself out as a lover for this woman in her late twenties, never married, bathed in a kind of aura of virginity. Yet that evening just ten years ago—her own twenty-ninth birthday fête—as he moved down the long corridor from dining room to salon, she had appeared at his shoulder. Her lips were parted, as if on the brink of speech. But she didn't speak. Instead, she threw her arms around his neck, drew him close—she was, he realized on the spot, an inch taller than he—and kissed him hard on the mouth. Astonishing. As he awkwardly, almost reluctantly, returned the kiss, that was all he could think: Astonishing. Then she stood back and said, "Henri, I know you are old and a fright, but I love you." An unforgettable declaration.

He had written to her as soon as he returned to his small apartment in the rue de Richelieu. It was a guarded note. He asked for a two-month delay to think about it. Why such a display of caution and suspicion to this oasis of love offered in the desert of his existence? He was wary. He had suffered, more than he ever wanted to admit, from what had up to then been the love of his life, with Menti—the Countess Clémentine Curial—who after three years of wild passion had left him for a colonel of the Hussars, of all things. Did he really want Giulia? Did he trust her?

But the love notes continued to be exchanged. And it was almost exactly two months to the day, on 22 March, that, wearing a veil and deeply mantled, she came to the rue de Richelieu. Her beauty, her elegant simplicity, swept the difficulties away. As he wrote to himself in his journal the next day, at age forty-seven he became a lion for love.

Giulia wanted to marry, of course. And why should he not? With the new regime that took the place of the fallen Bourbon monarchs in July of that year, after a three-day revolution he had watched unfold from the windows of his apartment, he had been appointed to his consulate—not Trieste, where his credentials were refused by the Austrian government, and not Livorno, as he had hoped, but still a steady position—which allowed him to ask her guardian for her hand. He had refused, in a letter whose surface courtesy covered an insulting insinuation that Monsieur Beyle was merely an unstable and impecunious scribbler whose new position depended on a government of dubious legitimacy whose days in power might be numbered. He had felt the insult, but Giulia had insisted that nothing would change between them. And it hadn't—except that seeing her had become more and more difficult, even with her return to Florence. And then she had accepted the hand of the washed-out Martini, at her guardian's insistence—but made it clear that Henri maintained all his rights.

So Giulia on the 24th. Only a week here in Civitavecchia, then turn things over again to his wretch of a chancellor. Yes, that was dangerous, the man was becoming ever more powerful, entertaining his own relations with the ministry—and with the

Vatican—while keeping an insidious record of Beyle's absences. But for a lion in love, there was no hesitation possible.

Darkness was settling into the office. And there was still the matter of the urgent instructions concerning the news of the Emperor's body. He glanced again at Desages' account. The frigate *La Belle Poule,* escorted by the corvette *La Favorite,* was to sail from Toulon as soon as she could be made ready. She was to be commanded by the Prince de Joinville, third son of King Louis-Philippe, only twenty-two but already lieutenant commander in the French navy. A voyage halfway round the world, to dig up a rotting corpse. But what a corpse!

If he were a novelist of sea adventures, this would make a great subject—he tried for a moment to imagine it. He might finally be able to write something popular, adventure stories sold well, especially seafaring tales. You should try this, he told himself. Find out who else is going on the voyage, find a hero for your novel. Make it true to life, but free yourself to imagine it, too. You're after all a successful novelist, at least to the happy few who appreciate you. Could he pull this off? Up to now, he had only written—of what? Of the inner life, maybe. Of the complexities of the soul. Of love, especially, he thought with a certain bitter-sweet irony, though lord knows you've never quite got that right.

❦ 3 ❧

The Diplomat

I T WAS close to midnight, Saturday, 20 June, when the cab drew up before the portico of Hartford House. Philippe felt a sense of accomplishment and relief as he paid the driver and began to mount the steps of the embassy. Another official reception done, and he had managed five minutes of private conversation with Lord Palmerston himself—though it was only about shooting grouse, His Excellency had recognized him and shown a general benevolence, and even congratulated him on his impeccable English. He could no doubt count on Palmerston's good will, and that would be of prime importance if he decided to pursue this career. And yet, what ennui! He recalled a phrase from Stendhal's novel *The Red and the Black,* that French wit lost three-quarters of its value in England. Solemnity was the tone in Whitehall, and he longed for Paris. Longed, too, for another meeting with Amelia (he liked to anglicize her name, as a private joke between them), whom distance had made only more perfect, the woman he was determined he would marry.

At the top of the stairs, the footman was waiting. But Philippe's customary "Good night, Burton" was answered by the footman's stepping forward.

"Mr. Chabot, a word with you."

"Yes, Burton?"

"His Excellency the Ambassador is awaiting you, sir."

"At this hour?" François Guizot was hardly known as a night owl.

"Yes, sir." He moved closer, and spoke in a stage whisper. "He's received a pouch from Paris just an hour ago. Says he must speak to you without delay."

This was sufficiently mysterious to be interesting. Ambassadorial secretaries have no choice, anyway.

"Thank you, Burton. I go at once."

So he turned into the right-hand staircase, leading to the Ambassador's cabinet. On the second floor, the footman bowed, opened the door, and announced him.

Guizot was behind his massive desk, his severe face knotted in a frown. Without rising, he waved the young man to a seat, and picked up a sheaf of papers.

"Good evening, Chabot. Let me come to the point at once. I have received curious instructions concerning you. The King wishes to send you to Saint Helena as royal commissioner, so that you may write and sign the official affidavit. He requires your immediate answer. Your place in the ministry will be held for you, you'll in fact be entitled to promotion on your return."

"Yes, Excellency." Philippe was having trouble bringing Guizot's words into focus. Had he missed something? "But excuse me, sir. What affidavit are we talking about?"

"That concerning the disinterment of the body of Napoleon,

and its return to French hands." He stared at Philippe over the sheets of paper he held.

"Let me understand. I am to ship out to Saint Helena?"

"Under the command of the Prince de Joinville. You are to leave London at once, travel to Paris where you will stop only long enough to assemble your kit, and then make your way with dispatch to Toulon, where the frigate *La Belle Poule* is readying for departure." Here he paused, and the lines of his austere face relaxed slightly. "I don't think a refusal is in order."

"Of course not. On His Majesty's service." Still, Philippe hesitated a moment. "Excellency, may I inquire, why me?"

This brought something close to a smile to Guizot's lips. "I don't know. Certainly an extraordinary mark of confidence in a man of your age. I suppose because you have established cordial relations with the English, with Lord Aberdeen and Lord Palmerston. And you are a familiar of the Prince de Joinville—the two of you make a kind of children's crusade. Not that I think this crusade is well considered." Here he lowered his voice. "I may tell you in confidence that I don't think much of this move. France without Napoleon, alive or dead, is better off. We have no need of tyrants. We have reached an age of true constitutional monarchy, like our friends the English. I would leave Napoleon's body where it is, seven thousand sea miles away."

"Yes, I understand. This risks stirring up factions. Couldn't it even put King Louis-Philippe's regime in question, Excellency? I mean, there's the Bonaparte nephew waiting in the wings. There are still those remnants of the Grand Army grumbling about their pensions."

Guizot waved his hand wearily, in the gesture of a man who has thought of it all already. "Yes, yes. But still you cannot refuse. If His Majesty has let himself be persuaded by Monsieur Thiers, we can only loyally carry out orders. See that things are done fittingly. And I trust you for that."

Philippe felt a rush of pride. Of course, he had to go. And it wasn't the round of ambassadorial receptions he'd miss. Still, Amelia.

"Very well, Excellency. What are my further orders?"

"You must be in Dover by the end of the day tomorrow. We'll send a message by semaphore telegraph at first light. With any luck, you'll be met at Dover by the French packet boat. Rendezvous at the Ship's Arms in Dover. The man who will meet you will be wearing the badge of the French Mail. He will address you with the words: 'Place Vendôme?' and you will answer: 'Manchester Square.' Go on board immediately, you will set sail at once."

"Very well, Excellency. Permit me, before withdrawing, to express my gratitude for the confidence which you have shown me, Excellency. In my position, it—"

"Enough." Guizot managed a bleak smile beneath his frown. "I understand. But time is precious. Go pack, and be back here at ten in the morning to receive the pouch that I will prepare for Monsieur Thiers. I will profit from your trip to make you the messenger concerning the state of affairs in the Near East."

Ah yes. Philippe would have liked to ask more. Was the Saint Helena expedition devised to distract attention from the gathering storm in the Near East? But he knew he should not insist. He rose, bowed, and moved toward the door.

"Chabot, just one more thing." Philippe, his hand already on the massive doorknob, turned back.

"Yes, Excellency?"

"You may be followed, you know. This expedition is no secret. There may be some of our countrymen whose zeal in a mistaken cause would like to interrupt the voyage."

Philippe nodded. "The Legitimists, I imagine. Those who would like to see the restoration of the Bourbons, who will try to seize on the King's decision to discredit the regime."

"Precisely. And preventing the Royal Commissioner from reaching Paris might be an effective way."

"The packet boat is in sure hands?"

"I vouch for that. But on the high road, you are more exposed. No stopping. Keep your instructions safe. Caution and prudence, above all."

"Yes, Excellency. I understand."

In his small apartment on the top floor of Hartford House, Philippe decided it would not do to wake his valet—even assuming that the phlegmatic Reggie could be waked—and set to his own packing. Much of what he would need was in Paris anyway. But his two official secretarial uniforms would be required, as well as the ordinary supply of linen—what did you take on an ocean voyage anyway? And where was Saint Helena? What latitude, what climate? He was tempted to tiptoe back down to Guizot's office, to consult the Ambassador's magnificent globe. But no, he might still be at his desk.

He sat on the bed, contemplating his botch of a packing job. He was no good at it. Everything was in the trunk that stood at the foot of his bed, but the result was lopsided and messy. Everything would be hopelessly wrinkled. Better to catch some sleep, and call Reggie at dawn. He rose, and went to pull back the curtains from the window. Already a gray light, filtered through the morning fog, suffused the gardens behind Hartford House. Startled, he pulled out his timepiece. Five o'clock already. No time for sleep. Nap for an hour, then call Reggie.

He woke three hours later, when Reggie knocked at the door, then entered, bearing a pitcher of hot water. From then on, it was a rush of movement until he found himself—not until eleven o'clock—settled in the carriage moving at a fast trot out of Manchester Square. There was a suspicious incident during the second relay, when a rear wheel spun off the carriage. But it was quickly repaired, and who was to say it was not a chance happening. He reached Dover at eight in the evening. The man smoking his pipe on a bench before the Ship's Arms was so clearly a French mariner he scarcely had to speak his password. Philippe was on board the steamboat within minutes. The Channel crossing was surprisingly smooth. They slipped into Calais harbor toward midnight. The night was too dark to attempt an approach to the quay, so they anchored and the launch took Philippe in to land. The mail coach was waiting; he was to be the sole passenger, and they were under way at once.

As the coach jolted over the cobblestones of Calais, and then the low shuttered houses became more rare and the road opened before them, straight and monotonous through the pastures, Philippe began again to try to make a mental list of what was to be done, a map of what lay ahead. A visit to his parents in the rue Miromesnil, of course. His father wouldn't like the mission—his whole life was enlisted in hatred of Bonaparte—but he'd bow to the necessity of accepting the King's command, no matter how dimly he viewed the politics of the Emperor's body. What was one to think of those politics, anyway? Clearly it must have been Thiers who convinced the King that such a sensational undertaking would placate the Bonapartists. Their party was growing, alarmingly. Along with the Liberals, they played a dangerous game of undermining the regime. They played on nostalgia for past military glory—which his compatriots always fell for. They forgot the misery, the bleeding of France, the constant new conscriptions of soldiers, the bankruptcy. So the Emperor's body was really a token in a game of national glory, a gesture in which the King would try to make the glorified legend work to his own advantage. A bold stroke, typically Thiers—but fraught with peril.

As for his own mission, to look it square in the face, he was going to travel halfway round the globe to act as official undertaker, this for the unburying of a body. A dubious mission, a doubtful glory. The Channel steamer was the extent of his sea-faring, and nothing in the idea of endless days at sea appealed to him. And nights. Months at sea. Deprivation, ennui. He must pack an entire library.

So, his schedule for the few days before departure for Toulon, where the ship was to be found. See his parents, see Joinville, pay his respects in court. Then he must call on Amelia's parents, in the rue d'Antin, and be sure to do it at a time when Amelia would be there. They could walk in the Tuileries Garden, of course only with Amelia's mother in attendance. Wouldn't this be the moment to make the decisive step? He was certain Amelia wanted it—or almost certain—there was something that indicated a reticence in her, an unspoken reservation, or perhaps more accurately a reserve, something he couldn't get to. Does she love me? He found himself asking the question with some anxiety just a moment after knowing with total security that she did.

Amelia. Her intense young face was framed by dark brown hair, and on first seeing her you could not help but be struck by her rich dark eyebrows—not the eyebrows of your conventional Parisian maiden, but wide smudges above her piercing eyes, which might be brown or might be green, depending on the light. Those eyebrows above those eyes gave something savage to her expression, as if there were something locked inside that clamored to be let out, something that would be very different from the meek sweetness of her lips and her sweet chin and her soft voice. He had met Amelia two years ago, when he was twenty-three, she twenty-two, and at once he had sensed that she was different from all the demoiselles he had been introduced to. She was a bit older, of course, than most of the unmarried women, and he wondered why someone had not claimed her hand before now. But he could not say he had come to know her well—how could he, with never more than five minutes alone with her, snatched during a stroll or a tea party or at one of the routs in the Palace of Neuilly? And then his posting to London.

How did you get to know the woman you thought you wanted to marry? To marry: the idea of leaving to spend the rest of your life in intimacy with a woman you had never truly seen alone. To take her to bed with you. He had a sudden vision of Amelia removing her clothes. An impossible vision. She appeared to him only as fully clothed, though he could imagine her body as enchanting, graceful, supple. His sexual experience so far was limited to actresses from the Opéra, and one witty grisette from the Bal des Artistes a year ago, who as the dawn broke following a night of gently drunken revelry suddenly went slack in his arms, and offered no resistance when he began to kiss her shoulders. They had made love until noon, when they fell asleep entwined. And then he never saw her again.

His plans were becoming a jumble. He should take his tablets from his attaché case and try to write them down. Make a list of things to do. Make a plan for Amelia. What steps should he take? Should he talk to the old General, her father? Would he be in Paris, or off in the camp at Saint-Omer? He was in any event less redoubtable than her mother, the Comtesse Curial, who had a fierce intensity about her, and the reputation of having had adventures. But he had no more than a week in Paris, at the outside. And there would be the tailor, for shipboard clothing, and no doubt an interview with Monsieur Thiers, to receive instructions, and all the visits demanded by protocol. Including Lord Granville, the British Ambassador in Paris, whose good will it would be necessary to obtain if all was to go smoothly in Saint Helena. What, exactly, was he to do there? To watch grave-diggers fetch up Napoleon's coffin from the ground, then see it transported to the ship. What if the coffin were rotted away—it had lain nearly twenty years in the earth, hadn't it—and what would be inside? How long do bodies last in the grave?

A thought found its way through his sleepy brain. There were the rumors that Napoleon's body wasn't really there, in the tomb of Saint Helena—that the evil Sir Hudson Lowe, Napoleon's jailer and persecutor during his final exile, had poisoned his captive and then spirited the body away, burned it or thrown it into the sea, and that the coffin was empty. Or held a substitute body. So would they form a mission to bring back an empty coffin to France? Did this mean . . . ? He shuddered. Did this mean they should open the coffin, to make sure the Emperor's body really was there? Reach into the dark secret of death. It was horrible to think of—horrible if the coffin should be empty, the mere simulacrum of the Emperor's final dwelling, more horrible still if there were a suppurating body there. And if there were, how could anyone tell if it was Napoleon's? Decaying bodies must look pretty much alike.

Here was a question on which he would have to have explicit orders from Monsieur Thiers. How was he to ask it: Do we proceed, Monsieur le Président du Conseil, to the verification of the body within the coffin?

He fell asleep, to dream of a charnel house, bodies lying in open coffins row upon row, their faces swathed in shrouds, with a pestilential smell rising from them. Which was the coffin he wanted? How to tell it from the others? He had run out of time, and he must be somewhere immediately, with the coffin. He had to grab one, now, any one. He reached for the handle visible on the side of the coffin nearest him. It came off in his hand, with a tearing sound from the rotten wood, and the stench became unbearable.

He awoke, his throat tight, his body in a sweat. It was bright morning. The coach was rolling swiftly down the Avenue de Neuilly, into Paris.

❧ 4 ❧

One and Another

DESCRIBE THE port of Toulon, where they will be leaving from. Describe the ship. A frigate—what does that look like? He could do military things, he'd done the Battle of Waterloo, after all, in *The Charterhouse of Parma,* but the navy was something else. Were there any frigates down in the roadstead? Skip that for now. The persons. The Prince de Joinville: he had glimpsed him in a reception at the Tuileries two years ago, tall, brown-haired, muttonchop whiskers, a good-looking young man—certainly compared to his father, whose face looked like a pear—but he didn't seem to have any striking characteristics. Invent them? He must find an engraving of the Prince somewhere, that should not be hard to do. At least, if he were in Paris it would be simple.

But description in any event didn't amuse him. The objection of his critics, often enough, who claimed there were no pictures of what his characters looked like. But you see, what matters to me is not what they look like but how they affect you. It's like painting—it's how the face in the painting speaks to your soul. It's all in the effect. The reader's soul is the violin, you are simply the bow playing on it.

But still, Beyle told himself, you have to know these people you are going to put onstage. Philippe de Chabot, now, the Royal Commissioner. What is he like? Never met him. But I do know something about his family. His father, the old Vicomte, now. He was an émigré during the Revolution, he became an officer in the English army and fought against Napoleon. After Waterloo, he came back to France, and became a loyal ally of the Orléans family, the younger branch of the royal family that came to power when the last Bourbon king, Louis XVIII, was sent into exile by the Revolution of 1830. Was he with the Marquis de Lafayette and Louis-Philippe that July day in 1830 when they appeared on the balcony of the Hôtel de Ville, Louis-Philippe draped in the tricolor flag and proclaimed King of the French? In any case, from then on he was near the inner circle of power. How old was Philippe then? Fifteen? Good timing for him, so far as his career was concerned. All the doors opened. And François d'Orléans, now the Prince de Joinville, had been his childhood playmate.

So this was interesting. In the great game of national politics, the retrieval of Napoleon's body fell to the scion of a royalist family that detested the usurper, the ogre as they no doubt called him. What a splendidly ironic muddle. It must have been Thiers who convinced the King that such a sensational undertaking would disarm the contentious—and growing—Bonapartist party. They now had something of an alliance of convenience with the Liberals, both set on undermining the regime. Napoleon the tyrant had in their scribblings—and in the popular imagination—become once again Napoleon the heir of the Revolution. France was being swept by a wave of nostalgia, for revolution, military conquest, empire. And Louis-Philippe was such a paltry figure, intent on keeping peace at any price, even when it meant the humiliation of France. The Emperor's body was a token in a game of national glory. A chance for Louis-Philippe to reconcile different factions in the name of the glorious past. To receive some reflected luster from the Man of Destiny. If it worked out that way.

But back to your novel, he admonished himself. The voyage out, the landing at Saint Helena—there's a chance to do something desolate, sinister, the prison created by nature and then made utterly despotic by Sir Hudson Lowe, the jailer who humiliated his illustrious prisoner over so many years. Then digging up the coffin, what might be left of it. Ghoulish, that. A kind of gothic scene, like something from one of those English novels from earlier in the century.

But he wasn't a gothic novelist. This had to depend on the reactions of his characters. Of Chabot in particular. What was he really like? Whom did he love? Tell me about how he goes about the pursuit of happiness in his everyday life, and I will tell you his character. Unmarried, so far as Beyle knew. Did he keep a mistress? Hang around with bit players from the Opéra? He needed someone for this character to love. A dalliance, at least. He needed women—how could you do a novel without women? His novels so far each had two enchanting women. Yet a sea voyage of several months hardly lends itself to much business with women. The stuff of adventure novels for boys. Definitely a problem here.

How does he feel setting out on this mission? Where is the happiness in it? Purely career ambition—after all, a high honor to be given such a mission at such a young age? Yes, but if that was all, he wouldn't be interesting. What's buried in the Emperor's tomb for young Chabot? What's he unburying in his own life? Probably nothing—too young. But perhaps a chance, in this adventure, to test himself, to see if he is more than a young man

born to every privilege? Yes, you could dislike the whole enterprise, find it distasteful, but find in it something that tells you
about yourself, discover some reality hidden beneath the surface
of things. This gravedigger's enterprise would be dark enough,
but it might shed a kind of light.

So: Chabot sets out as a kind of *farfallone amoroso*. He's had his
conquests, but they haven't amounted to much. Maybe, though,
he's just fallen in love—with someone he must leave behind. All
through the voyage he will be asking himself, Does she love me?
Worrying that she may not be there when he comes home. Then
does he himself meet . . . what? A Patagonian? A fair maid of
Cádiz along the way? Some woman smuggled on shipboard in
a man's disguise? Be serious. This is a men-against-the-sea kind
of thing. Where does love come into it? But love was all that
interested Beyle, really. He'd have to invent something, if only in
Philippe's memory, or his anticipation.

The real problem with Chabot is that he's too young. He was
bored with young men. He'd done them already. Julien Sorel—
he was of course exceptional, in his ferocity. Fabrice del Dongo, a
young aristocrat born with a silver spoon in his mouth, someone
who did not have to do anything to have all the favors of the
earth heaped at his feet. Yes, but he felt much closer to old Count
Mosca. That's what's interesting, what someone is like past fifty.
It takes that long to become a character of some depth. It is the
weight of past history that makes someone interesting, the accu-
mulation of past loves.

His own, for instance. Mélanie, Menti, Alberthe, Giulia. And
the unattainable Métilde: Did she love me? Could I have made
her give herself to me? That was still the great regret, which
other successes never quite assuaged. He'd become famous as a
novelist for his analysis of love, its stages, its crystallizations, how
it came to form, how suddenly you would wake up one morning
with your heart beating, asking yourself: Does she love me? But

the analysis of love was a poor substitute after a certain age—what you wanted was to be engulfed by it, have no other choice, give yourself to it utterly. He'd played at Don Juan—never very convincingly, to be sure—but what he'd really wanted to be was something like young Werther, suicide for love. Always playing the wrong part. I suppose that's why you write novels, to give yourself other parts. To distribute yourself in other people, peer out at the world through their eyes, possess their women in your imagination.

The paper before him still was blank. He set down his pen with a sigh. This wasn't working. How could he write such stuff? He began to suspect that someone else would have to write the tale of the Emperor's body. He couldn't see it, couldn't make it come alive before his inner vision, at least not yet. Maybe after the rendezvous in Siena he would be freed to write.

———

PHILIPPE DRESSED carefully before the mirror that stood atop the graceful old Boulle dresser. His room hadn't changed since his last visit—hadn't changed, he realized, since his parents moved into these vast old apartments twenty-five years ago, a couple of years before his birth. The Vicomte was thriving under the King of the French, but that didn't entail any sacrifices to modern taste. The apartment could have been the gathering place of old-regime notables—though never one of those places of free conversation that had done so much to undermine the old order of things. Respect for legitimate authority, order, ponder-ation, a sense of continuity with the past—that's what his parents stood for. If you knew their old château in the Cotentin, it was all displayed before you. That place, recovered in a state of dilapida-tion after the fall of Napoleon, then lovingly restored to its old condition—with scarcely a modern convenience added—spoke to the Vicomte's sense of eternal France.

He'd frowned, of course, when Philippe began his account of the mission to Saint Helena. He could hardly want his son involved in the resurrection of the ogre, even the ogre thoroughly dead. But he was fully sensible of the high honor done him. And the presence of Joinville on the mission made it all right—to be adjutant to the King's own son legitimated everything, however misguided he continued to think the mission itself. If the King had allowed himself to be persuaded by Monsieur Thiers, so be it. It might be folly, but it must be honorably executed.

So that was that. His father was squared, his mother had turned to ordering up tea and bonbons and other necessities to be packed in tin boxes for his voyage. Now the more difficult task lay ahead: Amelia. Did he want to try for an interview at her parents' place? Asking for a private meeting would be interpreted as meaning only one thing. The consequences unfurled in his mind. Wedding at Saint-Philippe-du-Roule. A reception hosted by the General and Clémentine Curial. Then a wedding voyage. He knew Amelia loved Italy, had friends in Rome, he believed. So should it be Lake Como? Sorrento? Long journeys.

What was that like, traveling with a woman, your wife? Again he tried to imagine Amelia in his arms, naked. This brought a rush of blood to his face as he gazed in the mirror. His heart was beating fast. But he couldn't picture it, couldn't see Amelia without her clothing. Couldn't quite see himself making love to her. What was wrong here—why couldn't there be some easier way to make her his own. What was marriage anyway?

In any case, he hoped for a chance encounter first, something less than a formal visit. With luck, she would be at the reception at the Tuileries, along with her father. She often took her mother's place in these official evenings, which her mother claimed to loathe—and at which she didn't quite behave properly. A woman who really was at home in a different era, in the freer manners of the imperial court. Philippe generally avoided thinking too much about Madame Curial's past. Rumor suggested that it was far from exemplary. Lovers, and not always from the best milieux. Military officers, adventurers, bohemians. Not quite the mother-in-law his parents wished for him. He knew that there would be some resistance from the Vicomte if he decided to marry Amelia. She was so charming she could overcome the resistance. If that was what he wanted. Do you, he asked himself again, do you?

He redid his cravat for the fifth time, and stood to study the effect. He looked all right. The black coat and white waistcoat, frilly shirtfront and white cravat, tied with just a shade of non-chalance—it was all correctly done. His face was still too red—diplomats should learn not to blush so easily—but his fair hair was set off well by the formal attire. The rosette of the Office of Foreign Affairs on his chest gave him an air of importance. If only he could wear a sword as well. But that was no longer the custom, except for the military. Now for his kid gloves, and he must be off.

Entering the vast reception room at the Tuileries, he paused to scan the gathering. The King and Queen at the far end, by the ornate chimneypiece, a circle loosely formed around them. At the King's left elbow, the Duc d'Orléans, his eldest son. No Joinville—en route to Toulon, to make ready the *Belle Poule*. He would need eventually to make his way to the royal family, to pay his respects. But before that, there was Amelia to be looked for—would she be there? And the important diplomats, especially Lord Granville. Yes, it was vital that he have a word with the British Ambassador, who certainly knew more about the history behind this expedition than most. And who might be more willing to tell some of that story than most.

Philippe moved forward into the crowd, making quick bows to right and left as he came upon remembered faces—couldn't put names to most of them, though. Bows to anyone in a uniform with epaulettes—there were a number of them. He noticed many medals representing service in the Algerian campaign. At least the uniforms relieved the monotony of the men all in black. The women were more interesting—though far outnumbered by the men. Anyone he knew? He recognized the old Duchesse de Parme, immensely fat and beflounced, like a large pouf. Her skirts spread so wide that the circle of men around her had to stand at a distance, leaving her like some grotesque idol in the middle. And the Comtesse de Lamballe. But no sign of the General, or Amelia.

Voices echoed in the vast room, in an unpleasant cacophony. And it was hot, airless. How long was he going to want to submit himself to this? Suddenly he had a vision of slipping out, making his way across the river on foot to the Left Bank, to seek out one of the cabarets where you found artists and students, and grisettes. Find a young woman, take her to one of the *bals publics,* spend the night with her. That's what he needed. There wasn't going to be any amusement of that kind on the endless voyage to Saint Helena. He owed himself a bit of indulgence, and experience. How could he become Amelia's husband without more adventures first? Maybe just spend half an hour here, then slip out. He knew he wasn't good at self-indulgence. He felt the weight of his puritanical childhood—his mother's English ways, his father's rigid sense of duty and virtue. Here he was, a rising young diplomat—charged with a royal mission—dressed in his finest. Why not allow yourself to live a bit?

He found himself already turning back toward the entrance—though no, not yet, he told himself, you must go pay your respects to the King and Queen before you go—when he became aware that he was being looked at. A pair of piercing blue eyes were directed to him. An older man, with white hair and handsome features, and tall—though slightly stooped, his shoulders rose above most of those in the room. He was . . . yes of course, Lord Granville. The man he must see. Who seemed to want to see him.

They exchanged bows, and then Granville took him under the elbow and with extraordinary dexterity moved him through the crowd, saying nothing while nodding curtly right and left, a slight smile playing on his thin lips, his bushy white eyebrows moving up and down in recognition and greeting. He steered Philippe toward the embrasure of one of the long windows looking out over the gardens. In the gathering dusk, Philippe could see across the Place de la Concorde to the Champs-Élysées beribboned with light, up to the vague mass of the Arc de Triomphe at the end.

"I counted on finding you here, Chabot." The Earl spoke impeccable French, though pronounced as if it were a slightly distasteful foreign invention. "May we use English?" he added, his eyebrows rising quizzically. Philippe nodded. "I'd prefer that our conversation not be overheard."

"Of course, Excellency. Be assured that I am aware of the delicacy of the mission entrusted to me. And appreciative of the cooperation of Her Majesty's government in this enterprise."

Granville waved his hand, as if to dismiss such formalities. "Of course, of course. Her Majesty's government in turn applauds your government's choice of emissary on this mission. Your ties to England, your knowledge of our ways, will smooth any problems you may encounter in Saint Helena. And I assure you that Governor Middlemore is the best of fellows who will do everything in his power to make the mission a success. With luck, this should mark a new stage in understanding between our two countries. We need to look to the future, not the past."

"To be sure, Excellency. And it occurs to me that this may be an advantage of my youth. That past means little to me."

"So much the better. There will, you know, be some sore points. Especially since I understand from Monsieur Thiers that you will be accompanied by some living relics of that past—Marshal Bertrand, General Gourgaud, old Marchand, I don't know who else. Men who were with Bonaparte on Saint Helena. Men for whom this may awaken painful memories, and dreams of conquest."

Philippe had not thought of this—in fact he knew nothing yet of his shipmates on the mission. His interview tomorrow with Thiers would make that all clear. He nodded, then, hesitating, asked: "What precisely do you fear, Excellency?"

"That's just it. There is nothing precise that I fear. It's impossible to predict what may occur. But it will be up to you—and to the Prince—to keep the possible resentments under control, to avoid embarrassing incidents, a possible flare-up of old emotions."

Philippe nodded again, but he felt more and more at sea. He realized he knew very little about all this other than the usual rumors—about Napoleon's years on Saint Helena, about the British as his jailers.

Granville went on. "You will recall, perhaps, that the governor of the island during the time of the captivity was the object of some . . . fairly venomous allegations on the part of the Bonapartists. I refer to Sir Hudson Lowe, of course."

Yes, Philippe did know that much, of course—that in French opinion, at least, Lowe was a cruel and vexatious jailer, reputed by some even to have brought Napoleon an unnatural death, by arsenic.

"Lowe was a hard man, no doubt about it, but utterly just and above suspicion," Granville continued. "He did his duty punctiliously. He has been much maligned. You must see to it that unfair allegations about the past are kept in their place."

Philippe nodded once more, trying to find the appropriate reply. What was his duty here? Did Lowe's actions matter, now, in the present, or not? But at this point, Granville reached inside his evening coat and pulled forth a sealed envelope. It was marked with the British arms, and addressed simply to Monsieur le Comte Philippe de Rohan-Chabot.

"Slip this into your breast pocket. And might I suggest you not break the seal until your voyage is under way?"

Philippe bowed, held out his hand. Granville, however, took him by the shoulder with his left hand, and managed at the same time with his right hand to slip the letter under Philippe's coat. Philippe reached to make sure it was well into the pocket. Safe? Yes, it was a thin letter, of small format. It didn't protrude.

"Now I think we've had enough of a tête-à-tête. I'll forgo the pleasure of talking further with you, in the interests of discretion."

Granville bowed to Philippe. Then he was gone, melted back into the crowd.

Now Philippe could feel nothing but the letter inside his coat. How to go off to cabarets, to dancing, to bed with that grisette— if she existed—carrying this document, whatever it was? He'd have to go home first, to put it in safe keeping. Damn. Why couldn't Granville have summoned him to the British embassy to give him secret letters?

He glanced once more out the window. The summer night was coming on. Lights everywhere, the pleasures of a Parisian evening inviting him. He turned back to the room, uncertain about his next step. More people had come in, the press was becoming intense, and hotter. Time to go to the King, then home. Then out again?

As he began to make his way through the crowd, he became aware of a tall figure in uniform with a young woman on his arm. Yes, it was. The General and Amelia. There she was. As he watched, he saw her intense eyes beneath their dark eyebrows search the crowd. Looking for him? Well, he was not going to avoid her. He would go to her. He would ask to see her at her parents' apartment. What came next he couldn't yet make out.

✤ 5 ✤

The Spy

T HE CAMPO of Siena spread its elegant fan shape
before him. Truly the most pleasing outdoor space
imaginable. A place where one should gather
all one's friends at nightfall, for a party with music—with
Mozart—and footmen carrying trays of sorbet through the
gathered guests. But now it was hot, too hot, even under
the café awning, and even the pigeons looked listless. And
besides, he knew that the man with the pomaded hair and
the dirty fingernails two tables from him was a police spy.
He was free to move in Tuscany and the Papal States, where
he was diplomatically accredited, though still prohibited from
entering Milanese territory, yet even here in Siena he must
be shadowed. It dated from his early days in Milan, then his
travel books on Italy, and then of course that petty tyrant,
the Prince of Parma, he had invented in *The Charterhouse of
Parma* seemed too closely modeled on the real Grand Duke

of Tuscany. He was permanently a suspect in the country in which he would have liked to think himself a native.

He couldn't imagine what reports the police spy filed with his superiors. He didn't look like a reader of novels, somehow, or even of travel books. He didn't even have a newspaper, but sat over his coffee cup staring blankly at the campo. Beyle had often dreamed of a kind of personal invisibility, in which somehow the power to know and master others would be the correlative of one's own nonappearance. So the idea of someone spying on him, furtively looking into his life, alarmed and disgusted him. Did the man with the dirty fingernails peer through the keyhole when Giulia joined him for the night? A horrible idea. Though it was not clear that his relations with Giulia could in any way compromise him politically, hers with him were another matter, since he was defined as suspect. He should broach this matter with her. Was her guardian so highly placed that he could demand to see the police reports? An appalling idea. After all, it was Berlinghieri, her guardian, who had chosen Martini as Giulia's husband. He might feel compelled to do something about Martini's "dishonor."

This was a delicate question. Giulia made it seem a nonquestion, though. For her, Henri was her original and continuing lover, the man she wanted to marry. Just because she had been forced to marry someone else could not be allowed to infringe his original claim. Martini had a claim too, of course, but it came second. Did Martini himself understand this? She claimed not, and she always hid scrupulously her rendezvous with Beyle. Yet he wondered if the ease with which she seemed to be able to get away from the villa in Florence for the Sienese visits didn't mark a tacit acceptance on Martini's part.

He signaled the waiter, paid for his coffee, but then continued to sit before the empty table. When the waiter had disappeared back into the cool depths of the café, he rose, and walked slowly, deliberately to the spy's table.

"Good afternoon, Signor Spione." Saying it gave him a rush of energy.

Startled, the man looked up. His puglike face displayed anxiety. Poor fool, have I put him out of employment? Beyle wondered.

"To whom do I have the honor . . . ?" The spy rose to his feet, revealing a messy waistcoat and spotted trousers. The walking stick propped against his chair clattered to the ground. His face was flushed.

"Don't play the fool. You know everything about me. What you don't know is that I know everything about you. If you knew what I knew about you, you'd go hang yourself from the lamp-post over there."

Now the face was bitter, the little mustache twitched, the eyes became mere slits.

"And just what do you claim to know about me, signor?"

"That you exercise the most vile profession on earth, that you are a kind of worm, that you live in the dirt."

What was he trying to do? You couldn't honorably have a duel with a spy. Though Beyle prided himself on his dexterity with the pistol.

The spy pushed the table forward into Beyle's legs. They glared at each other.

"Watch yourself, Signor Beyle."

Beyle smiled with pleasure. He hadn't been completely sure until this declaration.

"And what are you going to do to me? I carry a consular passport, you know. You'll be in deep trouble if you try to arrest me."

"Just watch yourself. All your comings and goings are known to us. You cannot move without our being there."

Now he stooped, and grasped the walking stick in his fat hand. He pointed its brass knob menacingly across the table.

"Spies are supposed to remain concealed. I'll report to the

Grand Duke that his secret police give themselves away in broad daylight. You'll have to be rehabilitated, two years in the fortress."

The knob advanced, grasped so tight in the fat hand with the dirty fingernails that he could see the knuckles were white.

"Put up your stick. Disappear for a while. I'm sure we'll meet again."

The man hissed. "Beware of nighttime promenades with your signora. Beware of dark streets. You have impugned my honor, Signor Beyle."

"Very well, Signor Spione. We'll meet in a dark street, then, and we'll see about honor."

Beyle turned deliberately, and made himself walk slowly down the slope of the campo. *Finita la commedia*. That was childish, he said to himself. Childish and hardly worth it, since now you'll probably get another spy, maybe more competent. Still, he had to admit to a certain satisfaction at the scene he had created. Life was becoming too short for these ridiculous games. Yet it wasn't the height of maturity to confront harmless spies in public. At age fifty-seven, he should be a bit less adolescent in his behavior.

He didn't tell Giulia of the encounter with the spy. Instead, as they dined in the private back room at the Albergo del Campo and he sought to dissipate the momentary awkwardness that seemed to preside at each of their meetings after long absence, he began the recital of his griefs against Lysimaque Tavernier, his consular chancellor who had so insinuated himself into the position that he now insidiously combined loathesomeness and indispensability. As he talked, though, he realized his annoyance about the spy at the café was contributing to his spite against this other man who so constantly kept tabs on his business.

"You deserve better, dear friend." Giulia's graceful smile had a touch of irony.

"Deserve, indeed. What is it that Hamlet says? If each be treated according to his deserts, who should escape whipping?"

"Ah, but that is a gloomy Englishman speaking."

"No, a melancholy Dane."

"Yes, of course, even worse, I should imagine."

"The English aren't gloomy, really—that's just their weather. It's more that they are unsure what to make of our forms of wit. They look on us with suspicion, as if we were strangely frivolous creatures, not morally up to snuff."

"You have a strange anglophilia. You write for their newspapers, you praise their literature, their actors—you think Shakespeare the greatest event in world literature—you love their constitutional government, yet you loathe their politics, their statesmen. You've never gotten over Wellington, and Waterloo."

He bowed his head, in amused assent. "You are right, of course. But as for Wellington and Waterloo, have you seen the news, about the expedition to Saint Helena?"

She looked completely blank. "Saint Helena? An expedition? A war?"

"No, no. I see you don't read the French newspapers."

"When we see them—when they are not seized by the customs—they are two months old."

"Aha. No, Saint Helena is where Napoleon is buried—where he was the captive of the English, from after Waterloo to his death in 1821. Now the English are going to give his body back to us French. There's to be an expedition, commanded by the King's own son."

"And what are you French going to do with the dead body of Napoleon, for heaven's sake?"

"There's the rub. I understand everyone in Paris has a different scheme. Bury it under the Arc de Triomphe, according to some. Or place it atop the Arc, in the form of an azure globe topped by a golden eagle with outstretched wings. Or else, put it on top of the column in the Place Vendôme—that column's made of cannon from the Grand Army, melted down, you know."

"A body atop a column? How very odd."

"Well, in an urn, you know. But those are the proposals of the veterans, the Bonapartists. The government won't have them."

"Quite right. I still don't see a body on a column, urn or no urn, and as for digging under the Arc de Triomphe, I should imagine it might collapse."

"Perhaps. But that's not the point, you know. This is a political comedy. Where the body goes is a matter of high politics. Give it too much prominence—in one of those monuments to Napoleon's glory—and you whip up the enthusiasm of the Bonapartists too much. Bury it without honor, and you insult them. The government thought of the Pantheon, but that has seen the bodies of too many Jacobins go in, and out. They even thought of the Basilica of Saint-Denis, where the kings of France were buried."

"Why not?"

"But Napoleon is special in the imagination of my compatriots. He demands a place to himself. Anyway, it appears likely it will be in the Invalides, the old soldiers' home."

Giulia made a visible effort to seem interested. "Is that appropriate? A building from the time of Louis XIV?"

"I think not. They need a new building, a monument to Napoleon alone. I've sketched it out in my mind. Something imposing, classical. I would see it as resembling the Castel San'Angelo, in Rome. Round, impregnable, visible from afar. A citadel, dominating the city. So that when you come to a crossing anywhere in Paris, you see it in the distance, a constant reminder."

"A reminder of what? Dear friend, I did not know you were so caught up in past military glory."

It gave him pause. "Am I? Well, I don't know. Nostalgia for my youth, more than anything. For a time when anything seemed possible, when the eagles marched to Milan and Venice and Vienna and Berlin, even Moscow. When I wore a uniform. But you are right, as usual. I have no use for military glory. I detest the slaughterhouse. And Napoleon betrayed us all."

Giulia reached her hand across the table. "I think I like you better in your present incarnation. You may be old and something of a fright, Henri, but I love you."

This was a better kind of talk. He held her slender hand with his rough fingers, and smiled.

At some hour between midnight and dawn, he awoke from a dream. There had been confusion and smoke, shouts, horses in panic, then a strange noise of hissing. What was it? Giulia lay asleep next to him, the ringlets of her hair spread out over the pillow like some fantastic botanical ornamentation. Where had he been in his dream? He fixed his mind on that hissing noise. A soothing noise, not a sinister one, but laden with anxiety. Hold that sound in your head a moment. Then it came to him: the sound of sleigh runners on packed snow. Russia. The retreat from Moscow, that was it. But the sleigh had come much later, after he left Smolensk.

That greatest adventure of his life, the moment when he truly felt himself a part of Napoleon's glory, in the farthest reach of conquest—which was also when it all began to come undone. This was where his own life intersected with the Emperor's, with history. Sleep was forgotten. This was worth remembering, recording.

When they came out from dinner in the Apraxin Palace that night of 16 September 1812, there was a red glow on the horizon, like the afterglow of some magnificent sunset. Only it was near midnight, and this glow was troubled with swirling columns of smoke. And it was on the eastern horizon. Moscow was burning. Yet it was bitterly cold in the street.

There was a shout from the end of the street, then an infantryman came running, lurching from side to side. He staggered, dropped the carpetbag he was carrying, ran on, then slipped and fell. A guardsman in pursuit was on him in a moment, sword drawn, and started flailing at him, first with the flat of the sword, then with the edge. Drunken screams from the fallen man. Beyle and Bourgeois jumped forward, and wrestled the guardsman off.

"Hola! Save your blows for the Russians," shouted Bourgeois.

The guardsman turned, his sword now raised against Bourgeois. Beyle pulled his pistol from his belt and leveled it. The guardsman, his face flushed under his shako, looked confused and hurt. "But he was looting, sirs. Dead drunk. Against orders."

"Right. We'll take him to the post. Go on your way."

The guardsman sullenly sheathed his sword. Beyle and Bourgeois—an adjutant in the Supply Commission who had become Beyle's most reliable aide, an amiable Burgundian—then wasted an hour finding an officer to take charge of the drunken infantryman, bleeding now from cuts in his right arm. Everywhere in the streets there was a confused milling of soldiers; they looked dazed, disoriented. Others asleep on doorsteps, muffled in their cloaks. No one seemed to be in command. When they found the officers' billet, the colonel showed no interest in their captive. He said there was looting everywhere. On their way back to the palace, they passed a regiment of dragoons, standing guard by their restless horses stamping on the cold cobblestones. In the eerie quiet that reigned in the courtyard of the Apraxin Palace, they made themselves wearily test the pump. They hauled a dozen buckets from the stables in back, filled them to the brim. That would have to do for fire prevention. Then they made their way upstairs and went to bed.

Beyle awoke at seven, and began the business of packing his barouche. He had no orders, so when he was done he simply told his driver to go join the line of coaches belonging to Count Daru, the Emperor's High Commissioner for Supply, and his own commanding officer. The carriages stretched over half a mile down the wide boulevard. But there was no forward movement. They waited, it must have been five, six hours. Meanwhile, it was becoming clear that the fire was far from under control. It was coming closer. You could now hear it constantly, like the sea from the seashore, a low roaring, punctuated by cracks as walls tumbled. It would not be long before the Apraxin Palace itself went up in flames. He paced the boulevard, stopping where the wider side streets gave the best view of the flames. They could not be more than a quarter of a mile distant.

Then orders came from Daru to find him a house for the night. He was going to hold on, apparently in the hope that General Kirgener's men would arrest the progress of the fire. So Beyle, accompanied by Bourgeois and old Reynaud, the quartermaster, began searching farther along the boulevard. They stopped at the imposing Soltykoff Palace, evidently deserted. The massive door was locked, impregnable. They smashed a ground-floor window, crawled through, and began a quick inspection of its magnificent rooms. It would do. Then they set off for the Kremlin, to find Daru. Another couple of hours wasted. Troops everywhere, some of them formed up to march, others in total disorder. They saw looting parties carrying out sacks and even furniture from a dozen houses. Two grand pianos sat in the middle of a street, abandoned. Then, when Daru returned with them to the Soltykoff Palace, they realized the fire had now come too close for safety.

Daru sent them off again, in the direction of the French Club, next to which they found a lovely small palace, full of paintings and statuary, also a magnificent library. It was perfect. Beyle dispatched Corporal Deguy to carry the message to Daru. As they awaited his arrival, Beyle decided to break into the wine cellars

of the French Club. He didn't much like looting, but all of them
needed white wine, to stanch the violent dysentery that was making their lives miserable.

Bourgeois found a way into the French Club through the stables in its rear, which led into a garden, pretty though the Russian trees always seemed to Beyle poor and stunted compared to
those in France. With the help of their four scouts, Bourgeois
and Reynaud pried open a low door in the foundations. All
they found was some very ordinary white wine, but it would do.
The three of them sat in the garden and uncorked three bottles. Meanwhile, the scouts appeared from upstairs with dam-
ask tablecloths and napkins. They would do for sheets. François,
Beyle's valet, was by now hopelessly drunk, and staggered out of
the building with an armload of wine bottles, tablecloths, and a
violin he had stolen, and evidently thought he needed. With an
expression of self-satisfaction, he proceeded to carry his loot out
to the barouche.

The wine finished, they left the French Club to return to the
pleasant palace they had chosen for the night. Beyle was just in
the process of assigning rooms and giving orders on making up
beds, when Daru himself arrived, with the command that they
were to leave immediately. Beyle was by then in a pleasant haze
of white wine and fatigue. He felt his legs give under him. He
had been looking forward to food, and sleep. But orders were
orders.

The barouche was overflowing with the items pillaged by his
servant—as well as the wine, the tablecloths, and the ridiculous
violin, there were two sacks of flour and two of oats, a couple of
loaves of bread, and other sacks of unidentifiable bric-à-brac. He
loaded in Bonnaire, the auditor for the Conseil d'État, who had
completely lost his nerve and was sniveling like a baby. Why this
good deed, he could not say. Then he went back into the palace.

A long road lay ahead. He needed something to read, he

realized. Quickly, he mounted the ornate staircase to the third floor, where he had come upon the library of whatever nobleman owned this lovely place. His boots made an echoing sound in the empty space.

The library, with its frescoed ceiling, its long mahogany table and impressive globe mounted in a dark, polished stand, its chairs upholstered in yellow silk, was the refuge he needed. He sat for a moment at the nobleman's desk. The blotter showed the traces of strange characters. Cyrillic, of course. The pen was still in the inkstand. He ran his eyes over the shelves of books that covered three walls, up to the moldings where the decorated ceiling began. The work of generations of collectors, no doubt. Three small ladders, on runners, lay to hand.

Shouts reached him from the street. Time to choose, and quickly. He moved to his left, scanning the spines of the volumes for whatever was not in cyrillic. There, a volume of Lord Chesterfield's *Letters*. He pulled it out. A beautiful Morocco binding. He set it on a step of the nearby ladder, and continued scanning. Now, here were the French authors. Montaigne. Montesquieu. Voltaire, in complete sets. Why not, Voltaire. But nothing too serious. He ran his finger along the line of some twenty volumes. Toward the end of the line was one with the title *Facéties*—that would be all the comic stuff. He pulled it out.

Holding the handsome volume—in half-calf with the nobleman's coat of arms stamped on the cover—he had a momentary pang of conscience. Spoil in this way his complete Voltaire? Would whoever it was ever be able to replace the missing volume? But this magnificent library was condemned to the flames in any event, wasn't it?

There was a muffled thud from the other side of the building, and loud cries. Don't be too much of a fool, he told himself. Time to go. He secured the two volumes under his left arm, and ran for the stairs.

The column of carriages had jolted into motion. He handed the volumes through the window of the barouche to Bonnaire, shouted to François to move on. He had no desire to squeeze in next to the white-faced Bonnaire in the overloaded barouche, despite his immense fatigue, so he fell into step next to the carriage.

It must have been about seven in the evening. Darkness had fallen already, and now you could see that the fire was blazing not more than a few streets away. You could feel the heat come at you in gusts as you passed the side streets. And now the smoke was coming thicker and thicker. Sparks, pieces of burning paper danced through the air. He found himself hoping that all the gunpowder had already been evacuated.

Their advance continued for only half an hour. Then they came up against a wall of flames. Some of the carriages ahead decided to make a dash for it though a side street. But just as they broke loose from the column and into the street, the wall of one of the houses went off like a torch, and collapsed in flames. There were piercing cries. Nothing to be done.

Suddenly Daru was at his elbow, furious. "Madness," he shouted. "Total madness. We'll all be incinerated. Back, turn back."

Beyle joined Daru in running along the column, shouting at all the drivers to turn around. Unspeakable confusion followed. The boulevard was wide enough for the turn, but no two drivers executed it in the same manner. Wheels locked with one another. A carriage overturned, with screams from the passengers within. Several trunks tumbled from overloaded coach roofs. Beyle continued plodding along the line—he recognized once again that he could keep his head in an emergency—shouting at the drivers—half of them appeared to be hopelessly drunk—grabbing the traces of the horses to turn them sharply round. The whole column swayed and regrouped, leaving a pile of debris—including a dozen carriages out of action—along the way. Then he quickened his step, and moved to the head of the column, where Daru, mounted next to his coachman, was urging his horses into a lumbering trot. He swung himself onto the side step of Daru's carriage, grasping the bracket of the side lamp, as they moved down the boulevard. Smoke everywhere now, and the sky was all a red glow, with from the left the sight of leaping flames, higher than the houses.

They came to an open place, where several broad avenues converged. In its center stood a figure on horseback, his plumed helmet and breastplate shining fiercely in the red glow, his sword raised. He was surrounded by a dozen foot soldiers, their bayonets extended in a protective circle. Beyle leapt from the step of the carriage, ran to the horseman, and saluted. Then he recognized him, General Kirgener. Evidently he had given up fighting the blaze, and was directing the retreat.

"General, Count Daru and his train. What route do we take?"

Kirgener pointed with his sword down an avenue to his left. "Down the Tverskoy. The only safe route."

Kirgener was one of the rare commanders who kept his head that night, Beyle later surmised. He ran heavily back to Daru's coach, and began passing the word down the line. Tverskoy Road. Follow us.

It was now past eleven o'clock. The road was indeed clear of flames, but after a half hour of rapid progress they ran into a French baggage train—Marshal Murat's, as it turned out—and there was more shouting and cursing and time lost in merging the two streams of traffic. It must have been three in the morning when the city began to fall away to the two sides. They passed through a gate, and then were mounting a wide avenue.

When they were finally clear of the city, Beyle turned back. What a sight. Moscow was now a pyramid of fire. Like prayer to the faithful, he thought, its base covering the earth, its point reaching to the heavens. The apocalypse come all unexpectedly. From where he stood, the roar of the flames was distant. The spectacle was purely visual, the most beautiful thing he had ever seen. So the Russians had simply decided to burn holy Moscow rather than letting the French have it. What was his name? Count Rostopchin, the governor. Would history rank him as a great villain or a great patriot? In any case, he had created one of the wonders of the world.

Moscow burned before his eyes. Flames danced from rooftops, like enormous votive candles. Buildings tumbled in crescendos of sparks. The pyramid of fire lit up the surrounding countryside in a strange theatrical light. Like the final act of some unimaginable opera. *Don Giovanni* with the flames on the stage rather than in the trap. Beyle stood aside from the laboring column of carriages and watched. Moscow gone. Where were they to go now? The Emperor had lost his winter quarters. Where would he lead them next?

At the top of the hill, they bivouacked for a few hours, and made a meal of raw fish, figs, and white wine. Beyle was slightly drunk on bad white wine. Afterward came the orders passed down from the High Command to Daru: he was to push on to Smolensk, to prepare the supply of that city for the retreating army. And then after Smolensk—by the time it got there, the Grand Army had lost half its men—on across the snow to the murderous Berezina, and Vilna, then Dantzig. And eventually Paris. He fought the Cossacks, he survived, he fulfilled his duties. Daru would tell him later his sang-froid had been perfect.

But it was the end of the army, and before long, the end of the Empire.

Beyle felt haggard. Is that what happens in old age, he wondered—our memories start weighing on us, literally like some heavy burden carried on the shoulders? Time is heavy, he thought, and as it accumulates on you, you step more slowly. You can't move forward with the same ease, with the freshness of the unburdened. A plague on it, he did not want to be old. There was too much left to do, too many books to write and publish under his pen name, Stendhal, too many women to love. He glanced at Giulia's sleeping form with something like gratitude. She made him feel a kind of suspension of time. They were always just as they had always been, she made lovemaking simple and pleasing. But since she had not been allowed to marry him, it was episodic. And the time between, in Civitavecchia, weighed more and more, with the weight of waste, of decay, of time that wore one down without taking you anywhere. And if he was going to waste his nights with Giulia in exhuming memories of his Napoleonic youth . . .

No, there was life in him yet. His story wasn't over. He still had time for more twists and turns, more reinventions of himself. He opened the shutter a crack. A cool breeze blew in from the Tuscan hills. The sky was beginning to brighten. He should find his place again next to Giulia in bed. For now, there was that.

❦ 6 ❦

Journey South

PHILIPPE'S EYES followed the wake, as it fanned out in two crisp waves, reaching toward the shores, giving the slow barges a gentle undulation as it passed under them, rocking more seriously the occasional rowboat. The Rhône gleamed under the July sun, like a polished pewter serving dish, hot from the oven. The slight breeze produced by the movement of the steamboat wasn't enough to cool him. The paddle wheels on the two sides threw up a fine spray, but that didn't quite reach him, whereas the black smoke from the chimney from time to time snaked down to the deck, making him cough and wheeze. All the other passengers appeared to have left the deck. He could hear voices raised from time to time in the saloon. It might be time to return to his cabin, to have a look at those papers. Maybe it was imprudent to have left them there, even with the door locked. Guizot had warned him there might be attempts to sabotage the mission.

Now he was anxious, as he made his way forward on the vibrating deck. His first major assignment in life, and he'd left the treasure unguarded. He sprang down the companionway ladder, and unlocked the cabin door. The attaché case was still there.

The small table that folded out under the porthole would do for his purposes. After making sure that the money sack was still wedged in the middle of the stiff, new leather case, he unbuckled the rear compartment of the case and drew out four letters. The one with the seal and the words *Présidence du Conseil* he set aside. This was the secret letter of instructions, to be opened only when they were at sea, and far from the French coast. He knew what it contained; the problem was that Joinville didn't. He didn't, and he was going to be surprised and certainly unhappy to learn that on this expedition, Prince Royal though he might be, he was out-ranked by his friend. The letter made it clear that Philippe de Chabot, Commissioner of the King, had full power to make any and all decisions concerning the conduct of the mission, during the voyage out, at Saint Helena, and on the return. Thiers had told him that the letter stated that any conceivable dispute would be resolved by showing the letter itself. It expressed the will of the government.

Philippe knew all this from the notes he had made during his second interview with Thiers, the long one. He set aside the second letter that came to hand, also from Thiers—these were his public, official orders, which he knew by heart and which had been announced in the Assembly—and picked up the three pages in his own hand, the notes he had set down from memory immediately following the meeting with Thiers. It was clear that the government feared above all some incident with the English, some unseemly and politically compromising outburst of French pride and Bonapartist nostalgia. Philippe was first of all to make sure that there were no stowaways on the frigate; he was to verify with Joinville everyone on the ship's manifest, both crew and the special passengers it was to carry. Then, he must make sure that the officers of the frigate and its escort would prevent any narrative of the events transpiring on Saint Helena from reaching France before their return. Correspondence to be surveilled and censored: only the official narrative of the mission would be acceptable. They were to manage—somehow—to return to Cherbourg between the 1st and the 10th of December, in time for the opening of the next sitting of the Assembly.

While on the island, ceremonial arrangements were to be left to the British. Only when the coffin was on the frigate would the moment come when "all the honors due to a sovereign will be given to the mortal remains of Napoleon."

Yes, but those remains. There was another page attached to the official instructions about sanitary precautions, the disinfection of the tomb. But he'd leave that to the ship's surgeon. Here was the core of the matter: Once they dug up the coffin, if it looked perfectly preserved and sealed, he was to have it opened, "with all the respect that such an act requires in the case of such a Deceased," in order to verify, by the authority vested in him, the identity of the corpse. Here, Marchand, Napoleon's personal valet who had himself laid the Emperor in his coffin, and who would be part of the expedition, would be the indispensable witness.

On the other hand, if the coffin was decayed, gnawed by animals, in a state of imminent collapse, and the whole grave—there was supposed to be a lead coffin within, then another wood one, then one in tinplate—a mess, he was to take firm measures against infection, and bundle whatever remained of the body into the coffin that would travel with them from France. The more probable situation, he thought grimly. Unless you are an Egyptian mummy, you don't last twenty years underground. But if all was rot and decay, how would they know they had the actual body of the Emperor? The British might have buried some insignificant peasant there. It was all thoroughly distasteful, in any event. A ghoulish mission.

Philippe set his notes aside, and reached for the fourth letter— the one slipped into his hand by Lord Granville during the reception at the Tuileries, with the polite but firm suggestion that he refrain from opening it until his journey was under way. Well, the steamboat down the Rhône was not yet the frigate *La Belle Poule* at sea, but he was under way, so he might as well open it.

He broke the heavy wax seal stamped with the rampant lion and unicorn. Inside the crisp vellum envelope, the letter it contained was yellowed, its folds worn. He opened it carefully, spreading out the brittle foolscap sheet—the folds were becoming tears—under the heel of his right hand. The ink was faded. *Saint Helena, 14 May 1821,* read the inscription at the head of the sheet. It was addressed to His Excellency Lord Wellington. His eyes moved down to the signature. What! Lieutenant General Sir Hudson Lowe. Napoleon's jailer, the man execrated in French legend as the tormentor of the fallen Emperor, the man some went so far as to suspect of having poisoned him. Literally—killed him with arsenic. It was his report to Wellington on the burial. He felt a thrill of discovery, but with a shade of the sinister.

The sinister impression was not dissipated by some of the details he painstakingly deciphered from the faded ink of Lowe's cramped handwriting. Napoleon's heart had been removed, preserved in vinegar, and placed in a silver vase; likewise his stomach, in another vase, and the two vases then placed between the legs of the body in the coffin. The body itself was clothed in the uniform of colonel of chasseurs. When the coffin was closed, the Count of Montholon, one of those famous (and few) companions of the exile, asked that the lid be inscribed: *Napoleon, born Ajaccio 15 August 1769—died Saint Helena 5 May 1821.* Here

Lowe proudly noted that he had said the name "Napoleon" would have to be replaced by "Bonaparte." Montholon categorically refused. Impasse. So the coffin went into the earth without any inscription at all.

Then came the details on the tomb itself. They had dug down twelve feet, and created a solid vault. When they had laid the coffin—rather, the coffin within the coffin within the coffin within the coffin, if he had the count right—in the vault, they had covered it with masonry. Then the hole was filled in with rubble and cement. Strange, Lowe's refusal to give the dead man the name by which the whole world knew him, while at the same time constructing this sarcophagus that seemed designed to withstand the ages, as if dealing with a pharaoh's body. As if he feared the body might escape—or else, thought Philippe, feared it might someday be dug up . . . to verify its identity.

He thought ahead to the excavation—all that masonry. Not something he could depend on the sailors to do. He'd need a small army of men with pickaxes and shovels. Recruiting his gravediggers would probably be his first act of high diplomacy with the governor of Saint Helena. What a bizarre mission.

He glanced out the porthole. Vineyards as far as the eye could see. He pulled out his watch. Another hour before they reached Avignon, where a coach should be waiting to take him the rest of the way, through Aix-en-Provence to Toulon. Time to write a short note to Amelia, though he didn't have much to recount since he saw her, yesterday. But just to swear his eternal devotion to her—were those the words he wanted? Could he assume a tone that implied they were now engaged to one another? No. No, that was far from clear.

They had stood in the conservatory off the salon in her parents' house. They had been there for nearly an hour, and no one had come to interrupt them, which must have indicated intention on her mother's part to leave them alone. Which he interpreted to mean she didn't discourage his suit of her daughter. Why indeed would she? The Comte de Rohan-Chabot was a wholly suitable match.

He had come close to declaring himself formally. They talked of his time in London, his longing to see her again, his apprehension at the five-month expedition that lay ahead, his hope that its successful conclusion would allow him his pick of posts in the ministry. Amelia listened intently, her dark brows contracted, her smile breaking on him from time to time like the cascade of something rare and wonderful. He asked her where she would be in December, and whether they might not find time for an extended visit if he prolonged his return to Paris until the New Year fêtes.

To Philippe, Amelia's face now appeared strangely veiled, inscrutable. "I can't tell, you know. It depends on Mother's plans. She's not been well lately. She may want a trip to Provence, to chase her black devils, as she calls them."

"Provence! How splendid. But then I could visit you there. I'll certainly be entitled to leave for some weeks, whatever happens after."

"I just don't know. We may want to be only the family, without any guests dancing attendance."

Philippe felt slightly wounded. "Well, I would not be a guest exactly like the others."

"So you say, but a guest nonetheless."

"But, perhaps, almost a member of the family? Amelia, you must know what I mean, what I want to say to you—"

"Don't." Her tone was peremptory, even cross, and she held out her hand as in military command: Stay back.

"But why? Surely we both know—"

"No, we don't. If you think I intend to commit myself concerning the rest of my life now, at this moment, you are mistaken. I am, thank God, still mistress of my actions."

Philippe reached for her hand in frustration. She let him hold it only for a moment, then gently slid it from his grasp.

"Philippe, my friend." She spoke in a gentle tone, but he saw her eyes as hard, bright not with consent but with resistance. "Listen. You have no rival in my affections. I admire you, I like your company. But do I need to give myself a lord and master at this moment of my life?"

"Lord and master? Say rather, a devoted friend, warm admirer—"

"No more." She paused, her face now contracted into something close to anguish. "I know what you mean, I appreciate the value of your affection. But not now. The time may come, but not now."

"May come? Promise me at least that when I return from this cursed expedition, you will listen to me."

"In December? Well, maybe. But I promise nothing. December is far off. Much could change."

"Change?" he echoed. He was beginning to feel stupid, "What do you mean?"

"Nothing. Simply that. We'll certainly meet in December—that's inevitable in any case—but I promise no more."

And that was all he could obtain from her. Why her delay? In Philippe's mind, nothing was quite explicable. There was something in her resisting, he sensed, something that suggested she hadn't quite made up her mind. Was there another suitor? He had no reason to think so. But there was something in her that he couldn't fathom. Who was she? he found himself asking. The idea of his long absence was more than ever disquieting. Could he count on her being there when he returned?

The coach journey over the parched and dusty roads of Provence went swiftly. He scarcely stopped. At the relays, while the horses were being changed, he took a loaf of bread and a wedge of cheese in the inn, then cried the order to move on. The coach ran on during the night, and Philippe's sleep was only a few hours, interrupted by the relays. Just after noon on 7 July, the coach slowed as it approached the walls of Toulon. His orders called for a first stop at the prefecture, where he was to receive a sack containing twenty thousand francs, to add to the twenty-five thousand in the sack brought from Paris. By midafternoon, he was at the quay. The launch was waiting. Four sailors sprang to the coach to take his trunk and cases, while Philippe stepped from the other door, clutching the attaché case.

He found himself face-to-face with a smartly dressed mariner, who saluted.

"Ensign Bazin, sir. At your service."

"Carry on, Ensign. Your orders?"

"Orders to take you on board at once, sir. You're the last to arrive. His Highness the Captain wants to get under way at once."

"Very well. I am ready."

Philippe suddenly realized he had now entered the world of naval discipline. Seated in the stern, holding the precious attaché case, his baggage piled amidships, he watched the sailors salute with their oars held straight up. Then Bazin gave the order to cast off. The lines came in, a gentle shove pushed the launch from the quay, the oars dipped in perfect unison, they were moving.

He hadn't until now had a chance to take in the roadstead. Ships of every description, rowboats, fishing boats, feluccas with their lateen sails furled at a rakish angle, a steamboat on the quay opposite beginning to make up steam, its smokestack belching black puffs. Then far out by the beacon light marking the entrance to the roadstead, the two tall ships. The smaller one, he knew, would be the corvette *La Favorite*, twenty-four guns, their supply ship and space for those of the official party who couldn't fit into *La Belle Poule.* That was the larger ship. As the launch approached, her sides loomed high. She was one of the newest fighting ships of the navy, sixty guns, a first-class frigate. Yet small enough when you considered she was to be your only home for months to come.

Bright white steps had been lowered along the gleaming black sides of the ship, and he could see on deck the marines assembled to welcome him on board. The bosun's pipe shrilled. They swung alongside in a graceful motion, the sailors backed their oars, bringing the launch to rest precisely below the ladder. Now to manage the steps, swaying slightly in the light breeze, along with his attaché case. As he rose, two sailors were on either side of him.

"You first, sir. We'll hand your case up after you."

With reluctance, Philippe loosed his grasp on the case—the only thing to do, he'd need two hands for the lifelines on the steps—and scrambled forward, and up the vertiginous steps. No moment to show yourself a landlubber, he thought. He reached for the deck, and a leathery hand grasped his, to pull him upright, standing on the deck. He glanced back anxiously, and a moment later the attaché case had been placed in his hand. Now he turned to face the deck.

The bosun was piping, the marines stood at attention in two lines, and Joinville stepped forward, Hernoux a step behind him.

"Monsieur le Commissaire du Roi, welcome aboard."

Philippe bowed. "My compliments to Your Highness."

Joinville smiled, then stepped forward to take his hand. "Here, I am called 'Captain.' You are now subject to the ways of His Majesty's navy."

"Yes, Captain. At your orders, Captain."

"We sail at once. But first let me present Ship's Captain Hernoux."

Philippe bowed to the white-haired Hernoux, who he knew

had long been Joinville's mentor at sea, as well as his personal aide-de-camp. Joinville then presented his second-in-command, Monsieur Charner.

To Charner's right stood two white-haired men whose uniforms, tight across the front and faded, nonetheless were like the sudden revival of a glorious past. The Old Guard. General Bertrand, a figure of legend, once grand marshal of the imperial court, one of the companions of Napoleon's exile, the man who was known to the whole world for having faithfully carried out the Emperor's last wishes, who had brought the sword of Austerlitz back to France, and who had refused all the honors offered him by the Restoration, out of fidelity to the man he had served so well. Bertrand's face was pale and drawn under his general's hat, his eyes deep-set and watery. For all his corpulence, he looked wan, unwell. Just behind him stood a young man dressed in black, his son Arthur, a silent presence at his father's side. Then General Gourgaud, massive in his light blue uniform, apparently still vigorous, still the fire-breathing military man who had been the indomitable spirit of the exile.

Joinville introduced him to several others, the old faithful chosen for the voyage. Then there was the fashionable young Abbé Coquereau—who had brought with him two angelic altar boys to assist in the mass—and Dr. Guillard, ship's surgeon and in charge of sanitary measures, and the master plumber Leroux, assigned to opening the coffin, if this were to happen. And then someone more interesting to Philippe, Emmanuel de Las Cases, son of the man who had set down Napoleon's reflections in exile in the *Mémorial de Sainte-Hélène,* which had done more than any other book to create the legend. Las Cases the younger, forty-one years old, had himself been page to the Emperor at the time of Waterloo, had shared the exile in Saint Helena for eighteen months, writing the history of the campaigns of 1796 and 1797 under the Emperor's dictation, until along with his father he was expelled from the island by Sir Hudson Lowe, under suspicion of having plotted Napoleon's escape.

Surrounded by these living reminders of a past which he knew only dimly, mainly through the harsh judgments of his father, Philippe felt a tightening in his throat. He was trapped, trapped on board a floating monument to something he couldn't feel sympathy with. How could he travel for endless months with these debris of a past he thought was long gone—and good riddance? What was the King up to, anyway? Did he know, or had he been taken in by Thiers' chauvinistic enthusiasms? Philippe had the sudden bitter taste that maybe he had compromised his whole career.

But there was no time for further reflection. Orders were to muster all men and search the ship for possible stowaways. Joinville insisted that they get under way first, then search—any unwanted passengers could be set ashore in Gibraltar.

Philippe followed his baggage to his cabin in the gun deck— large enough, and lighted by two open gunports—then was back on deck, as the bosun's pipes trilled and the crews went to work. The capstan turned to the stomp of twenty men at the poles. Sailors swarmed up the ratlines, and spread out on the cross yards. Canvas broke from its stops, brilliant white in the late afternoon sunlight. The wind filled the topsails with a cracking noise. He could feel the frigate shudder. Then the bow anchor broke through surface of the dark water, and gaffs reached to cat it into place. The sidelines came in. Yes, the ship was moving. Slowly, smoothly, it slipped down the roadstead. Philippe turned his eyes to the poop, where Joinville, in dress uniform, Hernoux constantly at his side, barked brief orders through a megaphone. Despite his baby face with its freshly grown whiskers, he seemed to know what he was doing. Philippe had never seen him in this role before. At least, Joinville knew what his role on this voyage was. The Royal Commissioner felt no such certitude.

The frigate was gaining speed. Now its bow was speaking, you could begin to hear the slap and rustle of water along the side. The quay, already in shadow beneath a Toulon now ruddy orange in the slanting sun, was quickly receding. Now they were even with the first of the warships drawn up near the mouth of the roadstead. First, the *Trident.* He realized that its sailors, there must have been two hundred or more, were standing at attention on deck. Then the *Généreux,* followed by the *Marengo,* also with all hands turned out to salute their voyage. Then, last in the line, the flagship of the Mediterranean fleet, the *Océan,* all flags flying. As the frigate passed the beacon at the end of the mole, and the breeze came stronger, a hum started up in the rigging, like some deep-throated harp. Then there was a crack and a boom. Philippe looked back to see a white puff of smoke billow from the deck of the *Océan.* Then again, the perfectly spaced rolling thunder of a nine-gun salute. They were off, the sea lay clear before them. There was no turning back now.

❧7❧

Meeting in Rome

AFTER PASSING the footman at attention by the door, Beyle paused on the magnificent stairway leading up to the *piano nobile* of the Palazzo Cini. He wanted to get his thoughts straight about the Countess. This was something he repeatedly told himself he must do during his jolting, sleepless journey back from Siena to Civitavecchia, without success. His mind was then too full of Giulia's adorable ways with him, and a debate on what his life would have been like had he married her—as he'd tried to do, only to be rebuffed by her guardian. Yet he could not help himself: What would Henri Beyle have been like as a married man? Past a certain age, marriage may be the only solution to certain intractable problems of life. Such as loneliness. Yes, he was lonely, and the three days spent in Civitavecchia following the rendezvous with Giulia made him admit it to himself as never before. The endless tractations over tariffs and trade, the undeclared but intensifying war with Tavernier, the bleak late August days in the dreary town drenched in unremitting sun, nights too hot to sleep properly—this was not what he needed. He had not written a line for months. His seafaring novel remained a blank page.

But even if this other Giulia—Giulia Cini, whom he dubbed Giulia^2 in his journal—had begun to show signs of interest in his assiduous attention to her, would a Roman liaison, with another married woman, serve his purposes? The Countess would be a flattering conquest, to be sure. And rendezvous in Rome were easier to manage than ones in Siena. Still, he realized that it was his imagination that was moved by Giulia^2's striking beauty, not his heart. He didn't find himself falling into those reveries, as in the months before the decisive moment with the first Giulia, where he would find himself asking anxiously, Does she love me?—and find, too, that his heart was pounding wildly. Better, then, to go cautiously, he thought. But could a lion for love refuse if the Countess declared herself any further? He realized that she did not make him feel very leonine. When he was honest with himself, he knew that his heart—alas—was at peace. Was it time to stop worrying about love—to make it simply something to reshape in the imagination, on the written page?

He resumed his trudge up the staircase, dimly aware of the mythological scenes unfolding on the coffered ceilings above him—the work of Giulio Romano, the family claimed—and nodded to the footman in scarlet and gold livery, who placed his fingertips together, bowed slightly, and stepped into the reception room to announce Signor Beyle.

The magnificence of the room never failed to make its mark on him. The lofty vaulted ceiling, with azure sky and softly billowing clouds gilded at their edges with rich Roman sunlight—representing the apotheosis of some Cini ancestor— lifted the room, and his spirits, to an exalted plane of existence. The frescoes on the walls, on a heroic scale that gave them a transcendent serenity compared to the mere mortals who stood and moved below them, recounted the life of Ulysses—from whom the Cinis claimed a legendary descent—with a kind of intense fidelity, evoking magical creatures—Cyclops, men metamorphosed into beasts by Circe—with a complete faith in their reality. As he paused just inside the wide doorway, across from him Nausicaa—blond for the occasion, and clad in the lightest of draperies that fell from her shoulders, exposing an enticingly plump right breast—greeted a bearded and disheveled Ulysses, covering his nakedness with the branch of an olive tree, on the Phaeacian seashore.

But he was not there as a pilgrim of art, however much he might prefer that role. He had rather to make good his reputation as the witty Frenchman, the diplomat who was *anche un scrittore,* the maker of phrases that would be cited in Roman society on the morrow. And the Count was approaching, his fine and agreeable features enlivened by a broad smile. With his high forehead, receding lustrous black hair brushed back, and his monocle dangling from a velvet ribbon, and his impeccably knotted cravats, the Count exuded a kind of generalized benevolence and security, a promise of unchanging perfection. The benevolence was particularly focused on Beyle, since the Count considered himself something of an expert in French politics.

"Beyle. What an honor you do us."

"What a pleasure to find you still in town, Count."

"We have overstayed this summer—my fault, entirely, too much to do—but we go Tuesday to Castelgandolfo. And you shall visit us."

Beyle bowed.

"But tell me, this news about the Bonaparte pretender, this Louis-Napoléon?"

"Ah, so you are already informed."

"My place at the ministry," the Count said, with a

self-deprecating wave of the hand. "I may not be the first to know, but news will out. But the details?"

"The details I have are few. Louis-Napoléon Bonaparte, the claimant to the Bonaparte legacy, made an attempt to capture the fortress at Boulogne, on the English Channel, on 6 August. His idea was apparently to gain the support of the garrison there, create an armed force that would then march on Paris. Or some say he wanted to march on Cherbourg, take it, and then capture the body of his uncle when it returns from Saint Helena—and use it as the trophy to raise the French in a wave of enthusiasm for the return of the Empire, under this new Napoleon."

"Astonishing."

"The most astonishing thing is that he almost succeeded at Boulogne. It was a simple colonel who showed some presence of mind, and thwarted the coup. As it turned out, Louis-Napoléon had to dive into the Channel and swim back to one of his landing craft. But they caught him; he'll be judged before the House of Peers next month."

"And what will be his fate? Shot, I suppose."

Beyle shrugged. "That would be logical. The man's an inveterate troublemaker. He tried a coup once before. But I don't know. I'm not sure that Monsieur Thiers' government wants to be forced to put a Bonaparte to death. The howls of opposition would be overwhelming. And it would rather spoil the triumphal return of the Emperor's body."

"To be sure, Beyle. But when will your compatriots have done with this cult of the Bonapartes? It can't be helpful to the King."

"My compatriots, as you so rightly suggest, can never rid themselves of that cult. It brings out their most childish side. They think the whole world should want them as masters, and love them for it."

The Count shook his head. "Ah well. But Beyle, I detain you, and I must not claim exclusive rights to you. The Countess will be fretful. Let me take you to her."

Did the Count suspect anything? Not that there was yet anything to suspect. And in any event, a Roman noblewoman was expected to have a *cavaliere servante,* a publicly recognized, though officially platonic, admirer.

Beyle let himself be guided by the Count through the press— though a sparser press than there would have been earlier in the summer, before Rome began to empty for country stays. As they approached the Countess, she was deep in conversation with the old Duchess of Monte Albano, and had her back turned to them—a back of infinite grace, Beyle noted, her waist slim and high, the lightest of dove gray silk falling from waist to floor in a line that marked the elegant swell of her hips, her burnished blond hair—she was from Lombardy—softly gathered at the nape of her neck. But next to hers was the back of another woman, all in black, which he did not recognize.

"Cara"—the Count touched the Countess lightly on the elbow—"it's Signor Beyle."

The Countess did not turn for a moment, finishing her words to the Duchess. The two women then embraced, then Giulia Cini greeted Beyle with the grave smile and serious eyes that reminded him of a Correggio painting. She extended her hand, he bowed and took it to his lips. As he straightened himself, his eyes were caught by the young woman in black, who had turned to meet him.

He felt submerged, suddenly as if drowning in a deep sea. The chattering Italian voices around him were muffled. What was this?

The woman was young. Her white shoulders and long, strong neck rose from her unornamented black dress, to a face of a kind of fierce, flashing beauty, with dark smudges of eyebrows, and dark auburn hair pulled back behind her shoulders. But surely he knew that face, knew her, intimately.

"Signor Beyle—a diplomat from your country," spoke the Countess. "Beyle, this is our young friend Amélie Curial, Amelia, we call her in Italy."

Amelia held out her hand in an easy gesture; her arm, thin and rounded and strong, nearly took Beyle's breath away. She smiled, her thin lips curling back charmingly. Her glance was intense.

"Signor Beyle will not remember me, but we met when I was a child. You knew my late mother, I believe."

Beyle's mouth was dry. "But of course, you are Clémentine's youngest child. But you say late?"

"Dear mother died three weeks ago."

The black dress. Why had he not heard of this?

"I am so sorry. This must have happened so suddenly . . ."

The Countess raised her eyebrows. "A tragedy. That is why our dear Amelia has come to us, for some rest in the Italian hills. She goes with us to Castelgandolfo on Tuesday."

"But tell me . . ." The Countess's eyebrows were now underlined by a frown. He was being warned off. He started again. "You look strikingly like your mother, you know."

"So I am told." Amelia had a charming, direct smile, one that set off tumultuous images in Beyle's memory. Clémentine—Menti to him—had been the most passionate woman he had ever encountered.

"An exquisite woman," Beyle went on, attempting to recover his composure. "She will be very much regretted. And the General, your father?"

Amelia's face was pained. "He suffers very much, you know. He says little, he is very stoical, but he worries me. I must go back to him soon."

"But not until after you have regained your strength with us," the Countess said. "And look, here is the sorbet we have been waiting for."

The majordomo, in a white jacket with gold epaulettes and white gloves, was at their side, holding out a silver platter bearing little glasses of pink sorbet.

He managed, sometime later, to have a word alone with the Count.

"Shocking news about the Countess Curial. I hadn't heard."

The Count glanced over his shoulder, and spoke in Beyle's ear. "Took her own life, it is said. In despair over some lover who had left her."

Beyle shuddered. "Tell me."

"I know very little of the details. I am told she had been in a state of despondency for some time. Dear Clémentine, she was, you know, always a bit"—he tapped his forehead—"a bit excessive. But you knew her well, I think."

Beyle managed urbanity. "Quite well, many years ago, close to twenty years ago. During the days I frequented Parisian salons. And yes, you are right. Clémentine was always a bit excessive."

"Amelia has long been our especial friend, our daughter Angelica's playmate when I was posted to Paris. Amelia's a bit older than Angelica, but they spent three years as schoolmates."

Angelica. Beyle realized he had forgotten to ask about the Cinis' daughter who, poor plain thing, never seemed to rise to the level of his conscious remembrance. "Ah, I looked in vain for Angelica this evening."

"Indisposed," said the Count. "Nothing serious. Amelia would have spent the evening reading to her, but the dear thing insisted on Amelia's joining the company."

"Please convey my wishes for her speedy recovery," said Beyle. Then after a pause he returned to the subject that interested him. "And you have taken Mademoiselle Curial in following the tragedy?"

"Yes. As soon as Giulia heard, she sent to the General, to request Amelia join us. She needs a woman's guidance. Especially now that she's at that critical age when she must be married."

"How old is she?"

"Twenty-four, nearly twenty-five, I believe. And I should think, a most lovely bride for the right man. Though her mother's reputation, and the stories circulating about her end, cast something of a shadow. Which may be why she is still unmarried. And I don't think there's much of a fortune there. The General was made a count by Napoleon, he's not the old landed nobility."

"I know. So the Countess intends to marry her?"

"Oh, Giulia has no one particular in mind. I think she may travel back to Paris with her in a few months, you know. There are perhaps not so many suitable matches here, in this backwater."

The Count spoke a bit archly. But Rome was a backwater at the present time, caught in the politics of the Papacy while the rest of Europe was marching to a more progressive step.

"Well," said Beyle pensively, "I shall help you if I can. She is lovely. She deserves a man of some quality."

The Count smiled. "I wouldn't think that most of your acquaintance would be quite suitable."

"You think them all old roués? Not entirely wrong, Count, but I do meet some promising young men in the diplomatic corps. At least when I get to Paris. Of Civitavecchia it's not worth speaking."

"Of course. But you must get to know her. Look, she's coming, I think, to us."

Beyle turned, and once again felt a kind of turmoil in his mind. Images of Menti's wild abandon on his canapé superimposed themselves on the image of the composed young woman who advanced toward them. The eyebrows and the eyes were the same, something in the mouth, too. She was not a perfect beauty in the Roman mode—not Raphaëlesque. There was something too abrupt in her movements, too intense about her face. Yet the open smile she wore didn't have that slight edge of insanity that made Menti so enticing yet always finally unreachable. So narcissistic in her pleasures, Beyle thought. She had led him to his greatest exploits of lovemaking, but never to a sense of peace. And she—she was never at peace. And now cold and dead. Killed herself. A chill ran through him.

He stepped forward to meet Amelia, as the Count tactfully turned away. And for the rest of the evening, he let himself slip into the role of kindly uncle, listening to her, speaking a word of friendly advice from time to time. She was, he quickly decided, wise beyond her years. The turbulent emotions that must have been a large part of her childhood with such a mother seemed to have given her a wise though slightly defiant attitude toward life. She evidently did not want to speak of her mother—nor, Beyle found, did he—as if this were a subject that would conjure up too many difficult issues, and perhaps a severe judgment. It was not the moment for judgment. But they did eventually come to the question of her future.

"I know the Countess thinks it her role to marry me. She has the kindest of intentions. But I'm not sure it's what I want."

"Everyone assumes of course it's what every young woman wants."

"That's the problem."

"But what other solution is there? How else can a woman lead her life?"

Amelia was somber. "I don't know. I've been pondering that question. It's not that the young men aren't charming, some of them. But to promise one of them eternal fidelity, to let him become one's lord and master?"

Beyle nodded. "I've never understood why we haven't arranged things otherwise."

"You see, mostly they bore me. There were moments in my

mother's salon when I would fall asleep on the sofa, listening to some young man offer the latest platitudes on Meyerbeer's latest opera. Or the French army in Algeria. It's all so predictable."

"That's what I used to think, as a boy in Grenoble. That's why I attached myself to the army. You never knew where orders would send you next."

"But that adventure is all over now. And it never was for girls, anyway. We are supposed to languish in innocence and ignorance, cultivating our piano playing and needlepoint until some man claims us. It's unfair, I don't even see how it can be good for you men. Do you really want your wives to be ignorant as carps?"

Beyle smiled. This was unexpected spirit. "So young, and already so bored?"

"Bored, yes. Not because I think life needs to be boring, but because it is all traced out for us, ruled with heavy ink lines."

"At least you get to come to Italy, to travel with the Cinis."

"Ah, that too. They are lovely, of course, and I am so grateful to them—I couldn't bear Paris just then, just after—but it, too, is wholly predictable. I can imagine exactly how every day in Castelgandolfo will unfold, from morning coffee to evening sorbet."

She paused, to take in once again the decorous reception beneath the high frescoed walls. Then she said: "I wish you'd take me to travel in America instead."

"America! Admirable place, no doubt, but what could be more boring than a democracy? You have to pay court to your grocer and your bootblack."

"But the undiscovered land. The wide Mississippi River, with the endless plains beyond. The wild redskins. The buffalo. Life in a tent. Waking at dawn to the sun rising over the mountains."

Beyle was amused, entranced too. "Dear girl, what have you been reading? James Fenimore Cooper, might I guess?"

Amelia brushed this off. Her eyes were shining with intensity, those magnificent eyebrows contracted, her brow furrowed. "Can't you arrange to take me away on some adventure? Get yourself posted to Lapland or Halifax or Minsk. Take me along. I'll organize your consular receptions."

What was he to think of this? It was evident that she spoke sincerely. She had wound herself up into a passion in which no doubt her imagination was dictating words and projects that reason would later repudiate, yet nonetheless he sensed she had the strength of character to make good on her proposals. He felt flattered she had said this to him, that he was chosen, if only in her imagination, to serve as guide and guardian for adventure. No doubt because she cast him in a quasi-paternal role: trusted friend of her parents, like the Cinis. Of course, she intended no more. Yet she made him come alive. He wished twenty years off his age. He would offer her his hand on the spot.

He thought for a moment, then risked a comment he knew to be not quite suitable. "Ah, but you know you would compromise your reputation thoroughly. I don't think I'd be considered a proper guardian for you."

She met this straight on, looked him full in the face, her own expression one of the greatest seriousness and concentration. "Oh, my reputation! I know that. I know more than you think I do. And I don't care, really I don't. I am not going to let my life be ruled by worry about my reputation."

He became aware that the Countess was on her way to join them—no doubt their tête-à-tête was beginning to appear somewhat unseemly—so he only had time for a few more words alone. He must choose them carefully.

"I believe you. There is everything about you that makes me believe you. I will think on what you have said. And I will come to see you in Castelgandolfo. And of course in Paris, when you return there—I must also make a trip there in the fall."

She stood looking at him. Her face was still eager and intent, but now a slight smile came to her lips. "Good. Then I believe you, too. I will count on you to help me."

The Countess was between them. Beyle realized it was time to say good night. He stayed only long enough to let the Countess repeat the invitation to Castelgandolfo, and to promise that he would make the visit.

❧8❧

Voyage Out

H E REALIZED that he loathed the sea. It was not that he was seasick, like old Bertrand and his new friend Las Cases. He was fine, even the pitch and roll that had started after they cleared Gibraltar hadn't bothered him, and the one squall they had encountered so far had been wet and uncomfortable, with his trunk coming loose and sliding across the cabin floor like a beast with a perverse will, but nothing worse. No, it was the sea itself he hated, the endless horizon without relief, the sense of a hostile element which bore them up only reluctantly. It was inhuman, that's what it was. No place for the paltry beings who tried to make their way across it. Wholly alien, indifferent.

Dreamlike. He had this strange sense that he was himself a character in a novel, as if someone else were writing his life. As if he were a puppet, with someone far away—back on land— pulling the strings. Of course that was true in a sense. He was really just a puppet in a political game, one that was fairly absurd when you looked at it. Someone charged with moving a dead body from one place to another, a pawn across the chessboard. But the feeling was worse than that. It had to do with Amelia, of course. Feeling totally helpless about shaping his life, leaving her without any agreement, open to the solicitations of god knows what other men. It was the suspension of the sea without horizon.

They called at Teneriffe, in the Canaries, last stop before crossing to Bahia. Joinville explained that since Saint Helena lay directly within the southwest trade winds, a direct approach to the island was out of the question. They had to get there crabwise: a long tack across to the Brazilian coast, then from there south to pick up the trade winds to Saint Helena, making their journey outward-bound some 2,140 leagues, whereas the return should be closer to 1,890.

There was no letter from Amelia in Teneriffe. He hadn't really expected one—there had been no promise of correspondence, the question had never come up, and it would have required ingenuity as well as passion to get a letter to Teneriffe in advance of the *Belle Poule*. But there were letters for some of the officers. He wrote to her—he ripped up several attempts before the deadline for the mail pouch finally made him complete one. It was the last letter to go into the pouch. He wasn't satisfied with the result, but he tried to put into it all the passion he couldn't express at their last meeting, to tell her he needed to see her again, that she was to make a place for him when he returned.

(Back in Civitavecchia, Beyle, looking out over the ships at anchor in the port—no frigates that he could detect, but some large sailing vessels—tried to imagine the voyage. The Commissioner of the King of the French, young Chabot. Fair hair, fair skin, blue eyes, excellent manners. A bit insignificant, no doubt, but earnest and well tutored. How did he go about the pursuit of happiness? Whom did he love, what poets did he read?

84

Victor Hugo, no doubt—Beyle grimaced—and Alfred de Musset. What books had he taken with him for the ocean voyage? What did he think of his mission? Of the great legend he was working to further? He was now entering the legend himself. It must be almost like a surrender: myself no longer myself but a ghostly visitor from a trivial present to a larger, engulfing past. That's what is interesting, not the monotonous voyage itself. Fix your mind on that: the young man suddenly faced with the visitable past, a past of the history books suddenly come alive, as in a waxworks that unsuspectedly began to move and talk.)

The morning they left Teneriffe, Philippe and Emmanuel de Las Cases shared a space they had created amidships, surrounded by packing cases that would not fit in the hold, which had been stripped of its cover for several yards to make room for the vast sarcophagus that traveled with them. As they watched the peak of Teneriffe fade to an uncertain form on the horizon, Philippe broke the meditative silence. "Do you remember anything of that first journey, on the *Northumberland*?"

"Yes. Everything, in fact. We followed very much the same route as we're doing now."

"But the mood must have been entirely different."

"The mood then, so far as I can recall it, was very different from what it later became on Saint Helena. The Emperor was stoic, even defiant. He had suffered a major reversal, yes, he was stunned and morose, but he did not believe the situation was hopeless, irreversible. He had come back from incredible odds before. He awaited something like Murat's cavalry charge at the Battle of Eylau."

"When did he lose hope?"

"Over the first year in Longwood House, I think. You'll see. The place exudes hopelessness. Never was a prison better chosen."

"You mean, Longwood House, or the island itself?"

"Both. Longwood somehow is the desolation within the desolation. The island itself, you know, is as close to the middle of nowhere as anyone could imagine. It's hard to say even whether it belongs in Africa or the Americas, it floats off somewhere in between. Once there, you soon come to know you will never leave. I think that is what happened to the Emperor. At first, he would ride restlessly around the Devil's Punch Bowl—as far as Lowe would allow him to go—then gradually he began to stay closer to Longwood and its gardens. You should ask Gourgaud, and Bertrand—especially Bertand. He was there to the very end. Gourgaud left in 1818, he couldn't face the idea of captivity unto death."

"Bertrand is very moving, in his stories of the last days."

"The replay of Waterloo?"

"Yes, how Napoleon toward the end would come back to it every evening. He would always pick it up at the same place, with Grouchy's troops moving into position against Blücher's Prussians, holding them so that Ney's assault on Wellington's line came off victorious."

"As if the retelling could alter the outcome, remake history."

"It would have required so little for the outcome to be different."

"So you say. So he thought, too. He never could understand how he lost at Waterloo. But I don't know. If he had won at Waterloo, he would have been defeated elsewhere, in the following weeks. There were too many nations leagued against him by that point."

"Maybe. And yet, doesn't Wellington's victory strike you as largely dumb luck?"

Emmanuel gazed out to sea for a moment before answering. "What I see is something else, some sort of an inevitability. Napoleon arose from the Revolution, at a moment when no one could bring it to an end. He fired on the Paris mob, and then gave strong institutional support to the ideas of the Revolution, all the while keeping the people under an iron fist. And exported those ideas throughout a Europe still largely ruled by feudal monarchs. He was necessary, like a scouring hurricane that cleans out the seaweed beds. He could not last, not in that form at least. Probably we are happier under our less than heroic current regime."

Philippe glanced round, though he knew there was no chance that Joinville was anywhere other than on the afterdeck.

"You're not afraid that this mission of ours won't be the doom of our less than heroic regime?"

"No, not really. It should work as a reconciliation. Louis-Philippe reaching out to say to his fellow citizens: the Emperor is ours, all of ours. He is no longer excluded from the march of French history, as the Bourbon Restoration tried to exclude him. You know, all those who referred to him only as *Buonaparte,* as the "usurper," as the "monster.""

Philippe knew only too well. "Remember, my father . . ."

"Yes, an émigré?"

Philippe nodded. "Yes, I was raised to loathe Napoleon, to believe only in *legitimate* monarchy." He smiled ruefully. "Nothing could be more unexpected than being emissary on a mission to fetch back his decayed remains."

Emmanuel's broad face now relaxed into a smile. "And you find yourself surrounded by these living remains, Bertrand and Gourgaud and the rest, all still babbling about what the Emperor said to them. Very strange for you. But I think they're harmless, these relics. It's just that they have never really awaked from the spell he cast on them."

"Was he so extraordinarily magnetic in person, then?"

"Oh yes. That is something you have to understand. He had a way of making everyone who followed him feel he was part of a kind of extraordinary family. He had a word for everyone, a smile even for the gardener. He knew their names, he knew their children's names, and asked after them, he knew what kind of tobacco they liked. He was . . . well, he was really an Italian *padrone* in many ways. He cared for the immediate family he gathered around him—those who were faithful to him. And of course the soldiers felt it also. He was their god on earth."

Philippe stared at this image a moment. "You must feel the difference between that and what you are part of now."

"You mean our fine constitutional monarchy, with its two chambers and its elections and its politics of finding the middle way in everything?" Emmanuel paused, then lowered his voice. "Chabot, I like you. I think I can be frank with you. I have thrived under this regime, and I like it just because it is not glorious. I think it's the best we can do. The kind of regime that divides us least, that blurs those fault lines and fissures that beset our countrymen. After Napoleon, after the attempt to turn back the clock and bring back the Bourbon monarchy, France needed to relax. That's what Louis-Philippe represents: a lowering of the tension."

Philippe considered. "No more eagles, no more trumpets."

"Exactly." Here Emmanuel reached out and put his hand on Philippe's shoulder. "And a chance for someone like yourself, descended from the old aristocracy, to sit fraternally with the likes of Thiers and Guizot and build a peaceful world."

Emmanuel was a sixteen-year-old page to the Emperor during the Hundred Days, that last campaign, following his escape from Elba, which ended at Waterloo. His father, the Comte de Las Cases, had stood among the few faithful when the Emperor left Rochefort to surrender to the English, and then volunteered to share the exile. So Emmanuel went to Saint Helena. There he stayed for some eighteen months, taking dictation from the Emperor himself—Emmanuel became his favorite secretary, the one who could stay up the latest without nodding off, as Napoleon refought from memory the glorious Italian campaign, the

Egyptian expedition. Then one day Sir Hudson Lowe arrested them both on the charge of carrying on a ciphered correspondence about plans for Napoleon's escape. As if you could escape from nowhere. So the two Las Cases were held incommunicado for a month, then shipped off the island and landed at Capetown, from where they had laboriously made their way back to France. There, the Comte finished writing and published the *Mémorial de Sainte-Hélène,* and almost by himself created the cult that gave the Man of Destiny a permanent place in the imagination of the nation.

Philippe was determined to understand. He asked Emmanuel over and over again to explain. Emmanuel had inherited the cult. He had even asked the British in 1819 for permission to return to the desolate Saint Helena—permission refused. Then, when Sir Hudson Lowe returned to London following his captive's death in 1821, Emmanuel decided the moment had come to avenge the insult done his father—and as well no doubt the six years of insult inflicted by Lowe on Napoleon. In disguise he traveled to London. He paced restlessly in Hyde Park for four days. Finally, Lowe appeared. When his carriage came to a halt in the press, Emmanuel leaped to its steps and struck Lowe full in the face with his riding crop, threw his calling card—on which he had penned in the name of his London hotel—into the carriage, and strode rapidly away. For the next week, he waited in vain for Lowe to appear in response to his challenge. Nothing. The coward turned instead to the law courts—Emmanuel learned that he risked being arrested for assault. So he donned his false beard and his cloak once more, and made his way back to France by way of Hook of Holland. That was not the end of the matter, though. Three years later, he was attacked one night in a Passy street near his father's home by two toughs armed with knives. He escaped with a minor slash on the thigh, and wounded one of the men. Lowe was known to be in Paris at the time. He had been expelled from his London club. He never reaped the rewards he thought his due for torturing the fallen Emperor.

I am not part of this, Philippe told himself over and over. This is someone else's story, another generation's story. What am I doing in the midst of it? Sometimes he felt as if he had wandered into the wrong novel, a military and naval tale whose heroes had swords dangling at their sides and whose idea of conversation was the endless debate of tactics. Tactics of the past— they were always replaying the battles won, and the ones that should have been won but were lost through some inadvertence that memory could correct. And always in this novel the figure of the Emperor, like the minotaur in the heart of the labyrinth, he thought, the unappeasable figure—monster?—who needed more flesh, whom they bowed down to in worship even in defeat. Even in death.

Emmanuel was a somewhat different case, though. He was younger—though still some fifteen years older than Philippe— and with a career in the new France, not simply the cultivation of nostalgia for the Empire. The Revolution of 1830 allowed Emmanuel to give up the role of condottiere of the Emperor's memory, to take up arms and then to enter politics. Elected to the Assembly, he joined the centrists around Casimir-Périer, and was returned at every subsequent election. So he traveled on the *Belle Poule* not only as a bearer of the glorious memory but as a part of the political caste. He and Philippe found common ground in the delicate balances of foreign affairs, especially the worsening situation in the Near East, where war seemed imminent. But the talk would reach a frustrating impasse from the lack of recent news. The newspapers they had seen in their stop at Cádiz had been useless.

And as the days and evenings wore on, Philippe began to let go of some of his resistance, to let himself fall under the sway of Emmanuel's explanations of the legend. He began to accept with more tolerance this practice of a pagan cult at which he was not a communicant. When, after the toast to the King that ended the captain's mess, Bertrand and Gourgaud and Las Cases sat over their cognac and evoked evenings in Longwood House, the words spoken by the Emperor, his judgments on history, on the nation, on his rise and his fall and his legacy, he sat back to listen, not to judge.

Over his companion's arm, Philippe could see that the Canaries had faded into a cloud bank. Alone again on the never-ending sea. He sighed. There was now something unpleasant to be done. Couldn't be delayed too much longer.

Emmanuel twisted round, to pull the bulky packing case that lay behind his left elbow forward in front of them. It was stamped with his name and, in several places, the word "Fragile."

"What's in that, if I may ask?"

"I was just going to show you, though now I'm not sure I should unpack it on deck. Or even at all before we reach Saint Helena. It's one of Monsieur Daguerre's cameras, a particularly fine one, with an extra-heavy walnut box to resist warping in the humidity."

"You know how to use it, then?"

Emmanuel nodded. "It's not difficult, just a bit fastidious. The timing is everything. Anyway, my idea is to set it up when we reach the tomb, and record all that happens there."

Philippe considered. "A rather macabre set of plates, I should think."

"But think how historic. And if the coffin is opened . . . and the Emperor really is there, in whatever form . . ." His gaze became intently focused on a phantom in his mind's eye.

"Very well, but be prepared for disappointment. Ashes to ashes, dust to dust. After nearly twenty years in the grave, there cannot be much left."

"To be sure, to be sure. And even if there is something worth recording, I'm not certain the coffin can stay open long enough for a satisfactory exposure."

Philippe looked out over the sea behind them. Was Emmanuel expecting that the Emperor's spirit would etch a ghostly image on the plate?

Teneriffe had sunk fully beneath the horizon. Time to obey his instructions.

"Now that we've made our last port of call in our own hemisphere, I have a difficult duty to perform. I think I'd better get it out of the way now."

Emmanuel raised his eyebrows. His mild brown eyes were quizzical.

"A sealed letter from Monsieur Thiers, to deliver to Joinville. His secret instructions. I'm not entirely comfortable with being Monsieur Thiers' messenger boy, I think he could have addressed himself to the Prince directly."

"Ah, but you know Thiers' motto: The King reigns, but does not rule."

"But it's not certain the King and the Prince see it that way. Anyway, I take leave of you now, though I very much want to continue this later. I need to know more about what to expect on Saint Helena."

Emmanuel gestured at the empty horizon. "We'll have time. Go do Monsieur Thiers' bidding."

Philippe rose. He stared for a moment at the open space amidships, where the decking had been removed so as to create a sort of hollow square on the gun deck, open to the sky. There it sat, the immense mahogany sarcophagus, with its inscription engraved in gold letters: NAPOLEON. The frigate was a kind of hearse-ship, bearing this empty coffin to the end of the earth, to stash whatever remained of Napoleon's body in it, to bring it back to France. A kind of primitive ancestor worship, he thought.

And he was in absolute command of all this, as Joinville would soon know from Thiers' sealed letter.

He descended the companionway to his cabin, opened his sea trunk and then the attaché case. He had a moment's anxiety as he opened the case. Yes, the letter was there, the seal intact. He grasped it and made his way back on deck, and to the poop.

Joinville was at his customary station, standing with Hernoux a few steps behind the helmsman. Philippe found himself wondering at Joinville's capacity to stand for hours on end, in a posture of command, scanning the sea and the sky and the sails—all sails set now, drawing well in the moderate breeze—without betraying boredom. He saluted.

"Captain, may I have a word with you, perhaps in your cabin?"

Joinville frowned at the request, then noticed the letter Philippe held at his side, and smiled graciously, fingering his whiskers. "To be sure. Hernoux, take the command while I go down with Chabot."

"Aye, aye, sir."

Down the companionway again, then a left turn and into the vast low-ceilinged cabin that extended across the whole stern of the ship. Philippe held forth Thiers' letter. "The President of the Council asked that I give you this letter in person only after our last landfall, when we were fully at sea. I obey his orders."

Joinville took the letter, broke the seal. He motioned to Philippe to sit, so they both took places at the long dining table, on opposite sides. Philippe knew the contents of the letter—though he could not tell with what diplomacy Thiers might have couched it—and knew it could not be a pleasure for Joinville to read. He rested his eyes on the ground, concentrated on the caulked seams of the new planking of the cabin floor as Joinville perused the pages.

Joinville brought the flat of his hand down on the table with a thud. He doesn't like it, Philippe thought. Didn't think he would.

"Cedant arma togae." Joinville spoke in a hollow voice. "Or as you might say, naval command humiliated by the politicians." He was fingering his whiskers again. "Damnation. This contradicts the most precise orders I had from my father. It's an act of insubordination to the ship's captain, as well as to a prince royal." He paused. "You know what it says?" He held forth the letter.

"I know its message, sire. Thiers gave me my instructions also."

Joinville's face was flushed. "Not to have said anything to me before, to have led me to believe that I was in charge of this . . . this mission of undertakers, grave robbers . . . and then to tell me, when I cannot reply, cannot protest, that you are his delegate plenipotentiary, that you are to command the whole land operation. Has he no shame?"

"Sire, please understand that I was formally forbidden from raising this subject with you until now. I must obey the orders of His Majesty's government."

Joinville turned, and moved to the windows in the stern. He stood with his back to Philippe, as if absorbed in the ship's wake, opening behind in glittering furrows.

He turned slowly, and threw the letter on the table. "And so must I," he said.

With a visible effort, he composed his face and straightened his shoulders. "Chabot, let us understand each other. I think we know and trust one another. It shall be as Monsieur Thiers orders. I command the ship, you command the expedition on land and all negotiations with the English. Let us never speak of this difficult matter again. And let our friendship not suffer from it."

He held out his hand, which Philippe grasped firmly, with a sense of relief. "Nobly spoken, sire."

"Curses on the political men, anyway. I'll never trust Thiers again." Then he changed the subject. "You and I haven't had a chance to talk since you stopped in to see me the day after you got back from London. Like shipboard?"

"Well enough. A bit of boredom, to be sure."

"And of homesickness, no doubt. Do you find yourself missing Amélie?"

Philippe felt the heat rise to his face. "Is the news circulating that we are engaged? Because, you see, we're not."

Joinville's face expressed concern. "I hope I haven't been indiscreet. It's . . . well, yes, I think it's generally assumed in Paris."

"Premature, at best. I just don't know where we stand."

Joinville's face encouraged further speech, and Philippe would have liked to make him a confidant. They were almost old friends, or at least men who had known each other as boys. But the young Prince—three years his junior—wasn't the counselor he needed, and besides, there were the issues of command separating them. Philippe drew himself up, smiled, and tried to pass it off lightly. "Women are a mystery, sire. I'll have to wait for our return for further explanations."

He moved toward the cabin door, to make his departure. Joinville stepped toward him, and grasped his hand. "To be sure. But Philippe, remember that while we are commissioners of the King and of his government, we still can be friends."

"Yes, sire. Thank you."

Philippe slipped from the cabin, and made his way back on deck. Still the unending horizon of deep green sea, the wind now freshening, flecking the waves with whitecaps. He would have liked to think of something else, but the parting from Amelia surged back into his mind. Nothing resolved.

Amelia. He now saw her face at their parting as both tense and determined. Above all, it just would not leave his mind. If social ambition were the thing, he could do better. There were all those daughters of the Duc de Broglie, the flower of French society, Protestants like his own family, with estates all over France. There were the lovely Scottish sisters, daughters of the Earl of Moray, he had met when he traveled to the Isle of Skye. He remembered an afternoon wandering the beach near Portray with Priscilla and Antonia, aged seventeen and nineteen, both utterly charming under their straw summer hats, their lithe and full bodies suddenly brought to his attention as Priscilla skipped a stone into the water, arching her back and flinging her arm upward, as Antonia unexpectedly sat herself on the beach, unlaced her boots, flung them aside, and, her skirts raised to her knees, trotted into the water with shouts of laughter. They were charming. And yes, there was a kind of naturalness about them. He could imagine—he felt his face flushing, and warmth suffusing his body. Yes, he had imagined it, pushing Antonia down on the warm sand. He felt a surge of arousal. Yet maybe Priscilla was really more desirable, taller, more muscular, with an utterly frank smile.

He could summon Antonia and Priscilla to mind, but always Amelia was already there, unbidden. How much was she her mother's daughter? he wondered. There was something wrong about the Countess Curial. There were rumors about her reputation—from long in the past, to be sure—and she had a kind of edginess to her. He was never at ease with her, she never seemed at ease with anyone, though she was charming and gracious with him. In fact, she had flirted with him, and that made him uncomfortable. The idea of a liaison with the Countess did not arouse, on the contrary. It was a somewhat fearsome thought. That would be . . . like going to bed with a tempest, he decided, something that would end in shipwreck.

So was that what was wrong with Amelia as well? A sense that love for her opened through some dark portal into the unimaginable?

He could not work it out.

Terrace at Castelgandolfo

THEY STOOD on the terrace of the Villa Cini in Castelgandolfo, watching the afterglow of the sunset. Down below them, to their right, the waters of Lake Albano had become a deep purple. A belated fishing boat, its sails slack in the nearly windless air, drifted toward the shore. When they turned to their left, they could see Rome, some fifteen miles distant, in a dusky haze on the horizon. Lights were beginning to appear. Then more flickered on. As they watched, the whole city became festooned with lights. They gradually merged into an orange glow.

The stones of the terrace held the heat, while the air was quickly cooling as night descended. It would be time to pass through the immense glass doors into the salon, where he knew the Countess would be pouring coffee, while Domenico passed small glasses of grappa. This perfectly orchestrated life of the Roman *villegiatura* was about to end for him—one more day of absence from his post and he knew the gathering storm prepared by Tavernier would be about his ears. He must go back.

Amelia spoke in unison with his thoughts. "You really must leave us tomorrow?"

Beyle turned to her. Amelia still wore black, this evening a long dress that fell from her shoulders in the back and was cut square in the front, showing the fine muscular form of her shoulders, and its waist was molded to the lithe slimness of her torso. The more he saw of her, he decided, the less she really looked like Menti. She was smaller than her mother, her face was softer, rounder, though with the same decided chin and fine nose. Her expression could be almost fierce at times, but never Menti's wild, disoriented look. Her eyes, under their rich smudges of eyebrows, glowed at him in the darkening atmosphere.

"Yes," said Beyle. "Neglect of duty is a finely tuned instrument I have learned to make the utmost use of, but it requires a certain discipline, you see."

"What great French interests are at stake in Civitavecchia that require the presence of Monsieur le Consul himself?"

"Trade in cod. An international crisis in the making. Contraband from Sardinia, utterly shocking, you know."

"I disbelieve everything you say. I think you are bored here, and want to go back to writing those wicked novels you sign with your pen name."

"No, no. I speak only the absolute bureaucratic truth. To maintain myself in my luxurious consulate, I am required to write twenty letters a day about fisheries, about pozzolana ash, to count the number of ships coming and going from the port with the greatest exactitude, and in general to perform a thousand stultifying tasks."

"And the novels?"

Beyle thought with a pang of his latest manuscript, about a young woman named Lamiel—Amelia in fact had something of her spirit—and his utter inability to bring it to a conclusion. "The novels. I think they have to await a leave from my post. It was only in Paris, on my last long leave, that I could finish the *Charterhouse*. It takes . . . a certain concentration of attention." He smiled ironically at his own sententiousness. "Or at least, you know, nothing else to do. Closing oneself in a garret."

"And here you waste your time in frivolities."

"Oh, waste! Where is the waste? Nothing more profitable. The food of the spirit."

"Really? Because you intend to put us all in your next novel?"

"Of course. It will begin on a terrace in Castelgandolfo, with a beautiful and mysterious young woman dressed in black, with glorious dark eyes and remarkable eyebrows, pacing pensively."

He could make out the sparkle of her teeth—with that curious and ever so appealing gap between the two front teeth—as she smiled in the darkness. She moved closer to him. "And then, a handsome young *carbonaro* appears, having climbed up the wall."

"Quite. All unshaven and unkempt. He's escaped from prison. From the Castel San'Angelo."

"In order to make the revolution, to unite Italy."

He smiled. "So that is the man you want, a dashing political prisoner devoting his life to Italian independence?"

She thought for a moment. When she spoke, it was not exactly to answer his question. "I should not mind being the heroine of one of your novels."

"Ah, but you see, the novelist knows everything that is going on in the head of his heroine. Her most secret thoughts, the wishes she cannot speak."

"So much the better. Then you might know how to please her."

"Please *her,* yes. Because she is my creature. Created out of my own desires. But does that mean I know anything about pleasing a real woman, one whose mind is walled off from me?"

Her face was now tensed, intent. "Do you think that in imagining your women, your heroines, you reach some truth about what a woman really wants?"

He thought of Lamiel. Did any real woman behave that way—hiring a rustic to teach her about love? A woman according to his own heart, perhaps, but never met in reality. "Can a man ever know that?"

"Men are so stupid. At least the ones my age. They speak of their eternal devotion, their desire for a future of domestic bliss. Slavery and more slavery. Boredom."

"But what would you have them say? Promise you a life of infidelity, of changing emotions?"

"No. Promise me adventure. Worlds to conquer."

"I begin to think you should have been born a man."

"You don't like me as I am?"

She now turned to stand square before him, her face pale and intent in the dim light. She was beautiful.

"Of course I do. You have the spirit I always dreamed of in a woman. If ever you can find the right man, he will be a most fortunate fellow. I envy him already."

Her face was searching his, he thought, as she stood silent before him. Then she said, "Why must you talk of another man?"

He felt a rush of desire, and at the same time a kind of tremulous timidity, as if he were forty years younger, falling in love for the first time. What did she mean? Could she really be offering herself to him, to his leathery old self, thickset and balding?

He stood stock-still for a moment. Then he said, "I am nearly as old as your father, you know, and all told hardly a suitable match."

"I know. But it doesn't matter. I find you more alive than most of the perfect and perfectly insipid men my age."

She reached out and touched his arm, then grasped it just above the elbow. He felt an iron will in her fingers. She didn't pull him toward her, but he felt her wish that he come closer. Still he did not move.

"Amelia, do you know what you are saying? It would be madness, you know."

"Do you mean you don't find me desirable? Not up to the standards of Stendhal's heroines?"

His resistance, which a moment before had seemed heroic, necessary, gave way, and he folded her in his arms. Her lips fumblingly sought his. They stood embraced for a moment. Then both of them, as if remembering where they were, broke from the embrace and stepped back from one another.

"Amelia." He paused. "I adore you. But can this be? I cannot let myself. The Countess would never forgive me, I would never forgive myself."

"But if it is what I want?" She tossed her head. "It's what I need. It's the only thing."

He nodded. "Yes, and it would be truly lovely. For now. But the consequences would be dire, for you."

"While there are never any consequences for men?"

"Oh, you have no idea. When you left me, when you were through with me—as would happen, you know—I would be destroyed utterly."

Her smile was radiant. "Am I then so desirable?"

"Completely. I am mad about you."

"Then why the worry about consequences? It is what you want, it is what I want. Surely we are not so stupid we can't make it happen."

His mind was a jumble of images, of Amelia in his arms, of the Countess in a rage, of Amelia standing alone and forlorn on a street corner in Paris. But still he could think with some lucidity. "My dearest Amelia, I don't say no. How could I? You are the woman I have always longed for. But we must reflect. Nothing can be done here in Castelgandolfo in any event."

She turned from him, frowning, and walked to the balustrade. He waited for her to speak, but she said nothing.

He moved to where she stood, gazing out toward the orange glow of Rome in the distance. "Amelia. We must meet again, and soon. In Paris."

She turned around, and he could see that she was anxious for reassurance.

"In Paris," he repeated.

"Will you really come to Paris? Can you? Soon?"

He now heard a rustle in the curtain window behind them. He spoke quickly. "Yes. I'll manage. We'll meet there. Then we'll see."

A footstep sounded on the tiles of the terrace. The Count was approaching. They both turned, and prepared to go in.

(This has been the most difficult of all so far. This had to be Beyle's scene, so I've had to hold back from asserting my own point of view. But I fear I may come across as a spoiled child, leading him on simply from boredom and curiosity. Curiosity, yes, certainly is part of it. I need to know. And he would be perfect for that. Even his irony suits my wish that it be love for the sake of knowing. But this isn't just idle curiosity. I want to know him better as well, to have some idea of what goes on in that inventive mind of his. There is some better form of life, some more challenging way to be, concealed here. It's just not open to young women of my society. To get to it—to get beyond the prescripted life that bores me in advance, no, that truly terrifies me—I need Beyle. As well as a pleasure for him, it's my own best chance. Egotists all, the best we can do is make sure our own needs don't get in the way of other people's pursuit of happiness.)

He replayed the scene on the terrace over and over again during
the night in his rococo bedroom, and then again during the long
coach journey back to Civitavecchia. He didn't see Amelia in the
morning. She had not come down before it was time for him to
leave.

When he reached Civitavecchia, night had fallen. So much
the better, Beyle thought. The place looks better when you can't
see it. And he turned from the window with a sigh that he recognized as theatrical. He was behaving like an adolescent in love.

Can it be that she loves me?

A difficult decision was before him. Supposing that he could
get another leave for two months—not impossible, if he pulled
the right strings—it still was not the wisest course. A couple of
months away, Tavernier would be in a position to denounce him
triumphantly to Latour-Maubourg, the French Ambassador in
Rome. Latour-Maubourg treated him with remarkable affa-
bility and tact, and seemed to understand that a man of spirit
could not live uninterruptedly in a hole like Civitavecchia, but
still there were limits. And then there was Giulia, always ready
to fix another rendezvous in Siena. That was the easy love, the
reasonable love, love consented to, a blessed oasis in the desert
of his existence, for her a chosen margin to her marriage. They
understood the limits to their claims on one another.

Whereas Amelia . . . The surge of excitement swept through
him again, followed by a tremor of doubt. Sheer bliss, and then
what? Well, there was always the solution of marriage. An
absurd idea. He would be a laughingstock. Something from a
Molière play, the old man cuckolded by the young wife whom he
had snatched away from the young suitors. But if Amelia really
wanted him? Yes, but despite her spirit and her knowingness,
wasn't she too inexperienced to be sure of what she wanted? Yet
why should he turn away from what she offered? He was not

going to start playing the altruist at his age. Still, do no harm. To be kind was necessary to his inner peace.

Next morning, as he stood before the shaving mirror—he had shaved himself ever since his campaigns with the army, finding this much simpler than waiting for the barber—he attempted an assessment of his face. He recalled the words of his first serious love, Mélanie the actress, who so many years ago had said to him: You are ugly, but no woman will ever hold that against you, because your face is interesting, witty, and kind. With what remained of his hair brushed forward, Roman style, he didn't look too frightful. The high rounded forehead did, he supposed, look intelligent, the asymmetrical eyebrows—one cocked higher than the other—might pass as witty, or grotesque in an unkind view. The nose was hopelessly broad, but it lent gravity to the face, along with the massive chin. The lips were maybe the best feature: thin, mobile, with a constant stamp of irony to them. Hardly the face of a romantic hero. It would do—it would have to do.

The shaving ritual scarcely over, as he sat with his morning coffee at the desk once again covered with neat but ominously high stacks of paper, Tavernier, with the inevitability of a figure in a Boulevard farce, scratched at the door. His rodent face appeared, then he edged into the room.

He began by making clucking noises over the piles on the desk, as if he hadn't himself put them there, or as if he expected they would have disappeared overnight. He mentioned the codfish problem, then wanted to discuss the accuracy of the figures on tonnage of ships entering and leaving during the past month. But his cunning face and restless manner suggested he had something else in view. He finally came to the point: word had come from the Vatican that some *carbonari* had slipped into the Papal States on the *Méditerranée,* bound from Marseille. These were, according to the papal spies, a group of ardent Bonapartist revolutionaries who had supported Louis-Napoléon's ill-fated attempt at a coup in Boulogne. Everyone knew, of course, that Louis-Napoléon was himself a *carbonaro,* part of a vast network of conspirators who wanted to overthrow legitimate governments throughout Europe—in Italy, to chase out the Austrians and wrest control from the Pope.

So there was a clutch of revolutionaries at large somewhere in the Papal States. Beyle could not bring himself to worry overmuch about that. A matter for the police, or rather, the polices, since there were several. He only hoped the poor fellows might stay out of their clutches. Imprisonment in the Castel San'Angelo was no joke. Few ever reemerged.

But Tavernier did not stop there. According to his sources, the French Consul in Civitavecchia, Signor Beyle—well known moreover for his revolutionary sympathies and his visits to Lucien Bonaparte, Napoleon's brother, in nearby Canino—had secretly conspired to let these undesirables land from the *Méditerranée.* Indeed, he was accused of having furnished them with false passports. Tavernier thought it likely a letter was on its way from the Curia to Latour-Maubourg, demanding that Beyle's credentials be revoked.

This was too much. Beyle brought his fist down on the table. "A pack of lies, as you know perfectly well. Why do you come in here with this nonsense to report?"

"Nonsense, sir?" Tavernier screwed his face sideways, his eyebrows contracted in a quizzical expression.

What a charlatan. Tavernier knew perfectly well that Beyle's visits to Canino were for shooting and to pursue the archaeological digs nearby. Or did he?

"Nonsense, to be sure, sir. But you will have to see the Monsignore, to clear this up, sir. To clear our name."

Our name? Tavernier now identified himself with the consulate? Decidedly, there was trouble in the offing. And there was the matter of Lucien Bonaparte's son, Pierre-Napoléon, who had barely escaped execution for slicing up a gamekeeper who had caught him poaching, and who made no secret of his escapades among the *carbonari*. He lived as a kind of brigand in the mountains. That he had something to do with the attempt on Boulogne wasn't altogether implausible. And Beyle had spent many an evening with him in the hunting lodge above Canino.

An immense weariness descended through his body. He felt old, abandoned. Was the one secure position he had ever won for himself to be lost because of his association with these remnants of the Bonapartes? They were harmless enough. Yet it was true that they had never accepted the post-Waterloo European order. They were always involved in one conspiracy or another, and it was just his luck to be implicated. The Bonaparte legacy seemed fated to keep him from happiness, one way or another. He knew it was the same for many men of his generation. They had come of age with Napoleon, they had entered the century with him, risen with his fortunes, fallen into platitude with his fall. A legacy you couldn't do anything with, but which wouldn't quite go away. They even had to send a young diplomat and a clutch of old relics to bring back the corpse.

Where were they now, those voyagers of *La Belle Poule?* In some hopeless immensity of sea still. Nothing he could imagine—he had never made an ocean voyage—and nothing worth imagining. Still, he must find time to think of that again, to create in the sphere of his mind the voyage out, and that young man surrounded by an alien yet living past. Worth a novel still, if he could only bring himself to write adventure stories. Stories that might even sell.

All right. He must summon Monsignor Delicata. Over tea, they would with all due circumspection move from the weather to the splendid ceremony in Rome for the new cardinals, to trade through the port to the question of the *Méditerranée* and her passengers. He would assure the Pope's legate that he was distressed to hear the rumors that . . . He would give assurances that his correspondents in Marseille formally denied the presence on board of anyone not on the *vapore*'s manifest—a well-regulated port, Marseille (here Delicata would raise his eyebrows, quite legitimately)—and that Monsignore should know the Consul of the King of the French exercised the utmost vigilance in surveillance of the comings and goings in his port. Why, he could show Monsignore ten thick folio volumes of spy reports—no, better not say that, even though Delicata must know of the counteragents funded by the Consul to keep tabs on the papal spies. The conversation would end inconclusively, but with Delicata exhorting him to greater zeal, and Beyle promising a thorough shakedown of the port authorities (as if that were possible, as if he had any power in the matter). And then they would talk again about the magnificent ceremony in Rome, quite the most splendid event either of them had witnessed.

He became aware that Tavernier was hovering, a habit he detested. It consisted of his shifting his weight from foot to foot while performing a slow, almost imperceptible shuffle that eventually would take him from the corner of the desk to Beyle's left to that on his right, all the while holding his arms in a kind of circle, fingertips pressed against one another, with his head twisted to one side. Why couldn't he hold his head upright? A sign of his deviousness, clearly.

"Very well then. I shall take care of it."

"May I inquire how, sir?"

By what rights did Tavernier deserve an explanation? Beyle fought back his temptation to collar the man and defenestrate him. "It's all right. I shall arrange a meeting with Monsignor Delicata, and we'll come to an understanding."

Tavernier's mouth cracked into something like a crooked grin, though it passed in an instant. His mouth returned to its usual obsequious yet exasperated and even slightly insolent expression.

"Allow me to remind you, sir, that the Monsignore is currently in Rome, and does not return here until the end of month. Will you be traveling to Rome to see him?"

Beyle sensed a trap. Yes, he supposed he should go to Rome to meet with Delicata to prevent this affair from festering. But now his heart was more and more set on another, longer trip: Paris. And why did Tavernier want him gone when he had just come back?

"If you go to Rome, sir, I imagine you could return by way of Siena?"

The viper. Beyle felt his face heating, from rage, from embarrassment, too. So that was it: Tavernier knew about Giulia Rinieri. How? Had he been reading Beyle's correspondence? More likely he was in touch with the Florentine spies. That man with the dirty fingernails.

"Siena? I don't take your meaning."

Tavernier continued his shuffle. He had now reached midpoint on the other side of the desk, directly opposite Beyle. But his shifty eyes would not focus on his interlocutor's.

"Only, sir, that it would be well to know in advance where I might reach you, should the need arise. Last time you were in Siena, His Excellency the Ambassador sent an express, you recall, and I was at a loss to know what to do."

The devil you were, thought Beyle. You managed to make the most of my absence, to put yourself forward as indispensable, and make me look irresponsible.

He said nothing. He sat looking grimly across the desk, with a face designed to discourage any further communication.

But Tavernier was not finished. "It would be better, sir, if we could understand each other. I am, you know, quite willing to act in the Consul's stead. But a clearer delegation of powers would be helpful. Or perhaps if you wished to remain here, or be else-where, I should make the trip to meet with the Monsignore."

For what does this knave take himself? Let him become the liaison with Delicata and the Vatican? Here at least, in this busi-ness Beyle was finding more and more unfathomable, was some-thing on which he could be decisive. "Where Monsignor Delicata is concerned, the Consul himself must speak. You understand, do you not, that you are in charge of current affairs, not diplo-matic missions."

"To be sure. And yet"—here Tavernier's quasi-grin reappeared—"you should understand that I have excellent rela-tions with the Monsignore. He honors me with his confidence."

What did this mean? Yes, it all fit together, as in the affair last year of the books and manuscripts he had shipped from Paris, which were searched by the Vatican's secret police. Who had tipped them off? He had always suspected Tavernier. If he entertained relations with Delicata, who surely had contacts with the Grand Duke's spies . . . and then his knowledge of the ren-dezvous with Giulia would come from this source too.

Beyle rose from behind his desk, and leaned forward. Sur-prised, Tavernier shuffled back a pace.

"It is indeed time to understand each other. Remember, then, that I took you on despite my predecessor's warning that I would regret it. Remember that I had you promoted from simple sec-retary to chancellor. That I gave you your decoration"—most unwillingly, he added to himself—"and treated you as a man of substance despite the mess you made of our accounts. Watch yourself. I am perfectly willing to allow you your full powers as chancellor. But I am the Consul. Absent or present. Diplomacy is my matter. And your spying will do you no good. I have the confidence of the Minister, and if I have to have you sacked, I can and I will. I'll handle Delicata in my way. Now go back to your accounts, and get them right this time."

By now he was bellowing, and he felt sweat begin to trickle under his shirt collar. But he read fear in Tavernier's eyes. The Chancellor bowed, and withdrew.

Like all insidious bullies, Tavernier was a coward. There was at least that to count on. Though as he settled heavily into his chair, aware that his heart was pounding, Beyle realized his victory was only temporary, and possibly costly. How was he now going to get to Paris? Well, that would have to be postponed. First, back to Rome—but a Rome now without Amelia. A circuit via Siena on the way back? He meditated, calling up the image of Giulia's curls spread across the pillow. But the image did not move him. He wanted to see Amelia again. Yes, a leave in Paris would be necessary. It should be possible by late November. He must go.

He found his heart pounding again, but this time not from anger at Tavernier. It was rather from the question that pushed its way into his mind despite his efforts to keep it at bay. Does she love me?

❦ 10 ❧

Visitor at the Villa

NGELICA HAD helped Amelia and her maid in the packing, and now everything looked ready. She was to leave early the next morning for Paris, while the Cinis made their way back to Rome, with the promise to visit her in Paris within a few weeks. Despite the tedium of the trip ahead, Amelia was glad to be traveling alone, accompanied only by her maid Berthe. She couldn't deal with visitors in Paris at the moment. Her father would be problem enough. She reproached herself with having left him alone for so long in his bereavement. Yet she also knew what it would be like. He would be gone all day to his club, home only for a slightly mournful evening meal, during which he would put forth pieces of the day's news between long silences, while she tried to be cheerful and interested.

And what was she going to do with herself? What was a young woman in her position to do—play the piano, read poetry, and wait for a suitor to ask for her hand in marriage?

That would presumably come soon enough, when Philippe came back in December. That would have to be faced. She wished she knew him better. No, that was not quite it. She wished she knew if there was anything about him to know, if she could ever get beneath his good manners, his reserve, his capacity to be perfectly the good-looking young man.

She turned to the window. It overlooked the Cinis' formal garden—they had carefully chosen this room for her—with its alleys of cypresses leading to Neptune's fountain, the god rising on a chariot from the basin, surrounded by half-clad Nereids. Odd, all this nudity, in a country so otherwise straitlaced. Nude women, of course, not men. Though now she called to mind Michelangelo's *David* standing in the piazza in Florence. The thought made her smile. Not so long ago it might have made her flush in embarrassment, but now it just seemed something to be curious about. That's something you need to find out more about. It is time for some knowledge of men's bodies. High time you had a lover, she thought, as she gazed into the soft vaporous distance beyond the fountain, the hills, and then the *campagna*. A place of sweetness and repose. Paris would not be that. But might there be a chance for something more arousing, something to wake her from this somnambulistic life?

Well, there was Beyle, promising to come to Paris. Would he really? Did she really want him to? Did she really intend to take him as her lover? He was a bohemian, a writer—a really good one, she thought, but not a popular success—a restless man with no fixed abode, a consul, yes, but in a forsaken spot, a man without any real social position. And there were the insinuations dropped by the old Duchess of Monte Albano. What had she been trying to tell her? That Beyle had been her mother's lover? Was that possible?

Of course it was. By what instinct do we know our parents' past? she wondered. She had gleaned enough, protected though she was supposed to be from such knowledge, to suggest that her mother had not been a faithful wife. She had not wanted to admit this into her conscious knowledge, but as she delved into memory she knew it was there, as some combination of rumor and her own observation. Of her mother with other men, of her father's progressive withdrawal from life at the rue d'Antin. She had always been satisfied to describe her mother as flirtatious. But now she needed to unwrap the veils from this image. Yes, her mother could very well have been more than a flirt. Have taken lovers. Taken her clothes off, stood naked before them, gone to bed with them. She could not remember ever having seen her mother naked, but she could almost imagine it. She had had a strong physical presence from beneath her clothes. And she was rumored to have killed herself because of some man—Angelica, poor protected Angelica, had picked this up somewhere, whispered it to her, blushing.

So if lovers, why not Beyle after all? Then what did it mean that she herself had been virtually making indecent proposals to Beyle? Was she attracted to him because he had been her mother's lover, if that was the case? She shuddered. Surely not. She had no wish to imitate Clémentine. She detested her. No, of course she didn't. She felt sorrow and compassion for her mother, a woman possessed, unhappy, driven by demons she could not understand. But she had not been much of a mother. Too many images of her childhood could be summoned against her if she let herself travel that path. And that wretched moment when against all her wishing to the contrary she had discovered she was becoming a woman, and had no other recourse than Berthe, scarcely older than herself. As a child, she had always thought of herself as a boy, she realized. When forced to face the contrary truth, it had taken her months—years, really—to reconcile herself. And maybe that is why a man, a man's body, seems so necessary now, so much what I want. Part of myself. She smiled ruefully.

Beyle and her mother. No, there was no need to dig up that past. Let it be. What is gained from exhuming past history when it can do you no good? An obsession of her compatriots, always replaying the past, fighting its battles over again—look at the stupid expedition Philippe is on. To live in the present—to live the present as it deserves, letting it unfold minute by minute, undetermined, without thought for how you were supposed to be. That came from the past, how you were supposed to be. Throw out remorse, throw out convention. Live as your imagination allows you to, in affirmation of an unknowable future.

At least there is this, she said to herself as she surveyed the trunks once again. I have signed no contracts, made no promises. I have still myself to count on. And I am young. Yes, but what good does that do you if you spend your youth in boredom? And getting older, soon twenty-five. Almost an old spinster, in the eyes of the Cinis. Why wasn't she allowed to do anything?

Berthe was in the doorway, and just behind her was Domenico, the majordomo, a calling card in hand.

"Signorina, excuse me. There is a man downstairs who says he must see you. On an urgent matter."

"Oh. Who? I was not expecting anyone."

Domenico held out the calling card. She took it and read: Signor Egidio Daponte. Nothing more.

"I don't know this person. But if he says it's urgent, send him up."

Domenico bowed, and withdrew. Someone with a message from her father? she wondered.

A moment later Domenico reappeared, followed by a short man with a puglike face and pomaded hair and mustache, holding a walking stick in one hamlike fist. His clothing looked rumpled and far from fresh. She noticed his fingernails were dirty.

He bowed. "Signorina Curial?"

"Yes. What do you want with me?"

The man glanced uneasily at Berthe. "Might it be possible to have the briefest of interviews with you, alone?"

This was audacious, but she nodded to Berthe. "Wait in the next room, please."

Alone now with the stranger, she found him uglier and more sinister than she had realized.

"Signorina Curial. Beg pardon for the intrusion." His speech was slightly slurred, and it seemed to cost him a certain effort. "I am in the employ of the Grand Duke of Tuscany. And I have many relations in the Papal States. In Rome, in Civitavecchia, all over."

She was puzzled, and increasingly impatient.

"Yes? Well what do want with me?"

"Ah . . . I believe you are acquainted with a certain Signor Beyle, Consul of the King of the French in Civitavecchia, also a writer of books?"

"And if I am?"

"A delicate matter. Certain persons with the signorina's best interests at heart would wish to warn you. The aforementioned Signor Beyle is best approached warily. He entertains unhealthy relations, politically speaking. He is protected by his diplomatic immunity, of course, but that only stretches so far. He is not considered altogether a desirable personage in certain of our Italian states."

What was this all about? She wanted to question him, know where this undue solicitude for her acquaintance with Beyle was coming from. As if she had anything to do with Italian politics. But she could not bring herself to speak to such a creature.

"And also, the signorina might be interested to know that Signor Beyle entertains relations, of a—ah"—his face now flushed—"irregular kind. With a certain Signora Martini. I could of course furnish details—sordid details—but I would spare the signorina."

There was a long silence. She felt the pulse throbbing in her temples. She waited.

"Is that all you have to say?"

"Yes, signorina. But I do not know if you grasp the importance—"

"Get out. At once." She raised her voice. "Berthe!"

Berthe stepped into the room. The man looked flustered, he managed a bow.

"Very well. I shall leave at once. But I beg that you will weigh my words."

"Get out. Never come back. Berthe, make sure Domenico sees him out, with orders that he is never to be allowed back in the villa."

Another bow, and he was gone, Berthe marching behind him.

Who, why, what in all the world was this? Someone—some vile lackey, something like a spy—come to tell her that Beyle was politically suspect? All the world knew that. And that he had rendezvous with some woman, with a Signora Martini? Well, that would not be strange. An unmarried man living alone in Italy. But who was this Signora Martini? Something serious?

That wasn't really the point. Who caused this visit to happen? Who were these "certain persons"? What sinister hand was meddling in her affairs?

But she felt more vexed by the information brought by the vile Daponte than she wanted to be. Beyle with another woman—his mistress. He hadn't told her that. Oh, of course, that would be just the kind of thing he'd tell you. Was that why he hesitated when she had spoken out—declared herself, really, she told herself, almost pleased at her shamelessness. Yes, I offered myself to him, but now it turns out he has a mistress. As well has having been my mother's lover. This was all too much. Better to erase Beyle from her thoughts.

But should she believe the man with the dirty fingernails? Beyle might be a man of loose morals, a bohemian—of course he was, he was a writer after all—but still he seemed sincere with her. Seemed to desire her. The Signora Martini might be only his amusement. She herself would be something else. Though she didn't quite know how to name it.

She had no one to turn to. She couldn't take the Countess into her confidence—couldn't talk to her about Beyle's interest in herself—and hers in him. She felt at sea. She needed someone to guide her in all this, someone she could trust.

She wanted to be able to trust Beyle.

❧ II ❧

Excavations at Canino

I T HAD seemed wise at first, but now Beyle was less sure.
The idea was to make a brief excursion to Canino before
going to Rome to undertake conversations with Monsignor
Delicata. At Canino, he might learn more about the reality of
those *carbonari* allegedly implicated in Louis-Napoléon's escapade. And forget the insistent memory of Amelia in the Etruscan
digs. To plunge yourself in the distant past—into this mysterious civilization buried under the Roman—that was his standard
cure when the present exerted unpleasant pressures.

But Lucien was absent—gone to town to purchase draft
horses at the annual fair, he learned from Principino Charles,
his elder son, the unadventurous one who lived placidly on the
estates with his wife Zénaide and more children than Beyle could
count. Charles was affable, invited him to lunch and promised to
accompany him to the digs late in the afternoon, after the siesta,
when it cooled off.

They sat over coffee after lunch on the terrace overlooking the wooded hills. Beyle tried a few questions about Louis-Napoléon's adventure at Boulogne, but it was evident that Charles knew nothing, or else was expert at playing dumb. Nothing at any rate was forthcoming. He risked a question about Pierre-Napoléon, but all Charles would say was that his younger brother was now released from prison, and thought to be living in Rome. He claimed to know no more than that.

Charles retired with Zénaide for the siesta—Beyle wondered if it was the habit of the siesta that led to such a proliferation of children. Beyle said he preferred to sit rather than lie down. But once his hosts had disappeared, he rose and began to wander through the estate. Lucien lived in truly princely surroundings. A winding path led him through stately groves of cypress and olive, where fountains plashed, their mist grateful in the hot afternoon. The place had once been the site of a Roman villa, and after a few minutes of meandering he came upon three columns at the head of a rectangular pool, once the bathing place of some rich Roman—what? tax collector? The shimmering surface of the water led his eyes out toward the hills beyond, forested above, with cultivated fields below, rich in tall sunflowers. This was the Italy he loved. Why had he landed in Civitavecchia? A place unimaginable for a young woman such as Amelia. As if that were any sort of real possibility. Don't become a sentimental old fool. Love snatched on the fly, as with Giulia—that is what you have always known, that is probably all you will ever know, until love becomes impossible. Leave Amelia to the novelist's imagination. Get back to that unfinished story of Lamiel. Or write your sea story.

What today, in the immensity of sea and sky? Drill on the frigate, no doubt. Target practice. Captain Joinville orders the launches from the *Belle Poule* and the *Favorite* rowed out with targets constructed by the carpenters from wood and canvas.

Then the decks cleared for action, the cabins on deck emptied of furniture and folded down, enormous effort for an exercise, but Joinville wanted it all to be properly done. Then the orders from the poop, "Fire on the roll!" And the shattering roar of the broadside, one cannon after another.

He continued his wandering, back now from the edge of the overlook toward the rear of the villa, itself a recent construction, an immense thing in the style of Palladio, but with the proportions all wrong. The path led back to the outbuildings. These were simpler, more the real thing—white plaster with red terracotta roof tiles, and dark brown shutters, closed now against the sun. Then he came to a magnificent stable, a building of noble dimensions, with its rows of doors, the top half of each propped open with a long iron hook. He heard shuffling, an occasional snort and whinny as he passed along the side of the building. At the far end, under the shade of the parasol pines, a door was slightly ajar. Gently, quietly, he pushed it open. Inside all was cool and odorous, with the strong smell of horses and hay. A long corridor ran the length of the building, the horse stalls opening on either side of it. Dark shapes showed over the doors to the stalls. A horse's head swung up to face him—its white blaze was what he saw first, then the soft brown eyes under the forelock, the ears twisting toward him. Then with a snort it was gone.

He moved quietly down the corridor. The rafters were high above him, floored over with planks. The hayloft, of course. He stopped, looking up at the lovely old woodwork. Then he had the impression of a murmuring of voices from above him. He listened intently. Someone in the hayloft? No, some two, one of them a man, the other clearly a woman. Siesta in the hayloft? Probably rather hot up there, but no doubt a noble, vast space for a tryst, if that was what it was.

Now he picked out, in the darkest corner at the end of the

corridor, the wooden ladder leading up through a hole into the hayloft. At the same time, he became aware that there was a wicker basket standing on the floor at the foot of the ladder. A rope was attached to its arched handle. Then as he watched the basket began to move. Someone was pulling it up, slowly, gently, so that it barely scraped against the rungs of the ladder in its ascent. He stepped as quietly as he knew how, and just managed to make out a stoppered wine jug and a blue napkin covering something as the basket disappeared up through the hole.

He had no desire to play the voyeur, but this lunch in the hayloft was intriguing. He just needed to have a look, then he would be gone.

The rungs of the ladder were thick and solid, and he found he could mount silently. Just two more steps and he should be able to glimpse the loft. No, three.

The high vaulted roof of the loft opened above him, with bull's-eye windows lighting it at either end. It was hot enough, but a cross breeze played through it from the open windows, raising the ends of the hay as it moved across the vast undulating light brown piles. The light in the loft was dim. He saw nothing but the hay, a sea of hay. Cautiously he raised himself one more rung. Now he could see across the loft. He could see that at the other end, near the round open window, a young woman was bending over a man propped up against a pile of hay, in a graceful posture. She was feeding him something. His forehead was wound round with a bandage. And his right arm was . . . yes it was in a sling.

The young woman—a girl really—was evidently a *conta-dina,* one of the farmworkers or the servants on the estate. Her hair was covered by a neatly folded blue scarf tied at the back of her head. Her homespun gray dress swelled over her breasts and was cinched at the waist with a broad red belt. The man's face was covered with several days of dark stubble, and his eyes were deep-set under the bandage on his brow. He looked haggard. But there were no signs of blood through the bandage. He could not use his right arm, though. He held the small wine jug in the left, from which he sipped in between the mouthfuls she was feeding him.

Now as Beyle watched, the man set down the jug and reached for the laces that closed the top of the woman's dress, loosened them, and slipped his hand under the dress. She giggled, and pulled back. The dress was now slipping from her shoulders. Again she leaned over him, and he again passed his hand inside, caressing.

Beyle was tempted to wait for what he was sure would be a magnificent breast to appear, but no, he was not going to play the voyeur any further. He wanted to know who the man was, but he wasn't going to be witness to their amorous sport. He reached downward with his foot for the next rung of the ladder. Then the wind wafted through the hayloft, raising a fine dust. Before he could take a further step down, he sneezed. And then he sneezed again. He had to hold firm to the uprights of the ladder. He felt another one coming.

Now the young woman was standing above him, clutching at the top of her dress. She raised an arm to strike him, and the dress fell away from her shoulders. She looked like a statue of some vengeful spirit. She stood above him bare-breasted, while he reached to stay her arm. The man was now with her, a knife clutched in his left hand. He pushed the girl aside.

"*Spione! Chi sei?*"

"I am sorry. I meant no harm. No, no spy. I am Signor Beyle. I—"

"Beyle! What are you doing here?"

Beyle scrutinized the face for a moment. Yes, it looked familiar. Of course.

"Pierre! My humble apologies. I meant no harm. I have just

been lunching with your brother. When he went to his siesta, I . . . I was just wandering, you know, looking at the estate."

Pierre still held the knife raised in his left hand. But he looked puzzled at what to do.

Keep talking, Beyle thought, it's the only thing. You've found his hiding place. He must have been part of the Boulogne expedition. And now it became clear that Tavernier, damn him, was actually right, they had slipped in on the *Méditerranée*. This one, at least.

"Listen, whatever secrets you have are safe with me. I'm with you, you know. I have seen nothing. In an hour I will be gone to the digs with Charles. And then home to Civitavecchia. And silent as the Etruscan tomb."

The knife slowly came down, but Beyle could see it was still clenched hard in Pierre's hand.

"Beyle. If you weren't my father's trusted friend, I would have to kill you. I should kill you. I have nowhere else to go, and now you know where I am to be found."

"I know nothing. None of this happened."

"How can I be sure?"

"Believe me. I have no motive to reveal anything. You have all my sympathy." He thought a moment. "Remember, I served in the Emperor's army."

Pierre hesitated. "But still, you serve the French government."

Beyle felt a certain hilarity at this. "Oh yes, I deal in codfishery and pozzolana ash for the French government, but I want nothing to do with political conspiracies. I am better off in ignorance. I declare my total ignorance of anything you're mixed up in. Truly."

Pierre continued to look at him somberly. "Beyle, your sacred word? How can I know I can trust you?"

"You can. Not a word. I won't mention anything, even to Charles, even to Prince Lucien when he returns."

"On your sacred honor?"

"On my sacred honor."

"On . . ." Pierre seemed to search for the most binding oath he could find. "On the memory of the Emperor?"

"On the memory of the Emperor. On his very body."

This seemed to satisfy Pierre. "Not a word, even to Charles."

"Not a word. Now I should go, before he and Zénaide reappear."

"Yes. Go. And understand that whatever I have done was for the honor of our family, and the freedom of our people."

"Yes, I understand. I am with you there." As he spoke, Beyle reached with his foot for the next rung, and began his descent. Then he paused for one moment. "But be careful. Don't leave baskets of food in plain view. There are real spies about. I met one the other day in Siena."

"Don't I know," muttered Pierre. "If anyone betrays me! It's why I really should slit your throat."

Beyle now moved more swiftly down the rest of the ladder than he imagined possible. As he stood again on the stable floor, breathing heavily, he realized that his hands were painfully chafed. He walked quickly down the corridor, as more inquisitive horse faces swung into view, watching his retreat. Out the door, which he pulled to behind him. He stood squinting in the sun, now beginning to cast long shadows but hot still. That did not happen, he told himself. Now back to the terrace, to be sitting there idly—snoozing even—when Charles and Zénaide reappear.

The long trenches lay deep in shadow now. There was very little daylight left. He wished he could stay for another day's digging—as Charles had hospitably proposed—but he considered it part of his promise to Pierre to leave. What he held was so lovely and so promising that it was hard to leave: a bronze hand. Though hardened earth still clung to it—he didn't want to chip away at it, it needed to be bathed clean—it was beautiful, sensuous. Surely a woman's hand, with delicate fingers. The fingers were barely separated, which no doubt gave the piece greater strength, allowed it to survive intact. He ran his own fingers along the palm. Just the hand and a bit of the wrist. The rest of it must be there somewhere, waiting to be dug up.

He reached for his pocket handkerchief, and wrapped it round the hand as best he could—the wrist still extended—then wiped his hand on the outside.

He shook hands with Charles, with his apologies: "My own hand's dirty, but with the soil of a more heroic age. My heartfelt thanks. This will be a splendid addition to my little collection. And if you find the rest, of course I'll bring it back."

Charles nodded. "Are you sure you can't stay? My father will be sorry to miss you."

"Tell Prince Lucien I'll make a longer stay the next time. And tell him . . . to be careful."

Charles's placid face now took on a darker look. "About what?"

"Well, you know, there are rumors. *Carbonari* implicated in your cousin's escapade at Boulogne. The police spies are on the alert."

Charles hesitated. "Do you know anything in particular?"

"Only that as His Majesty's consul, I'm somehow held responsible for their entry through my port."

"Do you know for a fact they landed at Civitavecchia?"

"No. Only vague accusations. But I am surrounded by spies."

Charles shuffled his foot in the dirt. "Then you should be careful."

"I am. I say nothing to anyone. Believe me."

This was enough on the subject. He turned to walk down the hill to his *sediola,* tethered under the parasol pines near the entrance to the estate. Darkness was gathering as he hailed his driver. Fabio saluted, and they placed themselves side by side on the bench, Beyle cradling carefully the bronze hand.

Just as they were turning out of the drive leading to the villa, Beyle saw something. Deep in a grove of olive trees on the sloping hillside was another light carriage, much like his own, with a single horse. A man standing beside it. He was short, with a face like a bulldog. Beyle's carriage was now moving at a fast trot, jolting over the rutted road. He saw that the man's right hand grasped a telescope. Yes, the man from Siena, the spy. Damnation. Had he been there all day?

Tavernier. He must have gone from spying himself to activating the network of spies employed by the Grand Duke and the Vatican. Damnation.

He was tempted to stop and confront the spy. But that would prove nothing—unless he killed him. And killing people was not his idea of happiness—too many haunting thoughts afterward. He needed to know what the spy had seen. He opened his mouth to question Fabio, then thought better of it. Find out from Tavernier himself. The thought of that conversation sank him into melancholy.

You need a respite from all this, he told himself. Deal with Delicata, then a trip to Paris. And a call upon Amelia.

Amelia. Her intense, serious face danced before him as the *sediola* gathered speed on the high road.

❧ 12 ❧

Bahia to Saint Helena

O N 14 September, they weighed anchor from the
roadstead of Bahia, and set forth on the last leg of the
journey.

Bahia was land, a respite from voyaging, but Philippe couldn't
find much else to say in its favor. A city of low houses, all on a
hill, where there were no wheeled vehicles to speak of, where the
Portuguese merchants were carried around in sedan chairs by
strapping black men wearing brightly colored liveries, who cried
aloud in warning as they trotted though the streets with their
passengers. A horrible place, really. Priests and churches everywhere, and so many slaves they could easily rise up and slaughter
their masters if they organized to do so.

Joinville led his officers upriver for bird shooting. A steamboat carried them up the estuary, then they embarked in two
canoes. They paddled for an hour or more, then landed to troop
into the forest, dense and steamy. It was all too easy—within a

couple of hours dozens of parrots and toucans lay together in a multicolored heap. Philippe stopped shooting early on.

They stumbled on a village, apparently deserted, on their way back to the canoes. Then, as they were about to push off again in their canoes, they were attacked. Night had fallen, and suddenly they were surrounded, on land and on water, by vociferating black men and indians, brandishing spears and a few rifles. There was a struggle, and they were disarmed. Joinville's hands were bound behind him. They were marched back to the village.

"I think Joinville came close to being executed, maybe we all did," Philippe told Emmanuel. "There was a very tense moment. They were yelling and dancing around us. Then the headman of the place—he was wearing a jacket and a stovepipe hat, though not much else—took charge. He decided we should be let go, I don't know why."

They tumbled back into the canoes, and paddled swiftly down to the mouth of the river, where the steamboat was waiting. The steamboat captain, who had evidently spent the whole afternoon emptying a bottle of rum and was totally drunk, proposed going back to slaughter "the damn niggers." But Joinville cut him short, commandeered the steamship, and headed out to the frigate.

"If our Revolution did one good thing in all its excesses, it was to abolish slavery," said Philippe. "Though your Napoleon let it return in the colonies."

"Yes," Emmanuel said, "there is that much to be said for the Revolution. Though it didn't have a lasting effect. Except maybe Haiti. You'd think the slaves of Bahia would have risen up, too."

The two of them were seated in what had become their habitual retreat, their backs to the longboat shipped aft of the foremast. They were out of the way of the mariners there, and could almost avoid looking at the sea, endlessly the same. Worse than ever, since two days out from Bahia they had entered the doldrums. Canvas slapped loosely above them in the light airs. The frigate advanced still, but so slowly its progress was almost imperceptible. It was better not to even try to measure it.

"Still, if Napoleon had managed to establish a universal empire, more of the world would now be free," Emmanuel continued.

Maybe, thought Philippe. But a freedom of the sword and the cannon, presided over by a despot. But he didn't want to argue about this again.

Instead, he said: "General Gourgaud is an odd bird. But I think I'm coming to appreciate his spirit. Nothing is ever over and done for him. He's still fighting the old battles. Still sticking up for his rights."

"I remember the day in January 1816—we had been in Saint Helena only a few months—when Gourgaud and the Emperor, on horseback, managed to give the slip to the English officer who was assigned their daily rides, and to get beyond the sentinels who guarded the perimeter of the 'riding ring,' as the Emperor called it. He and Gourgaud galloped all the way across to the south shore of the island, to Sandy Bay. There they inspected the shore batteries stuck into the cliffs."

Emmanuel paused for a moment. "It was the same all over the island, you see. A natural fortress doubled by an English fortress. That was his last escapade—Lowe made sure he would never again break out of the perimeter set for his exercise. But surely what the Emperor discovered on that gallop with Gourgaud was the futility of any attempt to break out of the encircling rings around Longwood House. Longwood was merely the cell within a prison, within another prison: Saint Helena encircled by the sea. There could be no thought of escape. Even that mind so fertile in tactics of siege and sortie could think of nothing."

Philippe nodded. "You don't escape from the end of the world."

"You know," Las Cases picked up again, "Gourgaud was a constant thorn in my father's side. He always wanted to be closer to the Emperor than anyone else, a kind of favorite son. He didn't want to share him with anyone else. He spent half his time in a funk. He would insist on amending the Emperor's versions of the battles he was recording under dictation, and then the two of them would refuse to talk to one another for hours on end. My father was much more tactful. A strange man, Gourgaud. And the Emperor would needle him unmercifully, tell him that what he needed was a wife, pick out various French princesses—thousands of miles away—for him to marry. But the Emperor never forgot that he saved the whole high command in Moscow by discovering the mine that was set to blow the French head-quarters sky-high. Made him a baron on the spot. But eventually he became too difficult. He left Saint Helena two years after we were expelled."

"Was your father really plotting escape, as Hudson Lowe claimed?"

"I never knew. Father had this servant, James Scott, a mulatto, who was planning to ship back to England, and proposed taking a secret letter to Prince Lucien. It was a long letter, setting the record straight—refuting the reports in the English press, telling the true story of our captivity. I copied it out for Father on pieces of silk, which we then sewed into the lining of Scott's coat.

"Lowe found it. The next day, we were sitting in the garden at Longwood. The Emperor had received a gift of oranges, from the Cape. He loved oranges. He was cutting them into quarters himself, distributing them to Gourgaud and Montholon and father and myself. Then a messenger arrived, saying that Lowe wanted to see us. Father and I went to the front door of Longwood. Lowe was there with a platoon of redcoats. We were seized, bound, and marched off to prison. We never saw the Emperor again.

"So Scott betrayed us. It was imprudent of Father to trust him. Or else . . . it's occurred to me that Father arranged it all on purpose. He wanted to be sent away, because he had enough material to publish. He knew that when he published the *Mémorial de Sainte-Hélène* things would begin to change. The rehabilitation of the Emperor would begin. Lowe would be seen as a nasty villain. Napoleon would live again—not in person, he was dead by the time Father published—but as the legend, the lesson to the future."

Emmanuel's voice was full of emotion as he recalled their separation from the Emperor, their long imprisonment, the final decision to put them on a ship bound for the Cape. But it was hard to believe he could really regret leaving Saint Helena. It seemed to Philippe as if Longwood House must have been slow torture. It preserved the hierarchies and rituals of the imperial court, with the Emperor the object of every attention, from the moment His Highness rose from his camp bed to the formal dinners at which the Emperor presided, Bertrand and Montholon and Gourgaud in dress uniform—when one or the other of them hadn't been banished to a private dinner—the valets in livery. Everyone vying for the Emperor's attention, with the most trivial incident magnified disproportionately. He more and more had the sense the Emperor was deeply selfish, childish really—intent on playing off against one another his faithful companions in exile. Constant bickering. A court in exile, where everyone ostensibly subscribed to the fiction of the Emperor's eventual return to power, yet with the simultaneous recognition that the only power left was that of memory, of a world reformulated in the mode of as-if. One day, Napoleon dictated to Gourgaud an entire reorganization of the army, with orders to prepare it as a formal report to the Grand Marshal, as if he were preparing a new campaign.

Philippe tried to focus his mind on those scenes of dictation, the fallen Emperor reciting to his faithful companions in exile the version of the past that he wished to impose on posterity. His last act of command. In the study of Longwood House, pacing restlessly, in his rumpled dressing gown, a foulard tied around his head, his right hand thrust into the flap of the dressing gown over his paunchy belly, his left reaching out from time to time to pick up from the table one of the orders of the day from the old campaigns, while Gourgaud or Las Cases, sometimes the father and sometimes the son, sat at the table under the window, looking out on the bleak landscape as the wind rattled the panes. That big head with the disquieting sensual lips, the face now losing its form, its composition, in the gathering certainty of exile unto death.

As Emmanuel talked, Philippe began to imagine Longwood House as something like Scheherazade's bedchamber, the place of endless storytelling. There was nothing else to do but tell—in this case, retell, go over the past again and again. Under the pressure of constant recounting, the past became malleable. History began to change. The Russian campaign no longer ended in disaster, since Napoleon arrested his retreat at Vilna, rallied his scattered troops, regrouped his command, and made a vigorous counterthrust at Kutuzov, one that broke the back of the equally cold, disorganized, demoralized Russian army. And then the triumphant vision of a united Europe, from the Atlantic to the steppes of Moscow, became a reality. No more wars, since there would be no need of them. A prosperous era of free trade and democratic institutions opened before the civilized world. When Gourgaud pointed out that it was at Vilna the Emperor left the army and posted alone to Paris with his personal guard, he was shut out from Napoleon's presence for two days.

The Hundred Days were recounted over and over again, from his escape from Elba, his landing in Golfe-Juan, his triumphant progress north, as the people acclaimed him in town after town, and one after another the regimental commanders deserted the Bourbons to rally to their true leader. And then Waterloo, a defeat that was so nearly a victory. He dictated several pages detailing the mistakes Wellington made on the eve of the battle, proving that he should have lost it. By all the principles of warfare, victory belonged to the French. If only it hadn't rained, turning the roads to mud. If only the battle had begun earlier than midday, there would have been time for victory. If only the artillery had been more effectively deployed for Ney's attack on Wellington's right flank. If only Grouchy had moved—he had orders to do so—he could have pinned down Blücher's 90,000 Prussians. The Emperor still had the Old Guard, they were fresh, he could then have thrown them against Wellington's center. The farewell of Fontainebleau blurred, his surrender to the English—they were willed away.

There was only one battle that was unmentionable—Eylau, the victory that spelled coming disaster, the unending butchery. Six generals dead, 20,000 troops. The day was saved by Murat's cavalry charge, the Russians ended by withdrawing prudently. But nothing was gained. And it all prefigured the Russian campaign: snow, endless snow, blinding Augereau's division as it moved to attack, the whole division simply wiped out. The Russians retreating, becoming unfindable. Later, Kutuzov would make this his whole strategy. You can't be beaten when you refuse engagement. Let the Russian winter take care of the French.

Longwood House was the temple of retrospective narration. Then there were days when the fiction seemed to fail, when the Emperor would spend three or four hours in his bathtub, without speaking, in a reverie. The Chinese servants would bring him his lunch in the bath. As the years went on and hope faded, the bathtub was his place of retreat. He dissolved in the warm water. He gave up his daily horseback riding. He began to long for the death that would come on 5 May 1821.

Philippe could now evoke it in his mind. There, in the

confines of the study at Longwood, fog and rain shutting out the world beyond—the endless ocean beyond that—the fallen Emperor paced and spoke. And Aboukir and the Battle of the Nile and the Pyramids, forty centuries gazing down sphinxlike at the French army, and the sun and the heat and the smells of Egypt rose to take possession of the damp room. The rulers of Europe hastened to make peace with him. There had been nothing like it since Alexander and Caesar, not even Charlemagne could claim so much. Now shrunk to this, the prison of the mind. The torture of Saint Helena was not just Sir Hudson Lowe, his petty restrictions on Napoleon's movements, his constant spying, his expulsion of the Las Cases. It was especially a mental torture, a prison of a mind inhabited by might-have-beens, by if-onlys, the man who once had encompassed the entire destiny of Europe reduced to utter impotence, at the end of the earth. Life at the last reduced to an intense bundle of regrets, and no way to counter them, nothing to be done. The mind's its own place, but that was the problem as well as the glory. You could create imagined worlds, but then the world outside the window would not make room for them.

He felt overcome by a vast melancholy himself, in the immensity of sky and sea, on the frigate rolling listlessly in its slow progress across the South Atlantic. Why had he allowed this to happen? He regretted the voyage. His career was interrupted. He was desperately apprehensive about Amelia. And all to go retrieve whatever was left—if anything was left—of this man who, when all was said and done, stood for everything he thought he detested. The tyrant, the butcher, the man who had troubled Europe for two decades, keeping the peacemakers—so he would like to be—from doing their work.

And what if the body wasn't there? If Napoleon had not died a natural death—Marchand continued to insist that he had been poisoned, that his end came too swiftly to be natural—Lowe might, as the persistent legend had it, have disposed of his body by dark of night, and substituted another. He wanted to question Marchand about this, after the conversation they had held in Bahia—but he sailed on *La Favorite,* now lagging behind *La Belle Poule,* a speck on the western horizon.

The ship's gong rang, summoning them to luncheon. Philippe and Las Cases rose, to make their way aft.

(Now Beyle at his desk asked himself how close they would be to Saint Helena. If they were really to be back in early December, as the French newspapers announced, they must be nearly at Saint Helena at this point. The idea of that novel of the sea voyage still gnawed at him, though he knew he'd never write it. Still, he could imagine it. Assume that the Prince de Joinville and young Chabot are standing at the rail, watching that godforsaken island heave into view. They are asking themselves what place their own volition has in this expedition. None. They are simply another result of the Emperor's revisions of history, come to carry out his commands, as if posterity could no longer refuse to listen to those instructions issued from Longwood House so many years earlier. A posthumous obedience.)

That night, the wind picked up. Soon it whipped into a gale. The frigate began to move swiftly with the following seas, dipping into the troughs of the waves, rising vertiginously on the crests. The new motion awakened Philippe well before dawn. He drew on his heavy sea coat and went up on deck. Clouds raced across the pale sliver of a moon. The dark sea churned into white at the top of the waves which rolled toward the poop, threatening to break, but then the ship lifted just in time, to begin its new dip and slide. Occasionally the clouds were whipped away long enough to see the stars, the unfamiliar constellations of the southern hemisphere, standing remote above them. On deck, the only light was the dark lantern by the helmsman's compass. Charner stood behind the helmsman, his head twisted back, watching the waves as they came up under the stern, ready to bark an order. But the helmsman had the motion, squaring the ship to the wave, then easing up as it passed under.

Three days of gale, then the wind moderated, followed by cold and intermittent wind. The evening of the fifth day, Joinville told them at dinner that their destination should come in sight the following afternoon. It was a long wait. Then toward five o'clock, the lookout in the crow's nest on the mainmast gave the shout: "Land ho!"

On an impulse, without asking the bosun's permission, Philippe grasped the starboard ratlines and pulled himself upward, up, up to the crow's nest. He had never done this before. The ship swayed beneath him. For a moment, he thought he had lost his balance, and would plunge down, not to the deck that now seemed impossibly small, but into the cold green sea. Then a hand reached down for his, and he found himself being lifted by the lookout's callused palm through the hole in the center of the crow's nest. Out of breath, he panted a thanks, and made a place for himself next the lookout. The man pointed toward the eastern horizon.

There on the rim of the sea was a form, something like a castle rising abruptly from the water, a fortress. It was all cliffs and hills, less an island, it seemed, than a piece of sculpted rock in the middle of nowhere. Their destination. Not the landfall you yearned for after months at sea.

Swinging slowly down the ratlines back to the deck, Philippe tried to console himself with the thought that the beginning of the end now was at hand. The problems to be dealt with on shore—the real test of his capacities—then the simpler, and shorter, voyage home. In principle, at least. Yet he could not rid himself of the feeling that this was not his mission, not his life. Someone else had written it all. He was merely the servant of Napoleon's will, his final revision of history, his orders issued from Longwood House, as if all posterity were summoned to bend to his dictates. In this story, he had only to endure.

It was not until the end of the next day—8 October, twenty-five years nearly to the day the *Northumberland* with its famous captive moored in the Jamestown roadstead—that the frigate rounded the rocks at the entrance to the harbor, came up into the wind, and was met by the pilot boat sent out by Governor Middlemore. Evidently they were expected. Strangely, a brig flying the French tricolor already lay at anchor off Jamestown, the swift *Oreste,* dispatched from Cherbourg, they learned, after the departure of *La Belle Poule.* The *Oreste* had sailed without ports of call to bring them a Channel pilot for the return home, but also further secret instructions. Philippe and Joinville opened the dispatch together. It was from Thiers. He claimed to have fresh information that Sir Hudson Lowe had plotted to replace the Emperor's body with that of a household servant who had died shortly before the Emperor himself. Whatever the condition of the coffin, His Majesty's Commissioner Chabot was imperatively to open it.

❦ 13 ❦

Her Portrait

BEYLE HAD become aware that Ingres had returned to Paris virtually the same day as himself. Why he had left his comfortable position as director of the Villa Medici, Beyle could not quite understand. His friend Bucci suggested it was because he wanted the commission to do Napoleon's tomb in the Invalides. A suitable project, Beyle thought, for an artist becoming more and more pompous and official. Though still the one living artist who had something of Raphaël's sublime. He admired Ingres, but he had never entirely liked him. He found him deeply provincial, with the narrow-minded pride of the arriviste. But he had relaxed his attitude somewhat after several encounters in Rome.

In any case, visits to Ingres' studio always held an element of intense sensuality. There was nothing wrong with Ingres' luscious modeling of the nude. He recognized a kinship in their appreciation of beauty, of the breathtaking revelation of the beauty that a woman could bring to one. Someone with such an eye for beautiful forms couldn't be anything but a kindred spirit, someone who understood how to exalt us above paltry life, to make the body sing to the spirit.

As for Napoleon's tomb, why not Ingres, after all? Since the Invalides now seemed to be irrevocably chosen as the place—so he learned from the diplomatic pouch that arrived on the eve of his departure from Civitavecchia. This, despite a hundred protests, from the Bonapartists, from the opposition newspapers, from Victor Hugo. Under the dome of the Invalides, Ingres' cold, marmoreal grandiosity might be just what was needed. He had after all achieved a kind of simplicity of line that was nearly that of the ancients. He was fussy, he was cold, but at least he wasn't like the pretend baroque painters Beyle found everywhere. Ingres was the best France could muster at the moment. And if he would listen to Beyle's notions of how the tomb should go, the result could be splendid.

He could walk to the Institute—he assumed that Ingres had returned to his old lodgings and studio there. It was still fine autumn weather, though already the end of October. He had only a few blocks to the Seine, then across the Pont des Arts to the other bank. He would go right now. He found himself truly absorbed by the question of what Ingres would do for the tomb. He tried to call up in memory the strange image of Napoleon on his imperial throne that Ingres had done shortly after the coronation, so many years ago, that now hung in the Invalides. A painting that almost no one had liked. Immobile, like a wax figure, the Emperor sits on a throne whose gilt circular top haloes his head, which is itself girdled with a gilded laurel wreath, and rests, almost as if detached, on a fluted circular collar. The face is nearly expressionless, indecipherable, the cheeks a bit jowly, shadowed by the beard—the Emperor is clean-shaven, but the shadow of the beard is striking. The eyes are penetrating, they look right at you.

But what is most peculiar about the painting is the superfluity of arms. It's as if Napoleon, like some Hindu divinity, had at least four arms. There is the imperial scepter, topped by a golden eagle, grasped in the hand of his extended right arm, then the strange hand of justice on the end of another long scepter, sticking up above the shoulder as a second left hand. It takes a moment to realize that the real left hand rests on the left knee. Then to Napoleon's right, where his right hand would be if it were not extended to hold the scepter, a strange globe—part of the throne—the same color as Napoleon's pale flesh, reads for a moment as his right hand emerging from the velvet, ermine, and gilt cloak. The image is somewhat baffling overall, almost repulsive, deeply inhuman, hieratic. Yet also unforgettable. What had Ingres been thinking of? Had he really considered this a flattering and friendly image of the Emperor? To Beyle in any event it spoke a certain truth, it said something about Napoleon from the moment he decided he would have himself crowned Emperor. That remained the moment of betrayal, the moment at which he passed from savior and necessary scourge to pretender, tyrant, someone who needed the simulacra of divine rule because he did not want to accept the limits to his historical destiny. He wanted an empire to pass on to his sons. At that moment his humanity ceased. And Ingres had captured that.

As he reached the quai and started across the Pont des Arts, a brisk autumn wind whipped down the Seine. A Paris winter soon, something he had not experienced in a while. But what a relief nonetheless. He stopped for a moment near the middle of the bridge. All his life he had been the champion of Italy, of its arts, its music, its opera, its kind of love, its passion. But ten years in Civitavecchia (with how many days, months, years of absence, though) was enough to make one renounce Italian allegiances. There was something to be said for freedom, even that afforded by this middle-class monarch who cared more for the stock market than for national glory. At least people in Paris looked happy. They didn't have to deal on a daily basis with Monsignore and spies.

He remembered perfectly the way to Ingres' studio, behind the kitchens of the Institute. It was rather a bleak place, Ingres must surely feel it a poor substitute for the vast, elegant spaces of the Villa Medici. But Ingres was a success now. No doubt he could move to a bigger studio if he chose. But he was always anxious about money, never a spender. Beyle felt some disdain for Ingres' provincial, middle-class attitudes, though he allowed that he might have benefited from a better domestic economy himself.

The narrow, uncarpeted back stairs leading up to the third-floor studio felt damp and chill, but when he opened the second of the two doors that led into the studio itself, he felt the suffusing warmth of the stove. Ingres kept the studio rather warm for his models. But as Beyle picked his way quietly among the armchairs and sofa, the flower pots and fragments of columns, the stacked canvases and piles of sketches, he became aware that the sitter beyond the plane of Ingres' canvas was not nude.

He was doing a portrait. Beyle saw the canvas before the sitter, and noted that the pose was typical: head and torso, to just below the waist. The right forearm had been heavily sketched with the brush, it propped up the oval of the face, which was turned just slightly from a frontal position. The face was blank still, just its oval marked, and the fall of the hair over the forehead. Too early to tell much about the painting, but already there was a stamp of grace on it, in the bend of the forearm and the gentle slope of the shoulders.

Beyle motioned to Ingres to keep at his work, while he scanned the scattered furniture for a place to sit. Had he realized Ingres had a private portrait under way, he would not have come. But didn't the painter usually do these sittings in his subjects' own drawing rooms and boudoirs? Why had this sitter come to him? Beyle carefully lifted a sheaf of sketches from a moth-eaten red brocade armchair with peeling gilt arms, sat himself, and pulled out his pocket watch. Quarter to eleven. If the sitting was still going on with this intensity at eleven, Beyle would take his leave, and return another time.

He permitted himself a glance at the sitter. He couldn't see her face, turned from where he sat, gazing slightly to the painter's left, resting on her right hand at the end of her bent arm. The image was one of delicate harmony, a dove gray dress, low-cut to show the sitter's shoulders. Behind her was a mirror, propped on an easel, so that what he took in first was the reflection of the back of the sitter's head and torso in reflection. The dark wavy brown hair with ruddy highlights was pulled back and tied with a black velvet ribbon at the nape of the long, graceful, muscular neck. That neck, and the squared shoulders with their fine matte finish—they reminded him of someone. He had seen that line before, rising from a black dress. He found his pulse suddenly beating fast. Was it possible? Surely . . .

He rose as quietly as he could manage, and walked on tiptoe to stand a few feet behind Ingres' shoulder. Now he could see the pensive face propped on the sitter's right hand at the end of the beautiful arm. Amelia! However did this come about?

Ingres turned to him, his face stern with annoyance. At the same moment, the sitter looked up from her pose.

"Beyle, you know you're not to do this—"

"Monsieur Beyle! You here?"

Beyle bowed. "Mademoiselle Curial, how delightful." Then, to Ingres, "A thousand pardons, my friend. When I noticed . . . when I thought I recognized in the mirror . . . I just had to make sure. An acquaintance from Rome, you see. I had no idea."

Ingres sighed. He reached for an oily cloth and began rubbing his brush. "Against all the rules. You know that. But now that will have to do for today."

Beyle was flustered. He was mortified at having interrupted the sitting. And his attention was divided between his desire to discuss the tomb of the Invalides with Ingres, and his more imperative need to find a way to detain Amelia, and speak with her.

Amelia had turned her back on them, and was arranging herself in the mirror. Ingres sank back on his stool, still cleaning the brush. His annoyance seemed to have passed. "An acquaintance of mine from Rome, too. When she called at the Villa Medici with the Countess Cini, we arranged to do her portrait. Here at my studio"—he looked slightly self-conscious—"because, you see, things are still at sixes and sevens at General Curial's. You know"—he lowered his voice—"about Mademoiselle's mother."

"Yes. Tragic. And I came here, you see—just come back from Civitavecchia—to talk about the Emperor's tomb in the Invalides. I hear you may be the one—"

Ingres shook his head. "No such luck. They've chosen Visconti."

Months of voyaging on the dark green sea, to return the decayed body of the Emperor to what? Some pseudo-Gothic gimcrack temple in the rotunda of the Invalides? Or would Visconti go for the neoclassical, a Greekish confection? Pity those voyagers whose journey would end in an eternal monument to high bad taste.

Aloud, Beyle said: "Visconti! That faker! That's bound to mean something in the pseudo-grandiose. Why, he's—"

Beyle's incipient tirade on the architect Visconti was interrupted. Amelia had moved to them. Out of mourning, in the simple dove gray dress, she looked softer than on the terrace at Castelgandolfo. But the face held the same intensity.

"Monsieur Beyle. How wonderful. Yet you catch me in what you must consider a vain and frivolous occupation."

"On the contrary. I can think of nothing more sublime than you represented by Monsieur Ingres. The model and the painter are perfectly in harmony. I shall have to ask Monsieur Ingres to do a reduction for me. If I can afford his prices."

Ingres merely smiled at this double flattery. Amelia flushed slightly. "You make mock, my friend. But, here you are in Paris and you have not called."

"I just arrived, three days since. After I last saw you at the Cinis', you know, I've had a thousand things to do. The codfish again. The spies. The most implausible affairs. I had to travel back to Rome, to negotiate delicate matters with the papal legate. Then I had to secure my leave. But you have been much on my mind. Why, I would have come to leave my card this very afternoon."

She looked at him intently. "Am I to believe this?"

"Don't you know that I am known to speak my mind, often to my own grief?"

She reflected. She seemed to hesitate in the choice of her words. Then she said: "I remember an unfinished conversation, on the terrace at Castelgandolfo. You departed early the next morning."

"Not so very early, but before your arising. Yes, I remember well."

"And?"

"And we must continue it. If you and Monsieur Ingres have really finished for today, let me escort you back. Do you have a carriage waiting?"

"No, I came by cab."

"Alone?"

"Yes. I know it is all quite unseemly, if Father knew he would be distressed, but where's the harm?"

He once again admired her spirit. What other young woman in Paris would come out unchaperoned and take a cab to an artist's studio? Even if the artist was the staid and reliable Ingres. She seemed determined to compromise her reputation.

Ingres helped Amelia into her coat, she tied her bonnet close around her face, and took Beyle's arm. Beyle promised a further conversation about Visconti and the Invalides tomb, but Ingres seemed uninterested. His attention was elsewhere. He explained that he had to be at the Tuileries after lunch, to begin the portrait of the King's eldest son, his heir, the Duc d'Orléans.

"Decidedly, you are becoming our official painter. So much the more curious about the tomb."

Ingres was vexed. "Yes, yes. The portraits keep me alive. But I didn't come back to Paris to paint portraits, you know. I've other dreams."

Beyle felt a pang of regret at leaving the painter looking so disconsolate. But after all, he was a favorite of fortune. The official portrait of the Royal Prince! Sympathy for Ingres was tinged with envy.

They waited outside the Institute for a cab. Beyle felt an almost illicit thrill of pride at having this young woman leaning familiarly on his arm. He watched the faces of the passersby, to see if they stared, as they ought, at this alliance of youth and age, of beauty and . . . whatever he should be called. But apparently no one noticed. One should never, he remarked to himself, underestimate one's own invisibility, not to say insignificance.

The cab ride to the rue d'Antin would take only twenty minutes. But before Beyle could find the words he wanted, Amelia looked him full in the face and spoke, her voice low but anxious.

"Just after you left Castelgandolfo, I had a strange visit. A certain Signor Daponte."

Beyle was puzzled. "Daponte? The name means nothing to me."

"A puglike man, in the employ of the Grand Duke of Tuscany. A kind of spy."

Rage seized him. "A little man with dirty fingernails?"
Amelia nodded.

"The vile worm! Yes, he's a spy—been following me. But to Castelgandolfo!" And where else? he asked himself. "I am so sorry. But why did he come to you?"

"Wanted to warn me, he said. That you were politically suspect—which of course I knew already."

"Poor Italy! If the spies need to bother with someone as harmless as myself, repression decidedly is everywhere."

Amelia didn't answer. Her gaze darkened. There was evidently something more.

"Yes?"

She blurted it out. "He said that you had a mistress. A certain Signora Martini."

Beyle felt himself flush. So this was a real plot—the spy Daponte—and behind him Tavernier, no doubt about it—meddling in every part of his life. How vile. How humiliating.

He took a deep breath. "Giulia Martini, yes. She is . . . a love from my past." He wasn't going to deny Giulia. But he needed to get this exactly right, both for Amelia and for himself. "A love from my past, for whom I have enduring affection, and tenderness. She has made my loneliness more bearable. But she's another man's wife. It is not love between us, it can't be, it's a kind of tender remembrance of the past."

Was he messing up everything? He watched Amelia's face as he made his explanation. Was she now going to loathe him, decide that he was nothing but an old womanizer she had better steer clear of? Entirely understandable if she did.

But strangely as he spoke her face seemed to relax. As he began to try again to explain the place Giulia had occupied in his life, she interrupted him.

"You don't need to say any more. I understand. I wouldn't have wanted you to live as a monk. That's not the way I want to imagine you. I want a man who loves women. But now, you see, it will have to be me."

It was the strangest scene of seduction he had ever experienced. Amelia was actually proposing that they set off together—to Switzerland, she seemed to have in mind, to some travelers' inn high in the Saint Gotthard Pass—there to become lovers. He could not help but smile at her romantic soul. But she appeared to be serious.

He reached out to take her hand. He stroked her long, strong fingers. They felt tense to his touch.

"My dear, dear Amelia. How can I undertake such a thing? It would be sheer bliss, of course. But think of the consequences."

She was agitated now, and spoke in abrupt bursts. "But I've thought it all through. It doesn't matter. Look at the Countess d'Agoult and Franz Liszt. They're an example. Love alone."

"But Marie d'Agoult was married before she ran off with Liszt. And ware the example. I've heard that he's left her. Bored with her, after their third child. Love conquers . . . only so much. Hardly all."

"But I think you are perhaps wiser and more reliable than Monsieur Liszt."

"Older, you mean. And yes, more reliable. You could count on me. But still, my dear, if I am to accept this wondrous gift offered me, it must be on another footing."

She glared at him. Did her knitted eyebrows and shining eyes show love, or something else? Determination, surely, but to what?

He made an effort to gather his thoughts into a sharp point of clarity. Did he mean what he was about to say? Was he in fact going to say it? He found his hand was trembling as it held hers. He clasped her fingers more tightly. He cleared his throat.

"Amelia," he began, "never did I think that at my age something so wonderful might come my way. Yet now that it has, I cannot put it aside. But I cannot accept the sacrifice you propose. I know the ways of the world too well. If you cannot envisage the sequel, I can. There is a better way. I have little to offer you, but I do have my eternal devotion, what may by this point in my life be some sort of wisdom." He paused. Was he getting it right? He continued with a smile he knew must appear strained, though he meant only tenderness. "Am I making myself clear?"

"Go on." She spoke tersely, under her breath.

"You must see, then, that I wish to marry you. I know, I know, the world will criticize us—will criticize me, mainly, will say I am robbing the cradle. That you are throwing yourself away. Burying your youth in the arms of an old man. But we can survive that."

He felt her hand slipping from his grasp. He had much more to say, but he paused.

Amelia dropped her hand into her lap and turned aside, to stare out the window of the cab. They were now coming into the Place Vendôme, rattling past the column.

"You're just like the young men, then. All you can do is propose marriage. Do you think that is the way to my heart? Why on earth should I marry you?"

"To be sure," he said uncomfortably, "you could do much better."

"Better's not the point. I want you now, as my lover, to show what the present can hold. I don't want to think about the future, marriage, children, all that." She hesitated a moment. "Mother was suffocated by all that, you know."

He did know, though Menti was suffocated by inner demons as well.

"I think I understand," he began. "It's precisely because I'm not suitable as a husband that you want me."

"Of course. Didn't you understand that before? Can't you take it as a compliment?"

Did he? In a way, yes, of course.

"Dearest Amelia. I do. I am overwhelmed with gratitude. I think you the most desirable woman I ever have met. And it shall be as you wish. But still, you should consider."

"If I consider much longer, I shall give you marching orders."

"Then I shall consider. The Swiss idea."

The cab slowed to a walk. He glanced out to see they were in the rue d'Antin. Their ride was at an end.

She stared at him in silence, biting her lip. He took her hand again. "I'll call tomorrow. We'll plan everything."

She nodded grimly. She looked as if she were about to burst into tears.

"One way or another, we will make things work out," he said.

The footman had approached the cab door. "Don't you men understand anything? I thought you were different, Beyle. Wrong again!"

She slipped swiftly out of the cab and through the open door of the building. Beyle was left sitting in the cab, a rueful grin marking his face.

❧ 14 ❧

Valley of the Tomb

A MOURNFUL STONE gate with a hanging portcullis loomed before them as they moved up from the quay. Night had fallen soon after they dropped anchor in the narrow roadstead, but after captain's mess, Emmanuel proposed taking the pinnace for a quick visit to Jamestown. Philippe sensed that he was fired by a strange nostalgia, the need to revisit a painful past.

Philippe tried to put himself into the mind of Napoleon as he was led through the gate, past its guard towers surmounted with cannon—cannon everywhere at the entrance to Saint Helena, the whole place was a fortress—twenty-five years ago. The gate—*Lasciate ogni speranza, voi ch'entrate*—to an underworld from which there was no return. A guard of a dozen redcoats presented arms, smartly. Then the Citadel, to their left, a small feudal-looking castle. More cannon. They came into the Parade, the one real street of Jamestown, mounting before them. The

150

town had nowhere to go, it was a narrow agglomeration in a narrow valley, walled in by abrupt basalt hills. A few large and agreeable houses, the rest nondescript, like a paltry English village. Except some ironwork balconies and porticos, giving it a colonial air. They paused before one of the larger houses. Porteus House, Emmanuel told Philippe, where Napoleon spent his first night after disembarking from the *Northumberland,* since it was too late in the day for the steep path into the interior.

Neither of them spoke after that. Philippe could see that Emmanuel was lost in reverie. They reached Side Path, which would lead them up, past Alarm House to Briars, where Napoleon stayed while Longwood House was being put in shape for his final residence, to Longwood itself, to the Valley of the Tomb. They took the left turn into Side Path, and began to climb. But the darkness was impenetrable. Emmanuel called a halt. They turned to look back to the harbor. The lanterns of *La Belle Poule* and *La Favorite* were just small globes of light on the black water.

They walked back in silence, past dark, shuttered houses. The moist wind blew up the Parade, tearing at their clothes, chilling their faces and necks. It was hard, in this pitiful and sleeping town, to think that they were on a mission of world-historical importance. And anyway, the man was dead, dead, dead. Philippe found himself feeling mainly annoyance. They had come for a decaying body. And tomorrow he would have to open all the formal negotiations with General Middlemore, the governor, for the exhumation—including Thiers' macabre instruction on opening the coffin—and then the proper formalities and ceremonies for bringing the body back to the ship. He was in charge. Joinville had decided that since he was not given command of the exhumation, he would remain on shipboard. There, his authority was undisputed.

All of us, he thought as he and Emmanuel climbed down into the waiting launch, all of us are moving like sleepwalkers in the mind of Napoleon, carrying out his egotistical wishes from beyond the grave. I need to escape, to find the present tense again, a life not held hostage to the past. Well, just a few more days. But then the alien sea again.

The negotiations with Governor Middlemore went surprisingly well. The old general was suffering an attack of gout. He excused himself for not coming in person to meet them at the quay, and invited Philippe to be his guest at Plantation House. There, Philippe gratefully accepted a cup of tea—only the English could get tea right—and exchanged impressions of the Surrey country-side with his host. For all his military training and stiff bearing, there was a sort of autumnal softness about Middlemore, and a bottomless nostalgia for an England he might never see again. The gaoler as prisoner, thought Philippe. He took evident plea-sure in his guest's familiarity with things English, and it required some adroit maneuvering for Philippe to bring him back to the business at hand. But then he was wholly cooperative.

He offered the services of Colonel Trelawney and Captain Alexander for all the necessary arrangements concerning the exhumation and transport of the body. He had himself received from Lord Granville a copy of Sir Hudson Lowe's memorandum on the burial, and the composition of the tomb. He offered to pro-vide a team of sappers, which could be reinforced by a dozen of the strongest sailors from the frigate, equipped with shovels and pickaxes and large cement cutters. Then he informed Philippe that he had already ordered the building of a large flatbed car-riage to carry the sarcophagus—with all those coffins within coffins, it was going to be a considerable weight. Affably, without dissension, the two of them decided on the order of the proces-sion: a detachment of a dozen artillery officers leading the car-riage, followed by the French delegation, with the 91st Infantry of the Line drawn up along the line of march. The Valley of the

Tomb would be sealed off during the exhumation by the local militia. An officer on High Knoll would give the signal when the procession came in sight, and then the cannon would fire at one-minute intervals.

Now came the delicate point. Philippe explained to Middlemore that his government had issued the most formal instructions to open the coffins, to the very last one, in order to inspect the Emperor's body, to make sure that it was not a source of infection, or . . . an imaginary corpse. He used Thiers' own expression here, strange though it was. Middlemore's weary gray head snapped up at this last remark. He fixed Philippe strangely with his faded blue eyes. The eyes had a kind of wounded candor. Philippe braced himself for a protestation of innocence. Would he have to explain the French view on Sir Hudson Lowe?

But Middlemore kept silent. "Very well," he said at last. "Proceed as the King of the French directs, with expedition and with all due precautions."

Philippe drew a sigh of relief, and then asked permission to make a reconnaissance of the tomb, along with the Prince, whose sole visit on land this would be. The permission was graciously accorded.

It was early afternoon as they set off: Joinville, Hernoux—always at the Prince's side—Coquereau, Gourgaud, Marchand, Emmanuel, and Philippe, under the escort of Colonel Trelawney and his guard. Joinville and old Marchand were on horseback, the rest on foot. Up the narrow rocky road, over the crest of the hill, down into the Devil's Punch Bowl—Napoleon's Valley, the locals called it. A barren, rocky landscape. Glimpses of black-green sea at every turning of the path. The sky was gray overhead, with the threat of rain—there was always the threat of rain on Saint Helena, except when it was actually raining—and the wind tore at them in gusts on the high ground. They walked in silence. He noted that Las Cases had not brought his daguerreotype camera—the day was too dark for an exposure. Would he ever get the chance to use it? When they descended out of the wind, they moved at a good pace for close to an hour, across a kind of blasted heath, then into a more fertile valley. Willows ahead of them.

"We're nearly there," Emmanuel breathed at his elbow.

Five minutes more walking, and he could make out a guard-house, at the entrance of a large enclosure surrounded by a wooden picket fence, and behind that an older, more majestic weeping willow. The sentinel stepped forward from his shelter, a stubby pipe clenched in his teeth, his uniform rumpled, his head bare. He stared for a moment at the approaching party, then retreated quickly into his shelter, and reappeared, shakoed and without the pipe, to give a rusty salute. Joinville returned it. Then he and Marchand dismounted, handing their horses' reins to the sentinel.

Colonel Trelawney gestured to the Prince, inviting him to approach. In the middle of the enclosure, near the foot of the willow, was the plot, protected by an ironwork fence. Joinville doffed his plumed hat. Coquereau sank to his knees on the grass, and bent his head in prayer. Gourgaud strode forward, then stood rigid at attention, his hand raised in military salute. Marchand joined him, his white head bent, tears streaming from his eyes. The English officer stepped discreetly aside. Emmanuel moved forward to the plot, and Philippe followed. As he stared at the ground enclosed by the iron fence, Lord Byron's lines came unbidden to his mind:

> *Stop!—for thy tread is on an Empire's dust!*
> *An Earthquake's spoil is sepulchred below!*
> *Is the spot marked with no colossal bust?*
> *Nor column trophied for triumphal show?*
> *None; but* the moral's truth *tells simpler so.*

That was the field of Waterloo Byron was talking about. But how true here also, he thought, as he gazed. Three slabs of fieldstone, utterly plain, devoid of inscription—since Lowe and the faithful French followers at the last had been at loggerheads on how it would read. Just these plain, melancholy slabs of stone. Here it was. The end of everything.

Joinville bent to pluck a red geranium from those growing as a border round the grave plot, and fixed it in his buttonhole. He replaced his hat. Coquereau rose. Philippe could see that his handsome face was streaked with tears. Marchand was sobbing like a child, whereas Gourgaud's face remained set, stricken. Joinville whispered to Hernoux, who reached into his vest and produced a handful of coins which he slipped into the hand of the sentinel, who bowed and then saluted again. That was it. There was nothing more to do here, for now. They'd return as gravediggers, Philippe wryly put it to himself. A brief colloquy with Trelawney, and they set off along the path to Longwood House, some two miles distant.

They crossed the Devil's Punch Bowl again. They came upon two derelict huts, the outer limit of the property, Emmanuel said to him quietly. Joinville and Marchand dismounted, and Marchand and Gourgaud fell into step next to the Prince, to serve as guides to the past.

They passed by the huts, and the profile of Longwood House came into view, a low horizontal building with faded yellow stucco walls. Something like a very modest English manor house, Philippe decided. As they approached the front door, Joinville paused, solemnly removed his hat, and then stepped across the threshold. The others followed, and stood blinking in a large empty room. No furniture, peeling plaster, a section of the ceiling hanging loose from its lathing. Their nostrils were assailed by an odor of damp and mildew. As they moved from room to room, it became clear that the place in which Napoleon had lived his final years, and where he had breathed his last, was a ruin. It had been rented to a farmer, who used it for grain storage. The door to the library was nailed shut, you could hear the coo of pigeons which had been given their roosting place within. The Emperor's study, where Emmanuel and his father had sat at the table to take dictation, was heaped with sacks of flour. And the bedroom—the room where the Emperor had expired in the arms of Marchand and Bertrand—now held a wheat grinding mill, its funnel rising through the ceiling—a rough hole had been cut through, to allow the wheat to be poured in, but of course allowing the rain to come through too. The floor was in a state of ruin.

Philippe could see Joinville's eyebrows shoot up as he looked interrogatively at Trelawney. The colonel shook his head and lowered his eyes.

And so it was as they continued through Longwood House. Ruin, collapse everywhere. A few years—not even—and the place might simply cave in, rot away, sink back into the earth. And why not, thought Philippe—like the body itself, ashes to ashes. But he could see that Marchand and Gourgaud were indignant. And Joinville appeared to feel there had been an affront to the French nation. Didn't he remember that everyone—including the rulers of France—once wanted an end to Napoleon, wanted him eradicated, wiped from history? Philippe saw no point in making Longwood House into a memorial—what pilgrim, even the most dedicated to the Emperor's memory, would ever visit this mournful place on this wretched island?

He felt restless and uncomfortable under the weight of the past thrust upon them. Surely there were better things to do—a better life for him to lead, at least—than this turning over of relics and ruins. If that is what the remnants of the Empire— Bertrand, Marchand, Gourgaud—wanted, so be it, that was understandable. But Joinville should have done with it, and he suspected Emmanuel felt the same way. He was, after all, a man who was thriving in the new age.

He escaped from the dining room—ruined, of course, with two beams from the ceiling fallen, at one end, to the floor—by giving a kick to a door that led outside. It wasn't locked. He found himself in what had been Napoleon's garden—in the years when he still could bring himself to be interested in gardening, before melancholy swallowed him wholly. Beyond the garden, a moor, over which the fog was now rolling toward him, a visible wall of fog. Moments later, it had engulfed him, and all of Longwood. Turning, he could scarcely see the door from the dining room. The wet, gray gloom surrounded everything. It was more than a mist, it was like living inside a rain cloud. His clothes were soon running with drops of water, his face was wet, the brim of his hat dripped.

"It happened nearly every day," Emmanuel told him on the way back to Jamestown. "It was as if the English had chosen Longwood House with an exquisite sense of its potential for depressing the spirit, even so indomitable a spirit as Napoleon's."

The climate of the place was insidious. You passed from extreme dryness, with the skin becoming dessicated from the dry prevailing winds so that the Emperor's persistent itch began to afflict him sorely, to the sudden arrival of this cloud bank, blotting out the landscape wholly, making even a walk in the garden impossible. Then after the cloud bank, very often the rain, as was the case during their trek back to Jamestown. Glacial rain. Philippe had to change into dry clothes when he reached Plantation House. And they were in October in the southern hemisphere—that is to say, in the springtime.

Over the next two days, nearly every hand on board the *Belle Poule* and the *Favorite* in turn made the pilgrimage to the tomb. Philippe learned that it had quickly become the custom to bring back a souvenir of the site. Joinville's geranium had set the tone. All the flowers were soon exhausted. The sailors brought back pieces of the ferns that grew along the outer fence, bits of bark shaved from the willow. And little bottles of water—the spring near the tomb, which Marchand claimed was pronounced by the Emperor to give the best water on the island, became an obligatory stop, and no sailor felt ready to reembark for France without some sort of a container—medicine vials, service canteens, mainly empty wine bottles—that could be filled and stoppered. Philippe felt as if he were witness to the origins of a cult. He found himself wondering if the water would later be called on to work miracle cures. But the cult existed already. He and his companions were merely servants to it.

Meanwhile, he worked with Trelawney and Alexander to prepare the exhumation itself, which would take place Wednesday night, or more exactly Thursday morning. Joinville had declared that everything should be completed by Thursday evening, so they could weigh anchor at dawn Friday. Already, that would be 16 October, and they would have to crack on sail to be back by their deadline. Philippe decided then that the excavation should begin during the night of Wednesday to Thursday, since it risked being long and arduous. Studying Sir Hudson Lowe's memorandum, he and Captain Alexander realized that not only had the floor and walls of the crypt been built of stone and masonry, but also after the coffin had been lowered into the crypt the backfill had been sealed with a layer of Roman cement, in which iron crampons had been set. Pickaxes and cement scissors should do it, but they would need time.

And then there was the opening of the coffin—or rather, of the coffins, the four of them, nested one within another. Philippe could hardly imagine that the first—the mahogany coffin— would have survived in this climate.

"At the very least, surely its screws—even though we're told they were silver-plated—will be unusable," Philippe said. "We will probably have to saw it open."

Alexander nodded briefly. "So once we cut through the masonry to the coffin, we'll have to lift it out, and place it, on trestles maybe."

"Yes. And given the weather, we may need a tent."

"To be sure. A tent, with the trestles set up inside. I'll see to it."

Then it would be up to Leroux, the plumber they had brought specially for this purpose, to open the lead coffin. After the lead coffin, they should find another wood one—this in local fruitwood. Encased within the lead coffin, they could probably assume that it was dry and intact—or could it have become dust? It could be unscrewed or sawed as necessary. And within it they would find the fourth and final coffin, this one in tinplate. Here again, it was a job for Leroux. He would have to undo the metal seal that soldered the coffin shut. And then . . . Philippe and Alexander looked at one another grimly. Alexander's nose wrinkled in anticipated disgust, and Philippe could not help laughing at the effect.

"O death, where is thy sting? O grave, where is thy victory?" He cited the apostle's words in English to Alexander. "Dr. Guillard will be ready with his chloride, in case it is all putrefaction. The main thing's to make sure the body really is there. We would look like signal fools bringing an empty coffin back to France."

Alexander shook his head emphatically. "That'll not be the case, I'm sure, sir. Lowe was a hard man, but not an unjust one."

"I'm not so sure. There may have been reasons for a switch of corpses. Marchand and Bertrand will have to verify the identity, Marchand especially—it was he laid the Emperor out."

Alexander's cheery round face now looked grave. "Those persistent stories of poison. No evidence whatsoever."

"We'll soon see . . . at least whatever is visible. And quickly visible. The tin coffin should lie open no more than two minutes. Then Leroux reseals it, it goes back into the inner wood coffin and the lead coffin—if those are intact—and then those go into the ebony sarcophagus we've brought. We'll set that up on trestles, too, next to the coffins from the grave, under the tent."

"Yes. Very well. And then your priest will do his rites and prayers, and then?"

"Then presumably General Middlemore arrives—at least he says he wants to be there to join the march back to Jamestown. Then the sarcophagus with its remains goes on the flatbed carriage for the march back to Jamestown. And I think you and I have to exchange official words. You have officially to convey the body, and I to receive it."

Alexander pursed his lips, and nodded. "Maybe we'd better write those words out now, to get them right." His honest face suggested to Philippe that this was probably the part of the whole operation that seemed the most daunting to him.

So they sat together to concoct Alexander's remarks: "Sir, As the Officer deputed by His Excellency the Governor, Major General Middlemore, Companion of the Bath and Commander of the Forces at Saint Helena, in the presence of the Senior Naval, Civil, and Military Authorities, to exhume and deliver to you, Monsieur le Comte Philippe de Chabot, Commissaire du Roi des Français, the Coffin containing, as has been duly ascertained, the Mortal Remains of the late Emperor Napoleon . . ." May it indeed be so, Philippe thought to himself. They finished Alexander's speech, and then Philippe quickly wrote out his own reply.

WEDNESDAY CAME—they had got through all the official dinners with the English, the toasts to the indissoluble union of France and Great Britain and the rest, the placing of the ebony sarcophagus on the flatbed carriage, the equipping of the sailors.

Philippe saluted Joinville, and ordered his troop to get under way. Along with Emmanuel and himself, there would be Coquereau and his two altar boys, Dr. Guillard, Charner and Captain Guyet of the *Oreste,* then Gourgaud, Marchand, Arthur Bertrand—his father could not make the night journey—the plumber, and the sailors who would do the digging. Alexander was taking with him Colonel Trelawney, Justice Wilde, Colonel Hudson, Lieutenant Littlehales, and then the sappers. It was ten-thirty at night when they turned into Side Path and began the trek from Jamestown. The night was black and windy. It appeared that rain would be falling soon.

❧ 15 ❧

A Box at the Théâtre-Italien

H E KNEW that his reason for another visit to Ingres was the hope of seeing Amelia again, and again finding a moment for conversation without the presence of others. He chose the day and hour of his previous visit, but the calculation proved in vain. Ingres was alone before a huge canvas, on which he had begun to block out in crayon what looked liked a three-quarter-length portrait of a man in uniform.

"The Duc d'Orléans," he explained, with a bit too much self-importance, Beyle thought. "A most affable gentleman, and a true connoisseur of art." One had to recognize that Ingres was something of an arriviste, like one of Balzac's heroes: the young provincial who came to Paris and made good. Though to be fair, it had taken Ingres many years, and no doubt he deserved his success. "I would like to have done with all this portraiture," Ingres continued, "and get to real art. But when the royal family solicits you . . ."

"To be sure. No doubt you're going to have to paint the whole family, all the sons—certainly, when Joinville comes back from Saint Helena with Napoleon's bones, you'll have to do him. In undertaker's dress."

Ingres looked grimly amused. "I believe I may, though I won't be doing any of the decorations for the Invalides and the ceremony."

"Bah, don't let that rankle." Beyle felt suddenly sympathetic to the disappointed vanity of his friend. It's something that hits you, past a certain age: a craving for honors, for titles, for recognition. They shouldn't need this, they were the elite of art—even if he, as Stendhal the novelist, didn't have Ingres' wide recognition, was appreciated only by an elite readership. It would be their honor—the only true one—to endure beyond the tasteless present age. To be looked at, to be read in 1940, for example. But of course, you can never, never know this.

To Ingres he said, "We both know this is an age without grandeur. We are living out a paltry transition, from that time of heroic revolution and conquest, to some unimaginable future. The best we can do is try to step out of time, or above it. To understand our place in history, but to make light of it."

Ingres looked at him with puzzlement. "I think I understand you. But have you really achieved such equanimity? Have you already concluded on your immortality?"

"No, no. Yours is far more assured. But I don't think we should assume that the era of the bourgeois monarch will last forever. Moneygrubbing has its limits. A new heroic age could lie ahead."

"With another Napoleon?"

"Not as such. Prince Louis-Napoléon is now in prison in the fortress at Ham, you know. Not much to be heard from him."

"Strange that he wasn't simply shot. With all this commotion about the return of his uncle's body, who knows what could happen?"

Beyle was not interested in yet another conversation about the Emperor's body and the ceremonies planned at the Invalides—Paris was talking of nothing else, it seemed, and he could recite every opinion on the subject along with all the stock phrases. He was engaged in casting furtive glances at the canvases stacked on the half dozen other easels, and along the walls of the studio. There was one in particular he was looking for.

Then he spotted it, against the rear wall. Evidently Amelia had been back to the studio since he last met her there. Much of the face had now been filled in, though detail was missing. The eyes were only roughed in, the mouth had evidently been redrawn more than once—Ingres was having difficulty getting those thin but sensual lips right. But the eyebrows were there, those glorious smudges. And he had already captured something essential about her expression, something tense and ardent and yearning. Now if he could get the eyes right, their piercing frankness shot through with a touch of anxiety. He found he could not help talking about her, though he had vowed not to.

"I see Mademoiselle Curial has been back to you."

Ingres set down his crayon, and moved to Beyle's side. "Yes," he said. "Two days ago. What do you think?"

The more he looked, the more Beyle felt a surge of hopeless passion, simply from the painted image. She was beautiful, no not beautiful, at least not by any conventional standard. But she was sublimely desirable, a woman who spoke to his very soul. "It's a success, my friend. It is truly wonderful, the way you have captured her. Get the eyes right, and it will be a masterpiece."

Ingres sniffed. "I think I can do eyes by now in my life. It's the mouth that's bothering me."

"Yes, a very special mouth." Beyle paused. "But how did this come about? Who commissioned it? Her father?"

"No. She suggested it herself. And with such a sitter, how

could I refuse? I wonder if she doesn't intend to present it to her fiancé."

Beyle was barely able to suppress a tremor that seemed to run down his whole frame. "Her fiancé?"

"Yes. Well, I don't know that anything is officially announced. But I heard it said at Madame de Castellane's the other night that she is to marry Comte Philippe de Chabot, the diplomat, the very one who's off with Joinville fetching the Emperor's body."

Beyle felt suddenly as if he were fighting back tears. Was this so? Why had she concealed it? Was he being used in some devious game?

"I didn't know. Tell me about him." Beyle tried to banish the tremor from his voice, but Ingres looked at him oddly. But he asked no questions.

"A rising diplomat, obviously—since Thiers entrusted him with this strange expedition. Stationed in London, a family that's part English anyway, on his mother's side. His grandfather was the Comte de Jarnac, who fled to England during the Revolution and married there, and died there. His father married an Irish-woman, joined the English army to fight against Napoleon, then became one of Louis-Philippe's closest advisers. I've never met him. Said to be good-looking, with perfect manners."

Nothing Beyle didn't know here. But hearing it put this way, he had to wonder at Amelia marrying into such a family. Was that what she wanted? It just didn't match the Amelia he knew—if he could say he knew her at all. What then to make of her proposals to him? Had she not meant it when she offered herself?

From feeling piqued, Beyle swerved to a surge of pride. Maybe it wasn't in spite of this Comte de Chabot, maybe it was because of him that she had declared her sudden preference for his old carcass. Maybe she was trying to escape. She was cer-tainly a being who seemed capable of fighting her destiny. If she was really fighting . . . what, an arranged marriage? Her father wouldn't be the sort for that. But a conventional marriage, in any event. Something expected of her, that she didn't want. What everyone would see as a solution, especially following Menti's suicide. If this were the case, then surely he couldn't abandon her.

How had she met this Chabot? And what was he doing— Beyle's mind flashed back to the Valley of the Tomb in the etching everyone knew, where those gravediggers must now be throwing up shovels full of earth—at the other end of the earth. Maybe he'd be shipwrecked—but not likely, alas. When would the *Belle Poule* be back? Perhaps that was why Amelia had spoken now—because there was this small window of time before her fate was sealed.

Chabot. A young prig he would make him in the novel (which he could imagine but somehow knew he would never write). An insignificant diplomat with perfect manners, charged with a mission quite distasteful to him. He saw him in the act of constantly pulling on dove-colored kid gloves, as his men dug a rotting corpse from the ground. His boredom at sea, as he dined alone, aloof from the sailors of the frigate. Shipwreck? No, no such miraculous intervention. He didn't go in for the melodramatic. It was precisely people like Chabot to whom nothing happened. He would fulfill his mission punctiliously, and arrive back in France at the appointed hour. And at the appointed rendezvous with Amelia. He wondered if they'd fixed the time and place. But his imagination could take him no further. Somehow Chabot resisted becoming a figure in a novel. He couldn't imagine his future, he saw no poetic invention there. But what was the use of fiction if you couldn't make it shape the world to your ends—couldn't make it bring the woman you wanted into your arms?

He felt the need for solitude, and deep reflection. He remained silent, gazing at the portrait emerging from the canvas in front of him. How could a young woman live, in any case? He meant that literally. His own heroines, the ones he had invented, the ones that came from within him, all were in revolt against their destinies. Lamiel—would he ever finish her story?—was merely the last in the series. Mathilde de la Mole, though she was haughty and too theatrical, too lacking in the natural, Clélia Conti—weren't they precisely young women who found ways to violate all the rules, in order to give themselves to men they knew were superior beings? He caught himself in a rueful smile. Yes, but Julien and Fabrice were beautiful young men. Whereas he . . . he was something closer to Count Mosca, but without even the Count's worldly power.

He took his leave of Ingres, who was too discreet—or more likely eager to return to the easel—to query his silent reverie. As he made his way back over the Pont des Arts, toward his rooms in the rue Godot-de-Mauroy, he realized he must see Amelia without further delay. If she wished to escape an eminently proper marriage through flight with him, how could he say no to that? Yet the idea of a trip to Switzerland presented some embarrassment. His salary on leave from the consulate was hardly princely, just enough to let him dine in style every evening at the Café Tortoni. Unless he could scrape together more money from his publisher, Buloz . . . but things did not look encouraging in that direction.

But at bottom, all that was secondary. The real problem was whether he had any right to wrench Amelia away from the promise of a comfortable marriage. She needed a well-established husband; surely General Curial wouldn't be able to give her much of a dowry.

Something close to panic gripped him. Isn't it time to begin to behave with the dignity of age, for once? Stop pretending to be one of your young heroes?

He didn't know what he would say to her when he saw her,

yet he had to see her, that was clear. He couldn't really call at the General's—a somewhat compromising idea in the present circumstances. At Madame de Tracy's? At Madame de Castellane's?

Back in his rooms, he found two letters. He immediately recognized the flourish of the script on the smaller of them. Giulia. She was wondering about a rendezvous in Siena, two weeks hence. Or should she find an excuse to make the trip to Paris, where they would re-create old times? He set the letter aside with a kind of tender regret. Giulia just did not seem relevant at the moment. There would be a time to think about that, later. The other letter was a fat packet from Tavernier. As he began to glance through its twelve pages, a sense of helpless rage welled up in him. What was the monster up to now? Evidently he had concluded that Beyle's tractations with Monsignor Delicata were inadequate, and had gone to see the legate himself. The audacious worm! He wanted to assure the Consul that the question of the *carbonari* was far more complex and serious than he realized, but that he, Tavernier, had all the intricate threads well in hand. The Consul was not to worry, but it would be inadvisable for him to visit Prince Lucien at Canino for some time. He was to enjoy his leave from his duties. Yet he would do well not to send any orders on the subject of the still-unlocated conspirators, since Tavernier was on their track.

So the outlines of the plot were beginning to become clear. Tavernier was using the Consul's supposed complicity with the *carbonari*—those involved in the Boulogne escapade—to undermine his position with the Vatican. Worse than this, he had clearly made an arrangement with the spies of the Grand Duke of Tuscany—or with one of them at any rate—so that he could demonstrate to Delicata and his superiors that his assertions were not simply rumor, that there were witnesses. But witnesses to what, exactly? Had Daponte of the dirty fingernails spied on the scene in the hayloft at Canino? He wasn't in the

hayloft—that he could be quite sure of—but if he had been following Beyle at that point, he could have verified Pierre's identity afterward. And he obviously had reported to Tavernier all
about Giulia. Beyle felt a new pang of regret for the scene in
the Campo of Siena—provoking spies is not profitable. Delicata
and the Vatican—which could well know about Giulia from
their own spies—would not see anything wrong with the Consul's liaison with an eminently respectable Florentine signora.
Unless that could be used somehow to blackmail him—say, if
he were to be courting another woman . . . planning a marriage,
something like that. Hence the spy's visit to Amelia in Castelgandolfo. Still, that was probably a tactical error on Tavernier's
part—wrong timing, wrong person—Amelia had brushed it
aside. And in point of fact, he was not courting her for marriage, not in her understanding of things. But nonetheless, Tavernier was compiling his list, chapter and verse, on the Consul's
unreliability. And if this list became too long, who was to say
that Latour-Maubourg wouldn't be obliged to sack him? Or
rather, Latour-Maubourg would no longer stand in the way of
Guizot's sacking him. That was a changed element in the situation: Guizot at the head of Foreign Affairs. Hadn't Guizot once
said—as reported by Mareste—that Beyle had too much wit to
be trusted?

It now stared him in the face—the loss of his position, Tavernier become consul, life on a miserable pension in the cheapest
garret he could find. Paris, to be sure, but not on the terms he
would ever want.

It was time for a vigorous counterthrust. A letter of official
reprimand to Tavernier, to start with, with a copy of it to Latour-
Maubourg. To Delicata also? Beyle started composing the letter in his head, but he could not concentrate enough to sit down
and write it out. And he was painfully aware that a letter wasn't
really what was called for. He ought to get back to Civitavecchia,

without delay. But he couldn't. Not just yet. There had to be some resolution with Amelia first.

He spent an unusually long time dressing himself for the evening. And after dinner alone, at Tortoni, he made an appearance at Madame de Tracy's. No Amelia. Toward eleven o'clock, he went on to Madame de Castellane's. No success there, either. And he found himself totally inapt for society at the present.

The next day was darker still. He tried to compose the letter to Tavernier, but he could think of nothing but Amelia. Five times he took his hat and gloves to go to the General's, but each time thought better of it. He almost set out for Ingres' studio again, just to be able to gaze at her painted self.

He dined early. As he was finishing his meal with a small cup of coffee—no dessert, since he needed to regain something like his old battle trim—he realized that it was too early to begin the round of the salons. So he wandered off to the Théâtre-Italien, and took a ticket for the parterre. He slipped into his seat just as the lights were going down. It was one of Marivaux's comedies, which they kept alive in their repertory, *La Surprise de l'amour*. All about two lovers who want more than anything to come together but are prevented over the course of three acts by their pride and misunderstandings, while their supple servants try to work things out. It was old stuff, which he knew practically by heart, but he found himself enchanted. The proud Comtesse, who had vowed never to love again, was utterly seductive as she fell hopelessly in love with Lélio. And it was a world in which nothing else counted but love. Any reality outside was rigorously excluded. Life was only a matter of a man and a woman getting things between them exactly right.

The first act ended, with the lovers hopelessly on the wrong course. But that would sort itself out, would lead in fact to a deep clarity in matters of the heart. As Beyle sat contemplating whether to stay for another act or go now to Madame de Castellane's—which would be acceptable, if just barely—he became aware of a pair of opera glasses fixed insistently in his direction from one of the boxes above him, in the second tier. How was it that one became aware of being looked at? he wondered. As he tried to make out the face behind the glasses in the penumbra of the box, a hand was raised, and waved tentatively in his direction by the woman holding the glasses. Could it be? She lowered the glasses. Yes, Amelia. Fortune was finally favoring him. He raised his hand to salute her. She smiled gravely in return.

No further hesitation was possible now. He moved toward the lobby, and found the narrow stair leading up to the boxes, at the same time reaching into his waistcoat for a coin for the usher, to persuade him to let him into the Curials' box. Who might be with Amelia? The General did not go out to the theater much since Menti's death.

The coin did its work, the door to the box was unlocked. Amelia stood with her back to him—though surely she must know he was on his way to her. The woman next to her turned round first, and he recognized the young Comtesse Louise d'Haussonville, daughter of Beyle's sometime minister, the Duc de Broglie. Impressive circles Amelia was traveling in. Some connection to the Chabots, no doubt. Beyle bowed, and Madame d'Haussonville welcomed him most charmingly. She was, he now recalled, a famous beauty, also something of a coquette, a woman who had left many a broken heart in her wake. Also, an amateur writer. She proclaimed herself flattered by Beyle's visit.

Amelia could in conscience no longer keep her back to them. But he sensed her reluctance as she slowly moved from the balustrade, still holding the opera glasses, and turned to face them. Did he detect the trace of tears in her eyes, or was this only a reflection from the chandelier? Beyle bowed in greeting, and she held out her hand.

"Monsieur Beyle. You honor us. How long it has been!"

It had not been long at all, unless you excepted that morning at Ingres' as something too private to be recorded, or at least alluded to. Did he detect a trace of irony in her tone? Or pique?

"Ah, but one does not see you in the habitual places." He tried for a tone of lighthearted banter, but he was aware that his eyes must be betraying him. Her own eyes pierced him, he sensed her desire to convey more than her voice was permitted to say. If only I could pass through into her mind.

They continued in this tone, aided by Madame d'Haussonville's easy chatter of the social season, until the interval reached an end. Then Louise d'Haussonville commanded him to keep them company during the rest of the play, and he was able to place himself just behind Amelia, with a view of the stage over her wonderful bare shoulder. Watching as Lélio and the Comtesse knotted and unknotted their loves, and discovered their true feelings, in a formal garden laid out in a labyrinth.

The second interval provided no more chance for private conversation. Beyle fetched cups of lemon ice for the two women, managed to avoid conversation with his friend Mareste in the foyer—he had more important things to attend to—and then watched love triumph, again over Amelia's shoulder. That shoulder was smooth and supple, it glowed at him out of the dark theater, it seemed to catch the glint of the stage lights. He had to restrain himself from leaning forward and planting a kiss on it. He wondered what would happen if he did.

The play ended, with Lélio on his knees holding the Comtesse's hand, all forgiven, all reconciled. He helped Amelia and Louise into their cloaks. The Haussonville footman had now appeared at the door of the box. Louise slipped out first, and Beyle and Amelia lingered, as by mutual accord, for one moment more. He knew he must seize this instant.

"I've been looking for you," he said. "We need a meeting, alone."

Amelia's face was anxious with inquiry. "You'll accept, then?"

Beyle hesitated for one instant more. "Yes," he said, "but we need to discuss matters."

She looked at him bleakly. "Haven't we said all there is to say? It's time to do something."

"Yes, but I need to know more about Comte de Chabot." As he said the name, he felt a sweep of wind through the willows in the Valley of the Tomb. The gravediggers forced their way into his mind.

Her face came apart at this, he thought she was going to cry. "Don't," she said softly.

"Don't? But . . ." He stopped. What, in any case, did he want to know?

She recomposed her features. "Very well. Come to me on Friday morning, at my father's, at ten o'clock. He goes every morning to his club. We should be alone then."

He bowed. "Very well, Friday at ten." That was three days hence. He must be armed with a decision by then.

✤ 16 ✤

The Body

ORK BEGAN in earnest shortly after midnight. Crowbars were placed under the iron railing on one side of the enclosure, to lift it off. Then the three flat stones covering the tomb were pried off and dragged to one side. A dozen men then fell to with pickaxes and shovels.

The night was dark and windy, and a fine glacial rain fell intermittently. At rare intervals a rent in the clouds gave passage to a cold, spectral moonshine, lighting the scene in a pale glow, showing the rugged hills surrounding the valley, the forms of the two white tents whipped by the wind, revealing the long line of sentinels wrapped in their cloaks who stood guard over the whole valley. But mostly it was only the illumination of the lanterns set around the enclosure, their flames guttering in the wind. The feeble light glinted from time to time on the head of a pickax as it swung up and down. No other sound than the thud of the pickaxes, the scraping of shovels, and the howling wind. A muttered curse from time to time from the diggers, in French or in English, or simply a grunt. Now a new team of diggers moved into place and took their tools from the exhausted men of the first team, who collapsed onto the wet grass, wrapped themselves in cloaks and sea coats, passing a bottle from hand to hand.

Philippe sat against the trunk of the willow, his hat pulled low on his forehead against the wind and the rain. The spectacle was like some witches' sabbath, he thought. The diggers were now well below ground level, you could see only their heads and shoulders, the high swing of the pickax, the brief appearance of a shovel with its load of earth, flung to one side. He could barely make out the identity of the watchers. Emmanuel was not far off, standing with a walking stick he had cut from a fallen tree, rain dripping from his broad-brimmed hat. Gourgaud, in full dress uniform and general's hat—like Napoleon's own, really—immobile, his eyes fixed on the hole before them. Old Bertrand—at the last minute he had insisted upon coming despite his enfeebled condition—and young Arthur, and Coquereau's two altar boys, had taken refuge in the tent. But Coquereau himself, in his black cassock and mantle and skullcap, stood in the rain. So did Marchand, Guillard, Charner, Guyet, and Doret and the others. A little apart was the knot of English officers, Alexander and Trelawney and Littlehales and Hudson, with Justice Wilde. They all seemed to need to watch, to bear witness to this moment. Though a sinister moment, he thought. What was the earthly use of this? Napoleon was well buried where he was. There was a fantastic dignity in this grave at the end of the earth, in this wild, forbidding landscape, this valley cut off by its natural escarpments from society and from history. A place in which to enter into eternity.

For the first time since leaving Toulon, though, Philippe felt he was emerging from a story written for him. They were finally at it, this was his business, he was in command. No one else could have imagined this. It was indelibly part of his life, for better or worse.

He heard a cry from Captain Alexander, passing word along the line of the sentinels. A click and thud as they presented arms, then returned to parade rest. Now the sounds from the pit changed. A ringing noise from the pickaxes, more curses, and he could even hear deeper breathing from the diggers. They must have come on the masonry.

He moved cautiously through the mounds of dirt to the edge of the pit as the team of diggers changed again. Four lanterns were lowered into the pit, and by the flickering light he could see that a grayish substance now lay exposed in several places. The pickaxes scarcely made a dent in it, and fantastic sparks glanced off as they hit solid rock. The workers groaned at every blow. The work now became tediously slow and painstaking. Several more blows of the pickax to open a slit in the masonry, then they would take the scissors to the slit, and try to enlarge it.

Captain Alexander was at his side. He cupped his hand to speak in Philippe's ear. "Five o'clock, sir. We'll never make it at this rate. I'm going to put some of the sentinels to work on a lateral trench. Go in from the side, where the wall of the crypt will be less massive."

Philippe shrugged. "As you choose. But I'm not sure you'll have better success."

But Alexander, undeterred, soon had six redcoats stripped to their shirtsleeves and at work on a parallel trench, some four feet to the right of the pit. Philippe watched the intense activity with growing anxiety. The rain was coming harder now, and the diggers were soaked. The parallel trench was becoming a mudhole. At least in the main pit the water drained away off the masonry. But progress was agonizingly slow.

He became aware that dawn was breaking, a cold, gray dawn, bringing no comfort. The light of the lanterns faded as pale illumination spread across the strange scene before him. The crew in the main pit changed again. And then, just after eight o'clock, a pickax went through into vacancy below. A cry from the worker. Philippe approached the edge of the pit. The man swung again. He had now ripped open a hole about six inches square. He reached for a lantern and held it to the hole. As the flames leapt and danced, Philippe made out the edge of a black wooden box. The outer coffin.

The workers fell to with redoubled efforts. Coquereau now made his way to the spring just downhill from the tomb with the water jug he had brought, filled it, and retired into the tent. To perform whatever rituals would turn it into holy water, Philippe surmised.

Alexander was back at his side. "We've got it now, sir. We'll give up the side trench, and I'll put those men to rigging the block and tackle."

"Right. For the slab." As the workers hacked away large chunks of masonry, Philippe could see that the center of the tomb, as expected from Lowe's memorandum, was covered by a single large slab of stone. They'd definitely need block and tackle.

The workers struggled to plant posts to hold the block and tackle. Alexander ordered the remaining sentinels to approach, and form up in a solid line around the pit. Marchand disappeared into the tent, to reemerge with Bertrand, without their cloaks, in full military uniform. Gourgaud—who never left the graveside—simply threw back his cloak, displaying a chest covered with filigree and medals.

The rain was now driving hard, cold and penetrating. Another hour with picks and scissors, and the slab was freed from the masonry. Alexander's sappers rigged ropes to iron clamps, these attached to edges of the stone. Alexander gave the order to lift. Coquereau appeared from the tent, now dressed in white surplice, preceded by the altar boys, one carrying the basin of holy water, the other the cross, and went to the head of the grave. Slowly the stone slab rose, tilted—a gasp from the watchers, as it seemed it would crash back into the pit—then it was safely up, swung to one side, and dropped on the pile of earth.

In the gaping crypt revealed below them lay the coffin. Spontaneously, almost simultaneously, all hats were off—generals' two-cornered hats, shakos, sailors' caps—and the massed ranks stood bareheaded, rain streaming from their faces, and stared. The redcoats came to attention with a thud of their rifles. The coffin appeared to be intact. Philippe could just make out the silver heads of the screws on the lid. To each side still lay the ropes and straps used to lower it into the crypt. A kind of still life from twenty years ago. They looked brittle and dusty, though now the raindrops were beginning to turn them a soggy darker gray.

Now Dr. Guillard sprang down into the crypt with a pail of chloride powder and spread it on the floor of the crypt, to disinfect. Coquereau raised his wand dipped in holy water, then made the sign of the cross over the coffin. The murmured Latin of his prayer was the only sound other than the wail of the wind. Then Alexander and Philippe stepped down into the crypt.

Philippe hesitated a moment, then reached out his hand and touched the wet wood of the lid. It felt solid. He removed his hand, turned it palm upward, and looked at it with curiosity for a moment. Just a slight muddy slime.

A moment's pause, then he reached up to grasp Gourgaud's massive hand. With a heave, he was out of the crypt. He strode quickly to the tent, to scribble his note to Joinville. It was now nearly ten o'clock in the morning. A rough estimate suggested that they should be under way toward Jamestown by early afternoon. He summoned Penarche, a young sailor he knew to be fast afoot, and gave him the order to run the message to the frigate. Ducking under the tent flap on his way out again, he stubbed his toe on a box stowed in the corner behind the flap. He recognized with annoyance the polished wood of Emmanuel's camera apparatus, destined never to come out of its box in this weather.

Alexander had got the straps rigged under the coffin. The block and tackle strained, then up it came. Twelve redcoats of the 91st advanced, bareheaded, to array themselves on either side. With a great heave, they had it on their shoulders, and shuffled forward into the nearest tent, Philippe and Dr. Guillard following. A quick examination of the screwheads, and Philippe decided it would be better to saw the mahogany coffin through at one end, to extract the lead coffin that lay within.

The tent swayed and rattled in the wind. Inside, the light was soft and dim. Side by side with the coffin, on another set of trestles, lay the vast ebony sarcophagus they had brought from Paris, still closed, with its simple gold lettering, NAPOLEON. Charner now was working to open the lid, without success, his face vexed. Evidently there was a secret catch. Did anyone know how it worked? Thiers' elaborate instructions had neglected this detail. Philippe stepped to Charner's side, and fumbled along the underlip of the lid. How did the thing work? "I saw them do this in Paris," Emmanuel whispered. "Let me try." Philippe waited anxiously. Then Emmanuel found it, a spring mechanism. The lid lifted slightly, with a quiet sigh.

Philippe grasped Emmanuel on the shoulder, and turned back to the coffin. The saw had almost finished its work. Then a sudden new sound: horse's hooves, the jangle of a bridle, the squish of boots in the mud. The tent flap was flung open. Philippe turned quickly, in alarm and annoyance, and recognized Lieutenant Touchard from the *Belle Poule,* sent by Joinville for news of progress. Somehow he had missed encountering Penarche on his way. How could that be? Philippe dispatched him back to the frigate immediately.

With a final effort, the carpenters were through the end of the coffin, which slid gently to the ground. Peering into the open end, Philippe could see the lead coffin inside. He signed to the workers to slide it out. One layer removed. He steeled his mind to the task ahead. Putrefaction . . . or nothing at all? With a silent gesture, he directed that the lead coffin be placed in the ebony sarcophagus. Better to have things enclosed as they worked toward the remains. The six men staggered under the weight.

Now Leroux came forward with his metal scissors to unseal the join of the lead, prying the cover to one side, like the lid of a packing case. Within the lead coffin lay another wooden one—made from local fruitwood—perfectly intact, and dry. No odor was detectable. Dr. Guillard inspected it with his magnifying glass, then stepped back.

The screws were in good condition on this inner coffin. The carpenters soon had them loosened, and the lid removed. Now they had come to the final coffin, of tin. It, too, looked in good condition, despite a few patches where the metal was oxydized.

More noises from without the tent, a trampling of horses. This time it was General Middlemore, his son, and his aide-de-camp. They had arrived just in time. It was well to have them as witnesses.

Alexander stepped outside, and ordered the sentinels to admit no one else.

Leroux, his movements hindered by the three coffin walls in which the tin coffin nested, applied his scissors carefully to the seal, working methodically from head to foot. Utter silence now in the tent, except for the rain, drumming hard on the canvas roof. Then Leroux was done. He beckoned one of the sailors, and together they carefully lifted off the lid.

Philippe was pressed between Gourgaud and old Marchand as he craned forward to look. What was this? A formless whitish mass. Something like a giant slug. Philippe fell back, startled, and glanced at Guillard. The doctor looked puzzled. Cautiously, he reached out a hand. The satin cushioning inside the lid of the coffin had fallen in, covering the body.

Inch by inch, Guillard peeled back the satin. Philippe heard a great sob from Gourgaud at his side.

The coffin was not empty. And there could be no doubt: the Emperor was before them.

The body was remarkably preserved, dressed in the dark green jacket of the chasseurs, with nankeen trousers and waist-coat. The gilt epaulettes on the shoulders were tarnished, but the large red rosette of the Legion of Honor was still bright. The hat—that famous hat—lay across the thighs. His legs were encased in high boots, the leather mottled and mildewed. Between the legs were two vases, sealed with the imperial eagle, one containing the Emperor's heart, the other his stomach. At the point of his feet, the stitching of boot to sole had come apart, and one could see three toes of each foot exposed to the air.

The head lay on a cushion, which thrust it upward just a bit. Yes, as in some of the portraits, the head appeared enormous, out of proportion to the body. A high, rounded forehead over the closed eyes. The nose had fallen a bit, the chin and the mouth were unaltered. You could see the front teeth, perfectly white, through the slightly parted lips. The skin of the face was like parchment, with the shadow of a beard that had continued to grow after death.

Gourgaud was sobbing like a child, and Bertrand looked as if he were ready to throw himself into his dead master's embrace. Philippe realized that his own eyes were swimming with tears. Was it just relief at this end to doubt and anxiety? Something more than that, he thought. He had reached into the secret of death, into the silence of the tomb, and found history itself, at the same time real, and dead.

Guillard now leaned over the body, and palpated the

face, and the right hand, a fine white hand with long fingers. "Mummified," he pronounced in a whisper. "Perfectly safe."

He stood up again, and glanced anxiously at Philippe. How long had they been gazing at the body exposed? Maybe two minutes. Philippe nodded to Guillard, who took a brush soaked in creosote and dabbed it on the underside of the satin lining of the coffin lid, then stepped back, beckoning to Leroux.

Leroux shook his head, and turned to Philippe. "Can't resolder the tin, sir. It's too oxydized. But we can seal the lead one."

Philippe nodded, and moments later the Emperor's body was gone from sight. The cover of the fruitwood coffin was screwed down, the lead coffin was carefully resoldered, the ebony sarcophagus was locked with a plaque inside bearing an inscription in gold letters:

NAPOLEON
EMPEROR AND KING
DIED IN SAINT HELENA
5 MAY
MDCCCXXI

Leroux, with a bow, presented the key to Philippe.

Coquereau, flanked by his altar boys, stepped to the head of the sarcophagus and began the *De Profundis,* dipping his wand and sprinkling holy water from head to foot. Guillard seated himself at the end of the trestle and hastily began to write out his medical report on the body.

Now Alexander stepped forward, and spoke in English the words he and Philippe had devised together—he had committed them to memory:

"Sir, As the Officer deputed by His Excellency the Governor, Major General Middlemore, Companion of the Bath and Commander of the Forces at Saint Helena, in the presence of the Senior Naval, Civil, and Military Authorities, to exhume and deliver to you, Monsieur le Comte Philippe de Chabot, Commissaire du Roi des Français, the Coffin containing, as has been duly ascertained, the Mortal Remains of the late Emperor Napoleon . . ."

This was a bit long-winded, but he had got it right, at least he had used the title Emperor, thus sparing Philippe outcries from the old faithful. Philippe bowed, and spoke his reply:

"Sir, in my capacity as commissioner named by His Majesty the King of the French to proceed, in his name, to the exhumation and the transportation of the mortal remains of the Emperor Napoleon, I accept from your hands this coffin containing the mortal remains of Napoleon buried at Saint Helena the 8 May 1821 . . ."

Philippe concluded, they shook hands. Then in a sort of stunned silence they moved to the opening of the tent. Major General Churchill was there, according to plan, his uniform draped with a black band of mourning. With his two aides-de-camp, he stood bareheaded in the rain. Behind him was the funeral caisson, with four horses hitched to it. A detachment of twelve redcoats stepped forward, and entered the tent. They could not lift the sarcophagus. It took double that number to get it onto the caisson.

They were ready to begin the four-mile march back to Jamestown. Philippe stared for a moment at the sarcophagus on the caisson, and realized there was one more detail he had forgotten. The imperial mantle to drape the coffin. He signaled to Trelawney to wait, and stepped back into the tent. Where might it have got to? Who was supposed to be in charge of it? He found it folded across one of the trestles, and carried it out to the caisson. Bertrand, Gourgaud, Marchand, and Emmanuel stepped forward, to unfold the deep purple velvet cloth, and spread it over the sarcophagus. An embroidered silver cross in the middle, gold bees everywhere, and a border where the encircled letter *N* alternated with the imperial eagle, then a fringe of ermine.

Trelawney gave the signal. The soldiers of the militia and the 91st Infantry began the march, guns slung in reverse, their pace slow and solemn. Then came Coquereau preceded by his altar boys, one with the cross held high, the other with the holy water. Then the caisson, the four horses draped in black straining to get the weight moving, with Bertrand, Gourgaud, Marchand, and Emmanuel at the four corners. The remains of the Empire except for Emmanuel, who, there in his father's place, seemed to represent the new order. Philippe's world, which now was taking the Emperor into its embrace. Then came the rest of the French contingent, followed by the English.

The horses strained forward. The pace was slow. It took close to two hours to reach the steep descent into Jamestown. Now the road was bordered on each side by a row of redcoats—the militiamen had gone ahead on the double, and placed themselves at parade rest with their rifles reversed, the end of the barrel resting on the left foot, the stock held under crossed arms. And as they passed into the narrow main street of the town, the military band up ahead began a noble and majestic hymn, the *Dead March* from *Saul*. They were doing it all right, the English. They finally seemed to have accepted the idea that he was indeed Emperor, not simply an international outlaw.

The cannon began, first in the fort, then on the frigate and the other warships in the harbor. An alternating boom and roll of thunder every minute. The entire population of the island now was following the cortège, diving into side streets when it passed, to reemerge lower down the slope. The redcoats, both militiamen and 91st Infantry, now were aligned to the two sides of the cortège, which moved without obstruction down through the gate to the quayside. The tricolor flag flapped in the brisk evening breeze, and under it Philippe could now make out Joinville, standing at attention with his afterguard drawn up in two columns behind him. As the caisson came into sight, the Prince and his officers uncovered their heads. Behind them, the oarsmen of the launches lowered their oars in unison. And out in the harbor, the *Belle Poule,* the *Favorite,* and the *Oreste* in unison broke out their colors.

They reached the landing stage. Coquereau took the aspergill from the altar boy and handed it to Joinville, who solemnly sprinkled a few drops on the draped sarcophagus. For a moment, Joinville stood silent, his hand resting on the edge of the sarcophagus. Philippe watched him, at once sympathetic and detached. Coming to terms with the shade within, he supposed, the shade they now had to carry back to France. He summoned up that spectacle by the gray early morning light of the tent, Napoleon himself in his uniform, his face in repose, scarcely altered from life. But dead, wholly dead. Joinville had missed that. He would never view the Emperor's body. That was an experience for Philippe to hold close, to remember forever. To what account? Spooks and goblins. He shuddered at the remembered face of death. Suddenly he felt exhausted, wasted from the night's anxious vigil and the slow march across the island. Let this all be over.

Joinville turned from the sarcophagus, and the sailors stepped forward. This was the most delicate moment. Slowly, painstakingly, they inched the sarcophagus to the water's edge and moved it on planks into the launch. The launch settled deep into the water under the weight—Philippe saw in alarm that there couldn't be more than six inches freeboard left. Joinville, Coquereau, and the other principals stepped in. There were the launches of the *Favorite* and the *Oreste* for the others. In ten minutes' time, they were at the frigate, before a lowered harness that was placed around the sarcophagus. It was covered again with the mantle, and Joinville gave the order to lift.

The sarcophagus rose in the air, and the launch, unburdened, rose from under it. Up on the deck of the frigate, the sailors were aligned in dress whites, with black mourning bands. The officers' sabers glinted in the fitful light of the lanterns. Down below, the crews of the launches held their oars straight up. Silence, except for the creaking of the pulleys and the slap of the water. Then a shattering boom from the citadel as it began a twenty-one-gun salute. It rolled echoing across the roadstead, reverberating against the mountainous shore, and then was reechoed as the ships at anchor answered with their own salvos.

It was almost night. Just as the sarcophagus reached its highest point, as it started to swing into its place on the deck, a startling ray of the setting sun broke through the cover of clouds and lit the roiling billows of gunsmoke and the bare spars of the frigate. Then it was gone. Night was upon them.

The sarcophagus came to rest on the deck. The last roll of cannon fire rumbled back through the hills of the island. Lanterns were placed around the sarcophagus, sentinels were placed at each corner, Coquereau began a new set of prayers. The wake began.

❧ 17 ❧

The Love Problem

L OUISE D'HAUSSONVILLE had an expression somewhere between mirth and concern. "My dear, you could
end up compromising yourself."

"Why? I know he's a bohemian, but surely he's a respected
figure. A consul, after all, and a remarkable writer."

"Yes, yes. But also a bit of a roué, I think. His attentions to you
are a bit suspect."

Of course they were, and of course she wanted them that way.
But she couldn't really admit this to Louise. "I think he's atten-
tive because of Mother. They were friends."

Louise arched her eyebrows in the theatrical way Amelia
thought she must practice before the mirror. "Friends, yes. Maybe
more?"

Amelia willed her face into a blank. When she didn't respond,
Louise continued: "There were rumors, you know, that she and
Beyle . . . were quite intimate."

"People don't repeat those rumors to me directly. But I had figured that out on my own."

"And that doesn't shock you, my dear?" Louise's little laugh ended in a giggle.

"No. Yes. I don't know what to think of it. Mother will always be a mystery. The unsolved enigma of my life."

"Does Beyle help with that?"

"Maybe. But Louise, you know I don't know him so well as all that. We've had a few conversations, that's all."

"Well, you did seem rather . . . *intense,* the two of you, as we were leaving the Italiens, the evening before last."

Amelia was surprised. Was that so? And visibly so, to boot? "I can't think why we would have been."

Louise reached out her folded fan and tapped her friend lightly on the back of her wrist. "Is there something between you?"

"Nothing. My mature admirer, that's all." Suddenly she felt the temptation to confide everything in Louise—to spill out her whole dilemma. It would be a relief to be able to speak. Yes, there was something between them—but what exactly? No, she brought herself up. No surer way to have yourself gossiped about all over town than to confide in Louise.

She shifted uneasily on the unyielding Empire divan, and grasped for another subject. But Louise wouldn't let it go. "Ah well, but wouldn't it be quite lovely to have such a man as your lover?" Louise gave her most charming smile, dimpling her cheeks. "But of course you ought to be married first. It's the only thing." She herself had been married, what was it? For just over a year.

Louise arched her back, fluttered her eyelids, and said coquettishly, "He's very clever, you know. And he could write you into one of his novels."

"Not my life's ambition," Amelia managed to speak firmly.

"But I do find Beyle very amusing. And there aren't many amusements at present."

"My poor Amelia." Louise in a graceful movement was at her side. She wrapped her arm around her waist and gave her a quick kiss on the cheek. "How you have suffered. You must come to me more often. And when my cousin Philippe de Chabot is back, I'll give a dinner in his honor, and you shall come."

Louise's intention was only to be kind. But here she was on the dreaded subject. Amelia twisted to look through the windows masked with their muslin curtains. Gray and cold outside. Then she spoke, evenly and more curtly than she intended. "Thanks. But I imagine I will have a visit from Philippe as soon as he arrives."

Louise's eyebrows shot up again—she surely cultivated this expression of astonished ingenuousness—as she said: "Oh, you've had news from him?"

"From months ago. He wrote from Teneriffe, on the voyage out."

"And?"

"He said he would call upon his return." That was all she was going to reveal, Amelia instructed herself.

"Are you then . . . his *promessa*?" Louise asked, a bit archly.

"No. Nothing of the kind. I shall simply receive him, to hear what he has to say."

"Dearest, it would be such a wonderful match for you. And Philippe . . . well, probably he doesn't strike you as quite scintillating, but he is so kind. And with a great future before him now. Guizot thinks the world of him."

She ended her speech with a little hug. Her flushed and smiling face looked so pretty Amelia could only smile back. There were so many questions she wanted to ask her, about Philippe. But better not.

Louise ran on. "I should think that what you need is peace, a happy, peaceful, orderly life. After life with your mother. I have some sense, dear Amelia, of what it was like for you, growing up in . . . a household that wasn't exactly united. So much younger than your brother and sister you hardly knew them, and with Clémentine more and more possessed by her devils. It can't have been easy."

Amelia nodded. But she wasn't going to talk about it.

"I met your mother only a few times, at large receptions, but I always was somewhat in awe of her—I think everyone was. She had such . . . temperament. One can see her appeal to men, I suppose. And very beautiful—as are you, my dear—but somehow not easy for women. All of them her rivals."

Including her daughter? Amelia asked herself. Certainly not back then, certainly never consciously. But it's true that Mother tended to drive other women away, her daughter included.

"I do recommend the married state, my dear." Louise was now playing the experienced woman, speaking a bit didactically. "I mean, there are certain things that are *strange* at first." She giggled.

Amelia guessed she was supposed to ask about—how was it that silly novel on her dresser phrased it?—the "mysteries of the nuptial chamber." But she wasn't going to. That was something you had to find out for yourself.

But Louise went on without a pause. "I used to see Philippe at our château in the Cotentin sometimes, in the summer. I was even sweet on him at one time. He was a sensitive boy, almost placid, but with a very kind disposition. Never pulled my hair," Louise said, with a toss of her blond ringlets.

Still Amelia said nothing, though she could imagine their summers in the Norman countryside, Louise and Philippe in straw hats, running across the dunes. It was easy to imagine Philippe as a boy. He seemed still a boy in so many ways.

Louise now spoke with a touching earnestness. "Amelia, you

will be twenty-five the day after tomorrow. You know as well as I what people will start to say. You'll begin to be seen as one of the spinsters, one of those women who are considered . . . a bit odd, as if they must have some character flaw because they aren't married. Treated with a kind of condescension. I know, I know—it's unjust. But it's the way of the world."

Amelia felt her face set in stubborn resistance. "Why must marriage be the only solution?"

"Oh, there's the convent. Or life as a bohemian artist. I do admire Madame Dudevant, who calls herself George Sand and publishes novels and lives a perfectly scandalous life. But that's not for us, I don't think."

But why not? Amelia wondered if she could ever find the strength to live a life Louise would think of as scandalous. To write, to create—like Beyle—worlds in the mind, so she could treat this world with the contempt it deserved. "Wouldn't that be wonderful," she said aloud, continuing her thoughts.

"Wonderful? To be a writer, you mean. Yes, I agree. Even I have my little scribblings, my memoir of the Cotentin. But women have to do that discreetly."

"Oh, I know. No scandal allowed." She wondered if she had the stuff to write—really write, not Louise's well-mannered and sentimental gruel. Yes, to do it right you probably had to be scandalous. Did she have the strength for that?

This was an important question, she decided. It came to her that this was something she wanted to think about. How strong was she? She had no way of knowing, she hadn't tested herself. Time to stop flirting with perhapses and maybes. Can I be something other than just a woman?

Louise rose, in a graceful billow of pale blue silk, and paced the worn Turkey carpet. Her companion's silence evidently persuaded her that there would be no further revelations from Amelia. She spun on her heel in a kind of charming pirouette that she managed so well, and started toward the door of the drawing room. "I must be going. I have my appointment with the dressmaker, then luncheon at Mama's. But you shall come to us soon, for that dinner. And think on what I've said."

"Of course I will." Amelia felt a rush of gratitude toward Louise, she had brought her face-to-face with a real question. Not that she could ever explain it to Louise. They kissed on both cheeks, and Amelia gave her an extra hug. "Come again soon. You do me good."

Louise's face was a study in harmonious beauty. "I'm so glad, my dear. And don't fret. Things do get better, you know. Marriage, for instance. It's not perfect, but it does improve life."

If this was another invitation to learn more about Louise's life with Haussonville, Amelia was not going to take it up now. She needed some thinking about her own life. She tried to cock her head in a kind of ingénue curiosity. "You'll tell me all about it— what it's like—someday soon?"

Louise rolled her eyes theatrically. "Oh but my dear. The corruption of innocence?" Then she laughed openly. "Of course. And there you and I certainly agree, innocence be hanged."

"Yes. Innocence be hanged, quite right." They now had moved from the drawing room to the front hall, and Berthe sidled toward them to open the door. They kissed again, and Louise was gone, leaving behind a scent of iris.

Lucky Haussonville, Amelia thought as she turned back toward the drawing room. A beautiful woman, and one who could not help but please. She must make an adorable lover as well. Whatever that meant. But Amelia was reasonably sure she knew what that meant.

She seated herself at the piano. Some Chopin to fill the empty time. Let's see, one of the nocturnes, yes, this one in F minor. But her fingers rested on the keyboard without moving. She was thinking about her courage, if that was the word. How far would it take her? Could she be like George Sand? Was that necessary—was there another way? Did this idea of creating lead her to Beyle's bed? Was that part of it, or merely a distraction?

She sat long in her meditation. It was a painful self-examination, yet filled with a certain voluptuous pleasure as well. For the first time in her life she felt something like a surge of power within herself.

ALL BEYLE's resolutions for the morning were proving useless. He needed to write to Tavernier. He had to get word to Giulia not to attempt a trip to Paris. And he had promised to get back to his story of Lamiel. Amelia had made Lamiel come alive again, given substance to that imaginary young woman, made her seem almost possible, as if he could conjure flesh and blood from his own writing. But Amelia herself was the problem, she blocked out everything else.

He found himself pacing before the window, looking down at the gray Paris street of a dull November morning, the wind buffeting the women on their morning errands. They wrapped their shawls closer, and with hands clutched to their bonnets, they pushed along the street like boats against the current.

What was he like, this Chabot? An insipid fair-haired young fellow, no doubt, with perfect manners and platitudes for every occasion. Hadn't Amelia said as much? Said that all the men of her generation bored her? One of those young men you met by the dozens at Madame de Castellane's, whose idea of pleasing a woman was to recount the plot of the latest novel by Madame de Krudener, with expurgation of anything bordering on the scabrous. But there wasn't anything of the sort in that kind of novel for chambermaids. But no, after all Chabot had been entrusted by the government with a major mission, however absurd and misguided. He couldn't be entirely negligible. The government must have future plans for him. Minister of Foreign Affairs. Who knows? President of the Council of Ministers one day. Amelia would be the queen of Paris society. Live at ease in vast apartments, keep her own salon.

Beyle grimaced at the slightly shabby gentility of his study in his rented digs. Despite the consulate, despite the unexpected success of the *Charterhouse*—all because of Monsieur de Balzac's generous, enthusiastic review (though it rather missed the mark)—he was nothing but a bohemian in fact, he would never be quite respectable. He had long ago thought he accepted this, but he was aware that something in his bourgeois provincial background revolted against it. He wanted status, he wanted ease.

He could not rid himself of an obsessive image that rose in his mind's eye, from a nightmare after he had finally dozed off, last night. Amelia in Ingres' studio, standing with her arms raised gracefully above her head, her hair undone and falling in abundant curls on her shoulders. She was naked—yet something blocked her from view, he couldn't visualize her naked. She was smiling with an intense, fixed expression, her lips slightly parted. And Chabot—he saw him only from the back, in a well-cut black frock coat, tapered to the waist, with blond hair and the ends of his mustache visible on either side—did he wear whiskers?—leaning toward her. This was absurd. Chabot was still thousands of miles away. Maybe at this very moment digging up the Emperor's body.

Beyle evoked in his mind the etching of the Valley of the Tomb, its weeping willows decorously framing the fenced plot of earth. He had long thought of it as the fitting site for Napoleon's final rest. He knew the temptation of withdrawal from the world, on the hard wooden bench of a charterhouse, for instance, or—he smiled wryly to himself—a consulate in Civitavecchia. But now, maybe at this very moment, the digging was to begin.

He had heard, too, the rumors of an empty tomb. He conjured it in his mind—the shovel striking a wooden box that gave off a hollow sound, the gravediggers looking at one another with wild surmise, young Chabot looking on anxiously as the coffin, much too light, was lifted from the hole. He saw them pry off the lid, and stare down into emptiness. Just a buried box. No treasure. That might really be the appropriate end of the affair. Napoleon's body gone, borne away somewhere on the tides of the sea, perhaps. He stared in his mind's eye into the empty box. Nothingness. That was it. That is what he faced, and soon. Amelia was simply a mask for the nothingness that lay ahead.

Or, no, they were probably on the voyage back by now, with that coffin, full or empty, on board. Chabot dreaming of his return to Amelia, of their marriage, of his wedding night. Beyle felt the heat of jealousy, of something that should be his that was not his.

His appointment with Amelia now lay twenty-four hours ahead of him. How was he to get through that time? A ridiculous question at his age, he knew. More important, that rendez-vous itself, at the General's. She had said they would be alone, but it would not be alone like Giulia and himself at the Albergo del Campo. He had never found resolutions to amorous dilemmas to take place in conversations in the drawing room. Not like a Marivaux play. Dénouements could only come, he thought, through two bodies coming closer, with a bed or a sofa nearby. Not in the resolution to travel together to Switzerland. At least that was his experience, which he had to admit was largely one of seizing chances where they lay. He cast a tender retrospect over some of those chances.

Did he really mean to take Amelia to bed? To risk all the impossible complications he had warned her of? They were real enough. But he wanted her, overwhelmingly.

The day engulfed him in an anxious grayness. By midafternoon, he finally made himself leave the apartment. He wandered through the streets until he reached the Tuileries Garden, then on across to the banks of the Seine. The water ran cold and green. Across the river, he could see wagons drawn up on the esplanade before the Invalides. Of course, workmen must be inside, preparing the site for the Emperor's tomb, a vast alteration project, which would not be completed by the time that coffin— full or empty—arrived. But at least they had to open the passage to what would be a vast open crypt, with a balustrade running around it. "I wish my remains to rest on the banks of the Seine, in the midst of the French people whom I loved so much," the Emperor had said in his last testament. Beyle was moved only for an instant. Noble words, yes, but really more of the propaganda machine, working overtime, working beyond death, in an attempt to control the future. An attempt that now would be met with success—if the body had been found. It was remarkable how they all did his bidding, even after death—as if they all continued to move within the vast circles of Napoleon's mind. That, of course, was nonsense in any realistic view. The return from Saint Helena was politics, he knew that. But still. Politics that served the Emperor's last wish. That might turn out to make the politicians themselves pawns to a dead mind.

He turned to his left, thinking he would go pay Ingres a visit. But he stopped after a few paces. No, Ingres was not what he needed now. What did he need? In the past he would have known. Something like those pleasure parties his friend Barot used to organize, where in a warm and elegant salon on the fourth floor of a house on the Boulevard Montmartre you would find half a dozen charming young bit players from the Opera and the Bouffes, aspiring actresses who knew that their careers and even their daily bread depended on the protection of a man. Love without consequence, venal love, of course, but charmingly offered. But that no longer interested him. He had over the years gained that much self-awareness: for all his aspirations to be Don Juan, he was really closer to Goethe's hapless young Werther. A lover, not a seducer.

There was nothing for it but to go sit in Tortoni's and drink coffee and read the newspapers—but these were ever more pompous and depressing and full of lies. Why couldn't his country ever have honest men in power? The rest of the day could only be wasted in any case. Then the night. Would he even be able to sleep?

❧18❧

Crossings

AMELIA IN her bedroom replaced the letter from Teneriffe in the drawer of her writing table, after rereading it for the sixth or seventh time. Why should this letter make any difference? she asked herself. It was only what was to be expected of him—the conventional response to their final inconclusive meeting before he left for Toulon. Nothing special about it, other than the exotic stamp. It told her nothing particular about him, it could have been composed by any of the young men in Madame de Castellane's salon.

The letter dated from months ago, but the man who wrote it must be close to home now. Things were too crowded. If she wanted to become Beyle's mistress and then Philippe's fiancée, in some implausible sequence, there didn't seem time for that now. At least, not the emotional time she needed. Things in her head were too compressed. She found herself resenting Beyle's hesitations. She had wanted him, that she knew. If only men understood.

She sat on the bed with a sigh. Of course Philippe will want me too—once we are properly married, that is—and I can imagine wanting him. Why was it Beyle seemed so different, though? Because marriage with him was out of the question? There would be no contract, no promise, no tomorrow—simply that lust to be satisfied, that sense of being a woman desired. If that's what it was, maybe she was being perverse. Yet how was a young woman supposed to live her life with such alternatives?

She rose again, and stood before the oval mirror. Her face was flushed, her features distorted in anguish. She tried to compose her appearance and her mind. Life was supposed to be all before her. Everything was her choice to make. The riches of the earth. She was twenty-five today, a mature woman, ready to become a wife, or spinster. She smiled wryly at this unappetizing choice.

JUST DOWNRIVER from Rouen, the massive sarcophagus was lifted once again, from the sidewheeler *Normandie,* too deep of draft to make it any farther up the Seine, to the *Dorade 3,* one of three swift steamers of the same name that along with seven other steamboats would continue the seven-day journey up to Paris, with orders not to stop. Philippe and Joinville received these orders at Cherbourg when the *Belle Poule* came to anchor on 30 November. They thought they were going to travel overland to Paris, in triumphal procession.

Instead, this. It was cold on the *Dorade 3,* and cramped—a summer pleasure barge, not a real ship. They all had to bunk down together, even the Prince, in the main saloon. No privacy. And cold, cold inside as well as on deck, as the monotonous winter landscape unfolded like a panorama on either side of the boat. Frost on the meadows, no livestock to be seen. The ruins of the

Abbaye de Jumièges, its honey-colored stone whitened out by the cold, wind sweeping though its broken arches. There was fear of early ice on the Seine.

Emmanuel and Hernoux had been more fortunate. Since there were important votes impending in the Assembly, they had been ordered to post to Paris as quickly as possible. They must be there by now. While he had days still of his undertaker's mission.

Philippe puzzled it out. Politics must lie behind the change of plan, this trip upriver rather than by the high road. Thiers had fallen while they were on their voyage, his place as prime minister taken by old Marshal Soult. Now, Soult was a man of the Empire, someone who would want to do the Emperor's body the highest honors. But he was only a figurehead. Behind him stood the man who now was the real power in France, Philippe's old master Guizot, become Minister of Foreign Affairs, and recognized by all as the King's lieutenant. Guizot from the start hadn't liked the decision to return the body. He feared its effects, the outpour-ings of popular sentiment—he had no use for popular sentiment in any case—the spontaneous demonstrations that were bound to take place in every town the cortège passed through, the cries of "Long live the Emperor!" that might quickly modulate into "Down with the King!"

Guizot was not in a strong position here. He was thought to have been a key negotiator of the return of the Bourbons twenty-five years earlier. He was close to the English, and highly suspect to the Bonapartists. So, insulating the return of the sarcophagus by way of the river route obviously made sense to him—this was his stroke, Philippe assumed. Yet how was he going to handle the Paris ceremonies? They couldn't be too low-key, or there would be a popular outcry.

Even the route up the Seine had its painful demonstrations. As they neared Rouen, he could hear all the church bells of the city going, as if sounding a general alarm. Then the cannon salute began, starting at the top of Mount Saint Catherine, and rolling into the town beneath. Where the English burned Joan of Arc—was that somehow part of Napoleon's return? They rounded the long bend in the river and found the suspension bridge had gained a bizarre excrescence, a papier-mâché Arc de Triomphe hung from under it, so that the *Dorade* had to pass through this strange festooned creation. A mass of frock coats and black stovepipe hats was awaiting them on the quay, and a brass band honked military marches across the water. They were beckoned to land. But since the orders were formal—no landing—the *Dorade* instead backed its engines, and drifted to a stop in the river, some fifty feet from the quay. Evident consternation among the greeting party, shouts to land, which Joinville refused through his megaphone. Then a figure stepped forth, doffed his hat—the mayor?—and began a discourse. Broken phrases reached them across the water. "Sacred emotions . . . last and final resting place . . . the man whom all Europe could not contain! . . . Patriotic enterprise . . . Eternal thanks . . . Frenchmen never forget!" A cold wind whistled up the river. The *Dorade* began to slew sideways. A clang of the bell, then a deep growl from the engine and a puff of black smoke, spewing toward the orator. The *Dorade* quickly gathered speed again, the welcoming party left stranded on the shore. Not the way to the hearts and minds of the people, Philippe decided, but orders were orders. He wondered what Emmanuel would have made of it. But he was no doubt once more absorbed in the parliamentary game. Trading votes. This government was by no means secure in power.

And so they continued on up the river, through rows of bare poplars on either side. Behind them, the empty pastures, rimed with frost. Then the steeple announcing a town. As it came into view, there was the inevitable gathering on the shore, the local notables in their Sunday best, then a straggling mass of peasants in black. All bared their heads as the *Dorade* passed. Occasionally a rusty brass band would strike up the *Chant du départ*. Then they would be gone abruptly, as the paddle wheels of the *Dorade* threw up a mist that obscured the view backward, and the river took another bend. The bleak winter landscape again, under a leaden gray sky.

Up toward Elbeuf, Les Andelys, Vernon, then Mantes. Toward Courbevoie, where the sarcophagus would be disembarked for the final procession into Paris. There was nothing to do on the *Dorade,* not even those routines they followed on the frigate at sea. Total monotony. Philippe had already written out for Guizot a full account of the business in Saint Helena—he had read it over twice, there was nothing more to add. Still, he sat at a small table in the saloon with paper and inkwell before him. He had to write to Amelia, but what? He had to see her right away, but could not think when and where. He realized it would have to wait—damnably—until after the ceremony at the Invalides was got through. Should he then make his way to her parents' apartment? Ask that she meet him—where? The weather wouldn't permit a meeting in the Tuileries. Perhaps Joinville could help him out with a meeting at the palace. No, that wasn't what he wanted. Best just a note to ask if he could call on her.

———

BEYLE ARRIVED at the apartment in the rue d'Antin too promptly in the morning. It was just striking ten. He was feeling a bit haggard, having slept little. Remember Napoleon before battle, he told himself. The plan made, advance on the opposing forces' weak points all arranged, the lines of retreat studied in advance. Yes, but which battle, he asked himself: Austerlitz, or Waterloo?

All these stratagems vanished from his mind when Berthe led him to the drawing room—a sad room, neglected and slightly shabby—and then Amelia was before him. She was wearing black again. Did she consider she was still in mourning, or had she decided that black became her? It did. She looked ravishing as she rose from the faded rose bergère to meet him in the middle of the gray room. Her face as she moved to him was grave, her rich eyebrows knitted in anxiety even as she smiled at him. She stopped before him and looked him full in the face, without a word.

"Amelia," he began. "I've come, you know, to say I love you."

Still she looked intently into his face, scrutinizing it. Still she said nothing.

"I love you, and I'll do anything to please you. We'll do everything just as you want it."

When she spoke, her voice was muffled and as if distant. "And what does that mean? What will we do?"

"Leave for Switzerland. Become lovers. Whatever we wish to do."

He opened his arms to her, and she moved into them gracefully. She reached her hands to his head, and brought it down to her lips. Then she stepped back a pace.

"I know. I believe you. But still. Now I'm not sure what I want."

Beyle found himself thinking that he must not let her go, must not let her escape from his arms, that if she did she never would come back to him.

"You've changed your mind? Now that I've decided you're worth everything to me?"

She shook her head. "You've decided. But just what have you decided? Here we still are, you see." She gestured vaguely at the room that held them.

He grasped her by the shoulders, then pulled her close against him. Something had to happen now, Beyle thought, or it never would. The stagecoach to Switzerland in order to take Amelia to bed in some Alpine hotel seemed a lugubrious proceeding.

She was in his arms now. He kissed her, and she responded passionately.

She stepped back, took him by the hand, and led him from the room, down a dim corridor. She stepped into a room—her boudoir—and closed the door behind her. They stood face-to-face in the small rose-colored space. Beyle noticed over her shoulder a canapé against one wall.

Amelia's face was intense to the point of anguish, but still she smiled at him. She let go his hand, and pivoted so her back was toward him. "Undo me," she whispered hoarsely.

His fingers felt too large as he tugged at the knot, it took forever to undo. Then it was loose. He parted the laces, the black dress slid gently to the floor in a circle around her feet. She stepped forward out of it, then turned to face him.

He thought he had never seen anything so beautiful as she stood before him. It was tenderness he felt as well as desire as he moved his lips over her shoulders and neck. He reached behind her to fumble with the laces of the corset, which slid to her waist. She was warm and lithe against him.

She took him by both hands and led him to the canapé. But as he placed himself next to her, she pulled away. Then she moved to the far end of the canapé. She was not embarrassed, sitting there half-naked, evidently proud under his desiring gaze. But when he reached out his hand toward her again, she shook her head.

"What is it?" he murmured.

Her face was grave. "I don't know. It's just that I can't. Not now, not here."

Anguish at her slipping away from him. He couldn't let that happen. "Amelia, I love and want you."

"I know. I want you too. Truly I do. I must be yours. But it's not the moment."

"But you were the one for decisive action." As he spoke, Beyle realized how absurd it was to argue in a situation like this.

"I know. But there is something unresolved now. Since the last time I saw you. I mean, I don't know why it should make a difference, but it does."

She rose, the unlaced corset falling away, slipping to the floor, and turned to the small writing table near the curtained window, slid open a drawer, and pulled forth a letter. She didn't give it to Beyle, but held it before him. He could see that it was dated from Teneriffe on 31 July.

He guessed before she told him who it was from.

"It's a letter from Philippe de Chabot, you see. It took forever to get here. He wants to marry me, you know. I'm not going to."

She paused, the letter held forth in her graceful hand before her bare breasts. Like some young messenger from the gods, he thought. An allegorical statue for the postal service.

"But if you have refused him?"

She shook her head. "That's just it. I haven't refused him, yet. I asked him to wait. I said I wouldn't listen to him until he came back from this voyage. Now he has written to beg me not to do anything conclusive until his return, until he's had a chance to speak."

"But if you intend to refuse him?"

"I do. But I feel—I don't know why, but this letter has made me think I owe him a refusal before . . . before you and I, you see. So that everything is square and honest. I'm not sure I could meet him and hear him out after becoming yours."

"But if you still want to be mine, what's the difference?"

"I can't explain. But there is a difference. There will be a difference, for us, once I've cleared the slate with him."

Beyle couldn't see much sense in this, but he could see that there was no point in arguing, and the serious talk had begun to cool his arousal in any case. He leaned back against the curved arm of the canapé and contemplated her with a smile which he feared might be too much marked with irony. "And so we stop here? And so you don't want to know what it is like, to . . . ?"

Now Amelia smiled enchantingly. "Are men so stupid really? Don't you think we know what we want from you?" She leaned down and kissed him quickly on the mouth, her breasts brushing against his chest. "Dear Beyle. I do want that, and with you. I think you would be the perfect lover for me. And I am not frightened, you know. I trust you."

Flattered, Beyle felt a new surge of desire. He reached toward her, but she stepped back, shaking her head again.

"No. I have decided. It can't be now. It will have to be after I've spoken with Philippe."

She bent to take her corset from the floor, and held it in place. "Here, lace me up."

With reluctance, with regret, he pulled the laces tight. Amelia stood for a moment before a small mirror, tying her hair back. She looked flushed and radiant, he thought. Is this all she wants of love, he asked himself?

But when she turned from the mirror and faced him again, her eyes shone and she clasped his hands. "It won't be that long, you know. Probably they'll be back in little more than a week. Philippe will call as soon as he arrives, I'm certain. And then we will have our meeting."

THE RIVER uncoiled before the steamboat. He had never thought about the Seine before, its extraordinary loops. Looking at the chart, you could see that between La Roche Guyon and Mantes it doubled back on itself, so that you had made virtually no forward progress when you'd done the loop. And before that, from Les Andelys to Vernon, the same thing. Philippe had watched the noble ruin of Richard the Lionheart's castle disappear as the *Dorade* churned on, black smoke drifting up to the severe pile of stonework on the bluff high above the river. Now they were past Poissy. The next loop to the right should start to open up the Forest of Saint-Germain to the left. Then Saint-Denis, and on up to Courbevoie. Joinville had announced their arrival at Courbevoie for the end of the day. There the sarcophagus would finally come to land, be transferred onto some sort of caisson for the trip into Paris the next day. One more day of this nonsense, and then normal life. He wondered what Guizot had in mind as his next assignment. Back to London? Surely in any case he had earned a leave for a few weeks. A few weeks in which he must settle things with Amelia. Must. This could go on no longer. What did she want? He found as he summoned up her image in his mind that her image was growing dim and fluid. He could see her face—that intensity was unforgettable, the dark brows, contracted in a near frown—but her body had become ghostly. How can this be? He knew he wanted her, but somehow her body was not there. He could not find anything solid to fix on. He felt no rush of desire. Was this all a mistake? Was Amelia just a figment of his imagination after all? Surely there were other women in Paris. In fact, he might find himself surrounded by eligible young women, fêted as something of a hero after the voyage and the return.

A heroic undertaker, he told himself. Ware being known forever as the man who brought back the body. Despite his resolutions, he fell back into the sense that someone else had written this story. He was a puppet, someone's wooden toy. This mission had compromised his independence, his career, too. He did not want to be thought of as the willing tool of those in power. He wanted to be among the powerful. Strange, that this mission, which should have marked his emergence into a position of command, seemed to have produced the contrary. This unshakable sense of lack of command, of his own life.

But this was no time for reverie. He needed to have a serious session with Joinville about arrival in Courbevoie. A message delivered at Poissy, written by Guizot's undersecretary, brought news that the European diplomatic corps would probably boycott tomorrow's ceremony. They were not about to offer homage to the usurper, the man who had tried to redraw the map of Europe and to put them out of business. Was this a serious matter? Guizot clearly understood their position—it was basically his own, after all—and would do everything he could not to envenom the situation. And anyway, this was a day for the French alone, a settling of their own scores, closure to an episode of their history. Yet surely Guizot would have all available troops on the alert, both in Paris and at the border posts. The Emperor might be a dead body sealed in four coffins, but still a potent force.

Joinville was seated at the long table in the saloon with the map of Paris spread before him.

"Here's our route," he said, tracing with his finger the way from Courbevoie into Paris, up the Avenue de Neuilly, on up to the Arc de Triomphe, then down the Champs-Élysées to the Place de la Concorde, across the bridge and along the quay to the Esplanade des Invalides. "Guizot has promised a massive contingent of police along the route. But I wouldn't rule out demonstrations nonetheless."

Philippe thought a moment. "The students especially, I should think. Plenty of liberals and Bonapartists there."

Joinville nodded, and went on to point out on the map where the likely gathering places for demonstrators would be. The essential thing was to keep the procession moving at a steady pace, not to let it be brought to a halt at any point. He detailed the order of march.

"It will be a long day. And then," he added, "we are done." He smiled at Philippe. "About time, eh?"

"Indeed it is. Normal life again—whatever that may prove to be."

"My dear friend." Joinville reached his hand to Philippe's shoulder. "Before we land, let me express my deep thanks to you. You've been a perfect companion-in-arms. I know there was that awkwardness about Thiers' orders. You've done everything right, spared my feelings. Let us not be separated by what lies ahead. I know I'll be caught up in life at the palace—my father wants me there for some time before I return to the Mediterranean theater—but you must know you will always have a friend there. I'll make sure you can always find me when you want me."

Philippe was moved. He knew that such declarations of emotion didn't come easily to Joinville.

"My thanks to you, sire. You've been an easy master to serve. And though it's seemed a long and weary journey, I don't anticipate that normal existence will be easier. Quite the contrary."

"Still the problem of Amélie to resolve?" Joinville's babyish face, now tanned a deep honey color from the voyage, was almost comic in its earnestness. "What do we men know about women, eh? But don't be too distressed. There will be scores of demoiselles eager to greet the hero of Saint Helena."

Philippe winced. "A strange heroism. But you're right, of course. There will be fêtes in our honor, bevies of young beauties. Every reason to be lighthearted."

"At least, reason to relax a bit. You are a good man, Philippe. But from your English ancestors you inherited a bit of that northern spleen. Perhaps too much of a conscience."

Philippe nodded. "True enough, sire. Though how one escapes that particular inheritance is not clear to me."

"Come see me at the palace. We'll think about Parisian pleasures together."

Philippe smiled ruefully. If only he could put the Amelia

problem aside in favor of Parisian pleasures. Still, he was deeply grateful for Joinville's effort, and for his friendship.

"Thanks, sire. I'll count on you." They clasped hands, and held them long.

———————

BEYLE EXAMINED his ashen face and stubbly whiskers—going gray—in the mirror. This would never do. You are too old to spend sleepless nights, he told himself. Writhing in agony over a young woman not possessed. All you need to do is go round to Barot's, and have him fix you up with one of the charming actresses he always seemed to know in large numbers. Someone to warm his miserable bed—he had been cold all night, despite a pile of blankets—and make his blood beat warm. This was totally ridiculous. Amelia was not the only desirable young woman in Paris. And besides, think of what a headache it would be—the scandal, the aftermath, her young life in ruins, his carefully arranged tranquillity gone. Peace is what you are supposed to be seeking at your age, he told himself.

Yet he was obsessed. Amelia had been before him all night, as in a hallucination, ready to give herself. Her image was fixed in his retina. No young beauty supplied by Barot would make the slightest difference. He'd be impotent. There was only one woman he wanted. And he had delayed too long.

Get yourself shaved, and out, he told himself. It would be cold and dreary out, but he needed to move about, wander, think this through.

He had just finished dressing when the porter was at the door, bringing the morning's mail. With a sigh he dropped it on his desk, on the increasing pile of things that must imperatively be dealt with. The new additions began to slide slowly from their place atop the pile. As they subsided onto the desk, he noticed a thick envelope from Rome, with the arms of the French

Ambassador. He reached for the letter opener and unfolded the three pages from Latour-Maubourg.

As he scanned the letter, his chagrin was almost matched by his admiration for how Latour-Maubourg had put everything together. The letter read as a concise narrative of his own—Beyle's—recent life. Tavernier had made his move, traveling to Rome not only to see Monsignor Delicata, but the Ambassador as well. To inform him that Beyle, now on yet another extended leave of absence, was part of that very conspiracy of *carbonari* he was supposed to have under surveillance. That he had lied to Delicata and the Vatican, and had been discovered consorting with the Bonapartes at Canino—but there was no mention of Pierre, thank God, no indication that the spy had seen into the hayloft—and furthermore that he was keeping a mistress in Siena and had traveled to Paris for the soft eyes of another young woman, protégée of the Count and Countess Cini. This was vile, preposterous—though irrelevant, of course, and Latour-Maubourg indicated as much. The tone of the letter was urbane, always the case with the Ambassador, but the conclusion was severe. Latour-Maubourg's protection was at its limit. Tavernier had stirred things up in Vatican diplomatic circles to the point that Latour-Maubourg would soon be obliged to make a formal report to the Minister of Foreign Affairs. And since that now was Guizot, Beyle should realize that his position was in jeopardy. Guizot had never trusted him, and he was determined to have a moral diplomatic corps. If Beyle were to return to Civitavecchia immediately, then after a suitable time there—a week or so—come to Rome to make the rounds of Vatican diplomats, beginning with Delicata, all could be set right. But delay would be fatal.

He knew he had no choice in the matter. He must go back. He sat down and scribbled a reply to Latour-Maubourg. His gratitude to His Excellency for warning him. He of course knew of Tavernier's malevolence. The man must be sacked. Using the Grand Duke's spies to pry into the life of his superior. The allegations about Canino and the *carbonari* completely baseless, of course. Beyle would remain in Paris only for the ceremony of the Emperor's body—fitting that he be there—then travel posthaste back to Civitavecchia.

He carried the letter downstairs to the porter, and went out into the cold Paris street.

———

STOP BEING such a self-indulgent ninny, then, she told herself. She left the bedroom with decision, and made her way to the drawing room, and took her seat before the piano. That difficult F minor nocturne she had been attempting to get through. But for the moment even Chopin had lost his power to console. Because, she thought, it was not consolation she wanted. It was passion. It was passion between a woman and a man, engulfing them, changing their bodies, risking all. She liked the way Beyle had looked at her in her boudoir. With lust, was that it? Well, she wanted lust.

She had told Beyle not until after she could see Philippe. She was stuck with that decision. Very well, let Philippe come—as soon as possible, as soon as the ceremony at the Invalides was got through—and speak his piece. Which she knew by heart. Unless he could surprise her? Then summon Beyle, and make yourself do what he wants you to do, she instructed herself. No resistance, no foolishness. Yes, he would know what to do. Just let him.

There was a solution, of sorts.

———

BEYLE WANDERED, aware that he was wandering. It was too cold to stand still, too cold to be out of doors, in fact, but he could not face the walls of his apartment. Amelia pursued him everywhere. He found himself looking for her face in the crowds of hurrying Parisians, bundled against the cold—as if she would be anywhere but at home. A pale December sun shone through the light cloud cover. His steps led him, as they always did, toward the Seine. So it was that soon he entered the Place de la Concorde. He became aware, beyond the usual traffic encumbering the great square, of knots of workmen in their blue blouses along the outer edge. Poles were going up, banners being slung from them. He shaded his eyes to peer up the Champs-Élysées. Banners at intervals all up the avenue, and then something being erected atop the Arc de Triomphe, some piece of statuary. He pivoted and looked to his left, across the Pont de la Concorde. There on the other bank, before the Palais-Bourbon, an enormous plaster statue had sprung up like a toadstool overnight. He turned to cross the bridge and face the monstrous thing, a kind of woman warrior in a hieratic pose, perched on one foot as if she were about to fling herself in the air—as if such a heavy weight of drapery and frumpery could ever become airborne. He read the inscription on its circular base: *Immortality.* So that's what immortality looks like, he thought. She brought a disdainful smile to his face.

All along the quay to his right there were statues, lining the route to the Invalides, each identified by the name carved in its base—Clovis, Charles Martel, Philippe-Auguste, Jeanne d'Arc. This was truly absurd. Charlemagne, Hughes Capet, Louis IX, Duguesclin—all the storybook heroes, looking like something from a schoolbook, all uncomfortably new in white plaster. François Ier, Henri IV, the Grand Condé. Then suddenly he had moved into recent history, here were Napoleon's marshals: Marceau, Desaix, Kléber, Lannes, Masséna, Mortier, Macdonald. So this was the government's idea of majesty, of how one welcomes back the body of the Emperor. What if it rained? The statues might improve if they melted a bit. What nonsense. An empire of plaster and pasteboard. That had nothing to do with what it was all about.

The day after tomorrow would be the big event. This whole thing was a mistake, the ceremony would be a pompous bore. No doubt it would be unimaginably tawdry, the whole thing done wrong—why didn't his compatriots understand simplicity, truth, lack of affectation: these alone were enduring. The whole of Paris would be crazed for a day. It would simply prevent his seeing Amelia. He was not to call on her until she had met with Chabot. His whole fate now hung on this young diplomat he couldn't quite imagine. Might the young diplomat be unequal to his task! Amelia belonged to him, to Beyle. But since he had to return to Civitavecchia, it made no sense.

But before that, the ceremony. Despite his disdain, he knew he would go. How could he not? This was a conclusion of sorts, to history—and it was his history. He needed to be at the conclusion, this entry into an entombed presence in the midst of Paris. He wondered again if Soult and Guizot—and the King—knew what they were doing. Already there were greasy peddlers along the quay, selling souvenirs of the Emperor, miniature swords and cocked hats and tin soldiers in the uniforms of the Grande Armée. There would be a crowd, despite the cold. He asked himself if he should get an invitation to the ceremony inside the Invalides. Mareste could surely supply one. Why not? Might as well go through with the whole thing.

He turned to walk back up to the Quai d'Orsay.

———————

THEY HAD steamed past the terrace of the château overhanging the river at Saint-Germain, with massed crowds and banners, cries and fanfares. Now, as the early dusk settled over the bitterly cold water, the town of Courbevoie came in sight. The *Dorade* was losing speed, the side wheels making a slow *chunk,*

chunk in the water. They stopped moving, and the boat glided silently toward the landing stage. Then the inevitable brass band burst forth, the *Chant du départ*. As they slipped toward the shore, Philippe became aware of a massing of shadowy figures under the trees behind the landing stage. Uniforms everywhere. He recognized the grenadiers, the lancers, the mameluks, the Alpine chasseurs, in their uniforms of twenty-five years ago. It was a ghostly Napoleonic army resuscitated from the shadows. A gathering of shades.

The *Dorade* was now feet from the landing stage, a belch of smoke and the paddle wheels went into reverse with a splash. The line of uniforms stepped forward, and Philippe scanned the faces. Old, lined, gray-haired, and gray-bearded. The uniforms were worn and some barely fit. But it was all the more impressive. A phantom army, come to receive a dead body.

The *Dorade* came to rest against the piles of the landing stage. The cries of the sailors making fast rang out in the cold air, then were swept away as a glacial wind whipped up the Seine. The gangway clattered into place. The coldest night yet was before them, Philippe guessed. As he was wondering how to stay warm overnight, the line of uniforms parted, and a tall figure stepped forward. He was wearing the plumed hat of a marshal of France, and his square shoulders were set off by epaulettes dripping with braid. Next to him, an old man in black who held his arm. Marshal Soult, Philippe realized, Duke of Dalmatia, now Prime Minister. And the other man was the older Las Cases, Emmanuel's father, the author of the legend, now almost completely blind. The honor guard on the *Dorade* came to attention, as Soult and Las Cases slowly made their way up the gangway. The military music fell silent as the two old men stood before the sarcophagus under its black canopy. Awkwardly—painfully, he could see—they both dropped to their knees, and bent their heads in prayer.

Night had fallen. On shore, fires were beginning to sputter

forth in the dark. Philippe could see tents among the trees. As more and more campfires flared forth, he realized it was a whole encampment, a bivouac. These remnants of the Grand Army were going to spend the night there, wrapped in their cloaks and overcoats. Something like the bivouac on the banks of the Berezina. The last tribute to the disasters of history. He felt he ought to be moved, but he was prevented by his irritation. Would his countrymen ever grow up? Would they remain forever caught in the fascination of war and conquest, forever in thrall to this tyrant-father? How could you build peace and constitutional government on such primitive emotions?

The clang of the ship's bell summoned him to their frugal dinner—the kitchens of the *Dorade* weren't equal to the numbers on board—and a last consultation with Joinville about the next day's ceremony. Then, as he prepared to bunk down in the salon, he cast a last glance out the porthole. Through the dark trees on the bank, campfires glowed. An occasional figure shuffled through the grove. A silent scene, under a cold sky, the moon barely visible through a veil of high clouds.

At nine o'clock the next morning, thirty-six sailors—those brave Bretons from the *Belle Poule*—lifted the sarcophagus and carried it down the gangway. A few yards inland Philippe spotted the carriage, a kind of immense gilded Roman temple on wheels, two storeys high. A gilded monstrosity, something like . . . the image of an overgrown wedding cake came to mind. Or something from a rococo painting. Whose taste was this? On either side two hundred of the Old Guard of the Emperor's Household drawn up in double file, guns reversed. The beating of a muffled drum.

The sailors, taxed to the utmost of their strength, succeeded in sliding the sarcophagus onto the carriage. The guard thumped the butts of their rifles on the frozen ground, then raised them to their shoulders. A salvo rang out. Philippe took his place in the black-draped carriage that would precede the funeral chariot, Coquereau was in a smaller carriage in front. Joinville would ride on horseback, just before the chariot. Philippe envied him, despite the cold. Better than being shut up in a box for hours. Then there was a cracking of whips, and the sixteen horses strained at the harness. The immense carriage slowly moved forward. They were on their way into Paris.

❧19❧

The Emperor Comes Home

THE DRUMS. Beyle had forgotten. It swept him back to the day when the Grand Army had marched out of the Austrian town of Essling, to a bloody and indecisive battle. He had been there.

A muffled thunder. The Champs-Élysées seemed to shake under their beat. Then from time to time a fanfare would break forth. The cortège moved slowly down the vast avenue, rank upon rank of the National Guard, the Troop of the Line, the cadets of Polytechnique and Saint-Cyr, rifles slung in reverse. Then the cavalry, swords pointed earthward, followed by the lancers and their brass band. On both sides of the avenue, amidst the plaster statues of *Victory* and the packed crowds, long tri-color pennants flapped in the cold breeze. Crepe-hung balconies overloaded with people—Beyle had heard these were renting for three thousand francs for the day. This was, after all, the France of Monsieur Guizot, where turning a profit was a patriotic enterprise. He made out the profile of Victor Hugo. Who will, thought Beyle, produce a bombastic poem to the occasion.

Filtering through the crowd behind the double file of gendarmes along the avenue were hawkers of all sorts, doing a brisk trade in hot tea and grog, served in tin cups covered with crepe. A kiosk near the foot of the avenue was selling pipes and tobacco pouches and mugs and other gimcrackery all decorated with the Emperor's silhouette. Someone had set up a sideshow in a tent near the rue de la Boétie, with a hand-lettered sign announcing a diorama of the Valley of the Tomb, Saint Helena, inside.

Beyle wrapped his gloved fingers around the cup of tea, wondering how much longer he could stand it out here. The snow flurry that began the day had ended, but now the cold was glacial, the sun veiled by a light cloud cover gave no heat. Everything bathed in a dim gray light. There was ice in the gutter.

He could make out now a riderless white horse emerging from under the Arc de Triomphe, draped in a dark purple blanket, boots turned backward in the stirrups, its bridle held by two veterans of the Old Guard. Cries of emotion from the crowd. This couldn't be the Emperor's own horse, which couldn't still be alive. Another bit of fakery, thought Beyle.

But now there were some real heroes to salute: the three hundred sailors of the *Belle Poule,* massive and awkward on parade. Young faces, burnt from the sun, under their round leather hats, pistols stuck in their belts, boarding axes held in their hands. Thundering applause. *Vive La Belle Poule!* Then two carriages. At the window of the first he beheld the solemn and beatific face of young Abbé Coquereau, the prelate of the moment. In the second, old General Gourgaud, and Bertrand, and next to him . . . he tried to get a better view of the young man on the far side of the carriage, fair-haired and flushed from the cold. Yes, it must be young Chabot. The real one, not the shadowy figure of his never-to-be-written novel, Amelia's suitor. Chabot looked about as Beyle expected. Nothing more to be gleaned from that face turned away from him. The carriage passed on down the avenue.

Now there was a cheer from the crowd above him on the avenue. Joinville on horseback, his saber pointed downward. Behind him, the funeral chariot emerged from under the Arc de Triomphe—itself surmounted by some hastily made statue of the Emperor's coronation, the last thing you'd think anyone would want to remember—and started down the Champs-Élysées. What was this? What were they thinking of? Beyle's lip curled in disdain. Behind the sixteen horses caparisoned in black, a two-storey construction of what? wood and papier-mâché no doubt, with various scrollwork and putti on the prow, and an absurd Greekish temple on top, held up by lightly draped caryatids. This was appalling. Would his countrymen never learn the beauty of simplicity? of truth? Had they never read Napoleon's bulletins from the battlefield—stated in the language of fact? Guizot was mocking them all with this operatic nightmare.

His thoughts were covered over by the shouts that began around him, swelling now in unison. *Vive l'Empereur!* They shouted, they clapped their hands. Hats were off, hats were thrown in the air. Then here and there in the crowd at his back other shouts: *Down with the English! Down with Guizot!* Some of the gendarmes swung round, and began to search the crowd for agitators. This day could end badly, Beyle thought. Off to one side, toward the entrance of a side street, a gas lamp shattered from a cobblestone heaved at it. He heard cries and the sound of a scuffle, but could see nothing.

And then, the moving spectacle of the Old Guard, what was left of it. Haggard faces, paunches protruding from tightly buttoned uniforms over their saddles. The men of Austerlitz and Wagram and Borodino and Waterloo. *Vive la Garde!*

Now, Beyle decided, is the moment to extricate myself, and

get to the Invalides. He calculated the side streets he would have to take to get round to the Invalides without using the Champs-Élysées or the Place de la Concorde. His consul's uniform seemed to help, as some of his frock-coated fellow citizens attempted to make a passage for him. But the crowd was several rows deep. When he finally made his way through to the rear, he came on a restless group behind. Young workingmen it seemed, and students, milling about.

LOOKING UP at the statue of Joan of Arc, which had sprung up overnight at the river side of the Esplanade des Invalides, Amelia could see that the plaster was still wet in places, and now covered with streaks of ice. Icicles on Joan of Arc, how strange. A bonfire had been lit nearby. Maybe the statue would start to melt. Her father had insisted on her coming with him despite the cold. Now she was wondering how much longer she could stand it. The crowd of thousands on the two immense scaffolds of seats on the Esplanade were stamping their feet against the cold, creating an unpleasant rumbling. Would it be any warmer inside? The sheer warmth of the hundreds of bodies should do something. Outside at least there was a pale sunshine. And if she stayed, she might see Philippe in his moment of glory. She wasn't sure she wanted to. If he saw her he would want some sign, a sign of love.

The cortège was now moving out from the Pont de la Concorde, down the quay. She could feel the drums and the marching feet in the cobblestones beneath her feet.

"Time to find a place inside," said the General, waving the two large cardboard admission tickets he had held clutched in his hand ever since they left home that morning.

She took his arm, and they joined the throng pressing toward the portico. Progress was slow, though now the gendarmes were urging them inside as the cortège began to make its turn onto the Esplanade. As they mounted the steps, they began to hear the cries: *Vive l'Empereur! À bas Guizot!*

Then just as her father was presenting his tickets to the guard stationed in the doorway, Amelia found her other arm taken by a large hand and pressed gently. Startled, she almost cried out. Then she recognized Beyle, resplendent in his consul's uniform with its gold filigree on the collar. He smiled kindly. She searched his face for some sign of what had passed between them. Was he annoyed with her? Had he consigned her to the class of young ninnies, no longer to be bothered with? He looked fatigued, but happy to be next to her. "Amelia! General! Well found! I can't imagine anyone I'd rather watch this tawdry business with!"

The General frowned, then laughed, with that curious roar of his. "What can you expect? These people couldn't possibly do anything worthy of the Emperor. Pygmies with their Gulliver."

"Whom they've got tied down all right, for good this time."

The General snorted. "They may be provoking the uprising that will turn them out of power. They give us Soult as a figurehead, but we all know it's Guizot in charge, and he can hardly keep the loyalty of the French."

"A fickle folk, to be sure," said Beyle, smiling. Amelia had the impression he was determined to be agreeable, whatever her father said. She pressed Beyle's hand under her arm as they pushed forward through the portico. A sideways glance. He was beaming at her, with pleasure, desire too, she thought.

There was a thunder of artillery just behind them, then a second and a third. Three batteries opened up from different emplacements. The noise was deafening. The chariot was coming.

———

To PHILIPPE, this was becoming sheer misery. Little sleep last night in the cold cabin of the *Dorade,* then this infinitely slow progress into Paris, and now down the Champs-Élysées. He turned to right and to left, in imitation of Gourgaud—seated opposite him—to salute the crowd. And his bladder was full. He would have to find a moment for the privy in the Invalides. He tried to recall where it might be. Would he be able to excuse himself from the procession for that? Wouldn't Gourgaud and Bertrand be in the same condition?

All hats were off as they passed down the wide avenue. The balconies above them, black bunting hanging from the railings, were packed with people leaning toward the avenue. He scanned them for faces he could recognize. Yes, there was the Duchesse d'Aumale, with a familiar figure next to her, someone he had met, or seen pictured . . . Victor Hugo, yes, the great poet, who had called for this day in his ode on Napoleon's death. The Emperor's return.

A shattering of glass. Bertrand flinched. The gendarmes at the four corners of the carriage sprang to attention, scanning the crowd. A knot of workmen in their blue blouses were struggling with the police under the lamppost they had broken. *À bas Guizot!* They shouted. *Death to the traitors!* Then: *Vive la république!* Curiously, he felt a kind of grim satisfaction. What did they expect? Bring back this storied body and you let loose all the pent-up forces of revolt in France.

There was a genuine riot under way beneath the lamppost, and no way their carriage could move any faster than its stately pace. The workers had been joined by a mass of students, it seemed. Black jackets and capes, velvet slouch hats. Suddenly the "Marseillaise" rang out—the forbidden song—as the students joined arms in an attempt to protect the workers. From the School of Medicine, Philippe thought. The gendarmes made a charge, batons flailing. The line of students buckled, then broke, scrambling to escape. The police pursued, clubbing where they could. Wretches were thrown to the ground and trampled by police boots.

Glancing forward out the window, he could see the Place de la Concorde was in sight, the cortège moving across it and over the bridge. Not too much longer now. He glanced back from the carriage window, to Joinville on horseback. The saber still in hand, pointed downward. His arm must be aching by now, Philippe thought. Damn this whole thing.

THE SWELL of the organ echoed under the dome against the background thud of the artillery salute outside. It was cold, even pressed between her father and Beyle on the hard wooden bench, and she could hardly see through the rows in front of her. But the King had arrived, with his entourage, and stood facing Monseigneur Affre, Archbishop of Paris, resplendent in purple robes and lace, with his acolytes in a swarm behind him. And now . . . yes, the honor guard was filing in, swords pointed to the ground. And here was Joinville, his saber out, and behind him the immense sarcophagus, borne on the broad shoulders of the sailors in their striped blouses and blue jackets, their leather hats marked in gilt letters *Belle Poule*. The Emperor's body had come. And Philippe? Then she made him out behind the coffin, under the doorway, a figure in simple back amidst the uniforms and the ecclesiastical robes. He looked thinner than when she had said good-bye to him, his face worn, but tanned and handsome under his fair hair. Yes, he was a good-looking man, she thought. Worthy of being the hero of the moment. Yes, I do admire him. She glanced sideways at Beyle's weathered and battered face. His piercing eyes were staring intently forward—at Philippe, she thought. Suddenly she realized her heart was racing with emotion. But she couldn't say what it was.

Now Joinville stepped forward to his father, and saluted with his saber. There was a pause. The organ fell silent, the vast assembly fell into a hush, with some coughing and scraping of feet. They waited. Wasn't Joinville supposed to say something solemn? It was the King who spoke:

"I receive the body of the Emperor in the name of France."

The sailors bent at the knee, and lowered the coffin onto the black platform in the middle of the rotunda. Then the King turned to an old man who was standing near Philippe. "Bertrand," her father whispered. Bertrand stepped forward, leaning on the arm of his valet.

"Grand Marshal, you are to place on the coffin the glorious sword of the Emperor."

Bertrand took the sword from the valet. Tears were streaming down his parchment-like face, losing themselves in his white beard. "The sword of Austerlitz," her father whispered again. Bertrand held the sword high in his two hands, trembling visibly, then in a long slow gesture he laid it gently atop the coffin. His knees buckled, as if he were going to collapse. His valet caught him under the shoulders, lifting him back from the coffin.

"General Gourgaud, you are to place on the coffin the Emperor's hat."

Gourgaud stepped forward to face the King, the famous, familiar shape cradled in his arms. He glared, as if challenging Louis-Philippe. To Beyle, it was like a final confrontation of the generations of his lifetime. Gourgaud was, despite everything, undefeated and defiant, the still-living glory of battle and empire, who had been in Moscow, like himself, at the farthest reach of the Empire. Louis-Philippe, all jowls and whiskers, looked like some placid shopkeeper imitating royalty.

Glaring still, Gourgaud turned to place the hat on the coffin, in a gesture in which he somehow managed to convey protest more than mourning. If Louis-Philippe regards this as a day of national reconciliation, Beyle decided, he is wrong again. Something new, a new resistance will come from this. Perhaps a real movement of Bonapartists.

Now the King knelt, and they all struggled forward from their benches to kneel, shoved against the bench in front, squashed together. Affre began the prayers of absolution.

Then the music burst forth again. Mozart's *Requiem,* he recognized with delight. A far cry from the anthems played as they entered the dome, evidently composed for the occasion by Adam and the other musicians of the moment. Mozart, that was more like it. That was his youth. He glanced sideways at Amelia. Her face appeared vexed. He couldn't read it.

———

FROM HIS place in the second row, behind the King and Queen, Joinville, and the Duc d'Aumale, Philippe anxiously scanned the faces in the seated crowd as the *Gloria* rang out under the dome. He was tortured by his bladder. How much longer now? And was she here? He had scanned the crowd twice, it wasn't easy to recognize anyone with most of the faces bent in prayer or meditation. He had found Emmanuel easily enough, since the members of the Assembly were all grouped together, Thiers proudly in the front row, Emmanuel also. Would they continue to be friends, or were they now, back home, members of separate castes? I must make a point of keeping in touch with Emmanuel, he told himself. They must not let politics divide them. Then a head jerked upward, and he recognized General Curial, his face flushed, angry, it seemed. Next to him, a woman, her head bent. Yes, it must be she. And to her other side, the square-shouldered man in a diplomatic uniform? Familiar. Who was he? Some friend of the General's, he supposed. Now, how to get a sign of recognition from Amelia? And ask her to meet him?

———

BEYLE CAST sidelong glances at Amelia's troubled face. It was clear by now that she was in some crisis. This was not emotion wrought by the Emperor's remains. As for those—Beyle glanced again at the immense coffin covered with its bee-strewn purple drapery—he found himself wishing he could peer inside, take a last look at the Man of Destiny. Joinville's expedition was said to have opened the coffin and found Napoleon himself, perfectly preserved. So he actually lay there in that box, himself, the man who had shaken the thrones of Europe, the cataclysm of modern history. And who now would lie there in the Invalides, forever, in this crypt—still unfinished, of course—with its inscription running round the base of the dome: *Je désire que mes cendres reposent sur les bords de la Seine, au milieu de ce peuple français que j'ai tant aimé.* Done. And yet, to what purpose? He had no sense now of where he was. A preserved piece of parchment, and even that would become dust. And shall to dust return. Then why this fuss about a piece of dust? It all seemed very primitive. Why did they need this dead body fetched from the ends of the earth and placed here in the capital? He had read that the Indians of America carried the bones of their ancestors with them on their travels. We're not much more evolved than that, he thought. For all our age of Enlightenment, here we are worshiping ancestral relics.

It was all a political charade of course, yet even there he still couldn't make it out. Was it just the rambunctious Thiers trying to gain personal popularity? His attitude in the front row displayed a certain self-satisfaction in this event which was largely his doing. So, was the King and his government unwittingly just smoothing the way for Thiers' return to power? Then there was the man in prison at the fortress of Ham, Louis-Napoléon Bonaparte. No, they had not executed him—as any intelligent government would have done for his bungling attempt at a coup d'état—but merely locked him up. Some idiots had even proposed letting him out, under guard, to attend this ceremony. Guizot had had the wits to veto that. Imagine what a living Napoleon would have done to the mob along the Champs-Élysées.

Beyle felt weary. Yes, his youth was in that coffin as well. No exhumation could change that. And to his left . . . the young woman born about the time of Waterloo, whom he proposed to make his own. That was madness. Yet wonderful. Maybe he would become a father—could he still?—and leave children to remember him. End as a comfortable bourgeois in retirement. Why not?

The *Amen* now rose majestically under the dome. Amelia's eyes sought the figure behind Joinville. What happened now?

An early December dusk was falling as the crowd made its way out of the Invalides. From down the quay, toward the Pont-Royal, they could hear shouts and the sound of scuffle. The cries again: *Down with Guizot! Down with the traitors!* Cries of *Alert! Arms at the ready!* Then a volley of shots, and a howl of rage. Beyle tightened his grip on her arm. Then suddenly Philippe was before them, his handsome tanned face drawn with anxiety.

"General Curial, Amelia!" He nodded curtly to Beyle. He was clearly in a hurry. "I can't stay, been summoned to the ministry. They smashed Guizot's windows, there's a regular riot. I'm called to service. But later."

Before Amelia could speak, her father intervened. "We're at home this evening. Call when you are free."

Philippe opened his mouth to say something more. But nothing came out. He looked flustered, almost in pain. He bowed briefly, and was gone.

Another volley, followed by running feet. Workingmen and students dispersing back to the Place de la Concorde and down the ramps to the riverbank. The gendarmes did not pursue. And as they cautiously made their way up the quay, there were no signs of casualties. No bodies, no gore. Darkness was gathering.

Beyle still gripped her arm tight, as if afraid to let go. What happens now? she asked herself. She wished her father would leave them, go to his club. But he walked on to her left, silent, deep in thought.

When they reached the bridge, the General roused himself. "We need to find a cab, if ever such a thing is possible in this crowd. Need to get home. I'm worn out by it all. What about you, Beyle? Where away?"

Beyle did not reply, but only stared intently into Amelia's face. She knew that she must give him some sign. She tugged on his arm. It had the effect of bringing him round face-to-face with her.

"You'll come to see me?"

"Yes. When? After dinner?"

But her father had told Philippe to come round then. Both of them together in her mother's drawing room? She had a sudden comic vision of them drawing lots for her hand.

She felt like a coward when she spoke. "Tomorrow morning. Say, at ten o'clock. I'll be there."

Beyle bowed, stepped back. Then he was engulfed in the crowd.

❧ 20 ❧

His Majesty's Commissioner Comes Home

P HILIPPE'S VOICE was hoarse, his eyes looked bleary. He thought he had caught an ague from the chilled hours of parade and ceremony. "After freezing all the way up the Seine, it was not what I needed. A nightmare of a day to get through in any case."

Amelia thought nonetheless he was very handsome, his face thinner, somehow more resolved in its lines than when she last had seen him. He was tanned from the sea voyage, his fair hair bleached further from the sun. Did he seem changed in other ways? Grown older, more mature? It was hard to tell, since he was insisting upon being so much the perfect gentleman. He had learned—maybe from Guizot?—of her mother's death, and she could tell he felt it was not the appropriate moment to press his suit. As if that were the real problem, she thought.

Her father had left them alone, claiming he needed to take his evening draught of medicine. So they sat face-to-face in the gray drawing room, circling around all that was left unsaid. He told her about the tedious days at sea, about his longing to see her again. He tried to describe for her the night of the exhumation itself, and the strange moment when the Emperor's body had been revealed before them. But he was losing his voice. And this was not the point, anyway. It was time for him to speak out. No, not even speak. Take her in his arms, however much he might be suffering from his cold. She was warm enough, she knew.

She had not meant to set him a test, but nonetheless she felt he was failing her. Decision, action, touch rather than words was what she needed. She'd never been sure who Philippe was, what he was capable of. His outline had always been a bit fluid, so you didn't know what lay beneath the perfect manners. What she needed to see in him was a new sense of resolve, an assurance that everything was right between them, that he wanted her and would make the future theirs. There needed to be some confirmation, something real, to conjure away Beyle and her other demons.

"You can't imagine the desolation of that island"—Philippe was giving the guided tour of Saint Helena. But she was not giving him her full attention. No, she said to herself, I am not weak. That's why I want a man as resolved as myself. Someone who knows what he wants, and knows that his future must include me, whatever I am. The feeling rose in her irresistibly, in a wave of certainty—she could do anything. Get me out of this stupid impasse, no longer a girl, not quite a woman, and I will show you my strength.

Philippe now rose from the armchair. "My dear Amelia, I must bid you good night. I'm summoned early tomorrow to Monsieur Guizot. Must get some rest first."

"Ah yes. Monsieur Guizot. He'll want to compliment you on your mission, I'm sure."

Philippe hesitated. "Yes, I imagine. It does seem to have gone off as well as could be expected." A pause. "I imagine he may want to say something about the future as well."

"Your future, you mean?"

"Yes. My posting."

"And promotion, no doubt. You certainly must be in line for a promotion. You deserve it, my friend, richly. An ambassadorship? Where to?"

"I know nothing. Not, I think, an ambassadorship—I'm considered too young still. But as chief of a legation, perhaps. North Africa? This is all speculation."

Surely there was never a better time than now for him to say something about her place in his future. Amelia rose and stood to face him.

"Whatever His Excellency has in mind for me, I shall ask him for two weeks of leave. I think I've earned that."

"Of course. Two weeks here in Paris?"

"Yes. And I shall be back, to see you. Just as soon as I know. And then we can talk seriously."

She scanned his face for any further sign of his intent. What she in fact saw was troubling to her: a certain startled look in his eyes, as if he wanted to get away, not be cornered, not forced to speak more. Hesitating still.

"I'll call on you, very soon."

She wondered what he found lacking in her. Oh, there was plenty lacking, even excluding the unmentionable fact of Mother's suicide. The world of the Rohan-Chabots could surely produce more desirable prizes.

I'm probably failing him, right now, she said to herself, and in ways I'll never understand. Just as he was failing her. She wanted to speak, to cry out that this was stupid, that they needed to understand each other. But she didn't. If he was trying to beg off, so be it.

She spoke with a smile she tried to make gracious as possible: "I'm very often here, you know, and I shall welcome your visit."

"Soon, then, very soon. My respects to the General." Philippe bowed, and was gone.

GUIZOT RECEIVED Philippe in his private secretary's office which opened through a hidden door cut in the gilded paneling from the main office, now draped in canvas as workmen carried in large panes of glass for reglazing the high windows that overlooked the Quai d'Orsay. Guizot's face was grim, even though he had dismissed Philippe's concerned inquiries about last night's riots with a wave of the hand. "If the sum of it comes down to a few smashed windows, we can consider ourselves fortunate," he replied. "Could have been a long sight worse. Every remnant of the Grand Army left alive out there yesterday, plus every crazy sect of republicans and socialists. The throne still is solid, God be praised. And maybe stronger for having survived this."

Philippe nodded. "My sense is it's mainly nostalgia, and that doesn't lead to revolution."

"Not unless there is a leader who could convert it into a movement toward the future. And their leader is a clown, who's now locked up in the fortress at Ham."

"Yes, Excellency."

Guizot evidently felt caged in the small office. He kept turning on himself, pacing the few steps from wall to wall. "Chabot, I have only a few moments. I haven't time to give you the praise you deserve. I read over your account of the proceedings with Middlemore in Saint Helena early this morning. Impeccably done. I've just seen Joinville, who heaps praise upon your performance. You have a true friend there, I must say. Your promotion will proceed immediately. And I want you back in London just as soon as possible. As minister plenipotentiary."

Philippe bowed. No North Africa, then. London was known territory, not exciting, but the center of power. For Guizot, relations with England were of key importance.

"You're too young to be made ambassador right away—that will be old Marquis de Clermont-Tonnerre. But you will be ambassador in all but name. The Marquis will be perceived by everyone as merely a graceful figurehead. And he'll retire within two or three years. Then I'll appoint you. Providing, of course, that I stay in office." There was a twitching at the corners of his mouth. Evidently he felt less secure about the political juncture than he wanted to appear.

So back to London. That was resolved. But the rest of life. He needed to say something about that. He had never spoken to Guizot about anything personal. There didn't seem to be any way to begin. "Excellency, you understand that I am most gratified by this mark of your confidence in me. A fine advancement for my age, I realize. But I must beg you for some brief moment for reflection. There are, you see, matters here in Paris that need resolution."

Guizot's restless and tired eyes now focused intently on him. "Ah yes. I understand. Is it marriage you are contemplating?"

Philippe found himself ludicrously blushing. "Perhaps, yes. This is certainly a possibility."

Guizot's eyebrows now arched. "Chabot, you know I like you. Think very highly of your talents. I care about your future. Go cautiously is all I can say. A future ambassador can make a very good match—and should make a good match."

"Yes, Excellency." Philippe hesitated. Did he know about Amelia? What did he know? Of course he had all the ministry's spies, if he wanted to know. He decided to risk it. "Are you trying to tell me something in particular, sir?"

"Your choice to make, Chabot, of course. But just realize that you could ally yourself to an important family, one that could make a difference to your future."

This was really risking it, but Philippe now felt a kind of recklessness. "You are aware of . . . where my affections are placed?"

Guizot's smile was grim. "Mademoiselle Curial, I've heard. The daughter of the late Countess. A very attractive woman. Though her life was not beyond reproach. Says nothing about her daughter, of course."

Philippe's mouth was dry. "No, of course not. But I do ask myself questions."

"Some streak of unhappiness in that family. I do feel sorry for the poor old General."

Philippe nodded. Then he blurted out: "How is one to know? How do you ever know what the woman you want to marry really is like?" Suddenly he found solace in speaking all this to the older man, despite his distance and his lack of warmth.

Guizot's face finally relaxed into a smile. "You never do, you know. Marriage is a mystery, a kind of wager. That's why I say choose a family, not a woman. A family's something solid."

And love? Philippe wanted to ask in reply. But he was now too perplexed to speak.

"Anyway, take two weeks to sort things out, Chabot. Report back here just after the new year. I can't talk longer, I'm expected at the palace."

Philippe bowed. "Thank you, Excellency." He would himself be going to the palace at lunch hour, at Joinville's invitation. But he had promised to return to his parents in the rue Miromesnil first.

As he made his way down the ornate staircase, he realized he ought to be going to Amelia's instead. That needed to be the first order of business. The General last night had made it clear he would welcome the marriage. And Amelia? Why could he never fathom what she wanted. Of course, he hadn't pressed her with an outright question. It seemed inappropriate, with her mother's death so recent. But he wondered if that was really what kept him from speaking.

What he needed now was to ask her clearly, decisively. Conclude things. That must be the right way. He was vexed by the promises he had made to his parents and to Joinville. But they had to be honored before he could make his way back to the rue d'Antin. And maybe he needed more time, anyway.

———

THIS CANAPÉ was decidedly too hard, unpleasantly hard. She should really have it replaced. Mother had always remained faithful to furniture of the Empire. None of the deep, overstuffed sofas that had now come into fashion. She rose, and paced across the gloomy drawing room. Nothing to be seen from the window. Gray sky—she would not be surprised if it started snowing. The street strangely quiet. No doubt people had chosen to keep indoors after last night's rioting, though that had quickly been repressed according to the news Philippe brought them last night.

Her father had gone out, much to her relief, after only the briefest of questioning about what had passed between Philippe and herself when he had left them alone. But of course nothing had happened. And it wasn't clear that anything would—that he'd make the step of calling on her father to ask for her hand. Surely he knew there was no opposition from the General, who was clearly relieved at the prospect of his daughter well married. But maybe he was put off by her own attitude.

She spun on her heels, and walked to the oval mirror over the smoldering fire. She found her face glaring at her, her brows contracted in vexation. Yes, Philippe had been the perfect gentleman. Probably he had held back from speaking simply out of deference to the news of her mother's death. She shouldn't be hard on him. He was the soul of honor and decency. Yet it wasn't decency she wanted at the moment. It was passion. Philippe was kind. He only lacked . . . he lacked something that would sweep away her questions.

And yet, she told herself, this could be your salvation, in disguise (deep disguise, the sardonic voice within her chimed in), the chance to find that independence that you want, that you know you can use, and use well. Yes, this was the astonishing thing. With every passing day it was becoming clearer to her that she had the strength to write novels in a garret, as Beyle had put it. She could do it. Though it must be a life filled with loneliness, herself a social pariah, and without a mate. That was part of it, certainly. Yet the problem was that the mate—a mate such as Philippe, in any event—wouldn't allow it, would give her no room to create. No, if you are going to insist on living as an independent bohemian bluestocking woman, whatever, you had to take the consequences. Including irregular mating, she concluded with a flourish that made her laugh aloud.

She returned to the window in time to see a cab pull up to the doorway. Her heart began pounding. Yes, it was Beyle emerging. As he replaced his hat, she could see the balding spot on the top of his head.

She took another moment to compose her features before the mirror. Then Berthe was before her, announcing Monsieur Beyle.

He stood before her with an anxious smile. As soon as Berthe had disappeared, she threw herself in his arms.

BEYLE SAT at a solitary lunch at Tortoni, his notebook, closed, on the table next to his glass of Clos Vougeot. The velvety burgundy was his only concession to celebration—that, and the note he had just encoded in his journal. It was mainly astonishment he felt, and a sense of happy lassitude. Amelia was his. No, don't be fatuous. Rather, she had given herself to him, in a gesture of wonderful abandon, and they had made love on her narrow day bed. First times were always awkward, but this had been quite extraordinary as well. There was simply none of that false pudeur you expect from a young woman. Once she had decided she was going to take him to bed, she had been completely natural and accepting. He couldn't really tell how much pleasure she had found in it—that after all took time, accumulated experience. The truly erotic only came with habituation, he knew, with coming to trust one another's gestures and movements. No, she had not exactly let herself go. It was as if she were engaging in an experiment more from curiosity than anything else.

Odd, he thought, how we bring up our young women in supposed ignorance of everything, even of what a naked man looks like—other than Greek statues in the Louvre, and they didn't have much relevance—unless she had seen some of the vases—and then expect them in one instant to accept the act of love as if it were something routine. How many bourgeois wedding nights must end in sobs if not screams. Yet maybe it was all knowledge inherited in the body, as it were. Amelia had seemed unsurprised by everything, ready for him. But of course, this had been no wedding night. For Amelia it was a kind of anti-wedding night. It was something she had chosen to do, for herself, not for any husband.

He sipped his wine. Nor for her lover. She hadn't made love with him to please him, or to declare her love for him, but for herself. Her birthday gift to herself, she told him. He should find that flattering enough, he decided. He understood, too, that she didn't so much want to enjoy, to take pleasure. She wanted to know. Well, fine. He understood, he applauded this. The sign of a superior woman. One might then ask what had she learned, other than the obvious facts of copulation. Maybe that "love" with a man was only that—was less than the great mystery it was supposed to be. It was as if they surrounded it with mystery in order not to recognize the truth. Love—that's all it is.

But that *all* was surely something rare, some kind of communication between a man and a woman that went beyond anything carried out in the salon. Some kind of truth in the vulnerability of nakedness, in the confrontation of desire. Some sort of recognition of the forces of life, of death. Yes, a kind of continuity of life and death—an affirmation of life toward death.

Beyle smiled grimly to himself. You are beginning to sound like a German philosopher.

His *boeuf en daube* suddenly appeared on the table before him. He discovered he was ravenously hungry.

What happened next wasn't evident. Amelia had made it clear that it was not marriage she wanted. Nor was a trip to Switzerland still in the picture—she had shaken her head and told him that was no longer necessary when he'd proposed it. And when he had asked if he could call that evening, she'd said no—her father was expecting company, and she didn't want to have to deal with Beyle at the same time. They had made no plans. He must call again, at least to find out what his instructions were. And just to see her again.

❧21❧

Duel?

HOW SHE had found the words to tell him she would never know. It hadn't been easy to make him understand. His handsome face hung for the longest time in puzzlement as she tried to explain that he must know she was not quite the maiden he took her for. As the meaning of her speech gradually became clear to him, the puzzlement gave way to consternation and affront. He was a fine, wounded creature, and he didn't know what to do. She wished now she could call back her words, assure him that they meant nothing, that it was all just to test him. Why had she spoken, she wondered, out of what perverse sense of honor? No, not that. Out of pride. She had sensed that he had come, after the lapse of a full week, to propose to her, though his whole manner made it seem he was performing an assigned task rather than anything he wanted to do. He was constrained, tense. And she felt she had to tell him before he spoke any fateful words—before he committed himself irrevocably, before his honor was at stake.

Well, it was clear she hadn't spared his sense of honor. That couldn't be helped. She was still surprised at what had happened with Beyle—she was not entirely transparent to herself. But she wasn't ashamed of what she had done, and she didn't want Philippe to be, either. Yet how could she expect him to be anything but hurt and outraged?

"Now what becomes of our future?" His face was anguished as he spoke. "Of my thought of a future . . . together."

"Nothing is changed in that regard," she spoke gravely and firmly. "What I did had nothing to do with you, or with you and me. It was something I did for myself. Now it's over, done."

"Did for yourself? Had you no thought for me?"

She drew a sharp breath. "Yes, I did think of you."

"And that did not stop you?" He gave a bitter little laugh. "Obviously not."

She tried again. "It was not despite thinking of you. It was because I was thinking of you, of a possible future together, of many years stretching ahead of us, when I might be—when you might want me to be—your . . . wife." The word stuck in her throat, she blurted it out in the manner of an insult—not what she intended. "That's why I had to do what I did, first. So that I could make a good wife, so that I wouldn't spend years wondering, regretting . . ."

"Regretting . . . you weren't in another man's arms? In his bed." Philippe's mood, she could see, was moving from anger and anguish to despair.

"Something like that. Now it's all over. I am fine. It's made no difference, really, to me. Now I am ready to listen to you."

"No difference? Really!"

If he was going to be a prig, so be it. Then she would be done with him. Or rather—she found herself smiling inwardly, in a grim sort of way—he will be done with me. That maybe was why she had gone to bed with Beyle—to set Philippe the ultimate test, to make sure that he wanted her, despite everything. Or else—her irony was still working—to make sure that he would leave her. But that really wasn't it. Testing him was not what she had had in mind. It was only about testing herself. But you see, don't you, that there are consequences that involve others as well.

"How could you?"

She shook her head. "I can't entirely say. But I did. And now I want to hear you out. I am"—she stepped toward him, her face now radiant though tears stood in her eyes—"I am ready for you now."

But Philippe made an impatient movement with his hand, as if to shake her off. He turned toward the window. She saw his face as less angry now than mournful.

There was a long silence. Then Philippe turned slowly from the window and their eyes met. Then each glanced aside, as though not finding in the other's face quite what was needed. But it seemed that anger had passed away. There was something graver now between them.

"I don't know," he said quietly. "I shall have to think."

Of course he would have to think. He would weigh everything as if it were a problem in international diplomacy. Let him do something—slap her in the face, or fold her in his arms. Just be something, she wanted to scream at him. But she was being unfair. Yes, he needed time to absorb this. It cast a new light on her—maybe new shadow is more like it—and he needed to come to terms with that.

She answered him gently. "Of course you do need time to think, and to decide if you can forgive me. I quite understand. If you can see your way to understanding and forgiving what I did, it may make you know me better, as I really am. That's important to know. I'm not made quite like the other eligible women of my age, you need to know that."

Philippe's blue eyes darkened. It was as if she had struck to the quick, to the real question that was between them. Who was she? She could ask the same of him, but in some outward sense everyone knew who Philippe de Chabot was. Why, now the whole nation knew. She remained the great perhaps. And she knew she would not remain content with that, in ways that he maybe could never accept.

Philippe opened his mouth, but then evidently thought better of whatever he was going to say. Amelia in turn became aware that Berthe was approaching from behind Philippe's shoulder. Had she forgotten to tell her they were not to be disturbed? Wasn't that obvious in any event?

"Mademoiselle, Monsieur Beyle."

What! She opened her mouth to say that Monsieur Beyle must be told to wait.

But it was too late. Beyle himself stood in the doorway.

"Amelia! My humble apologies for arriving unannounced."

As Chabot spun to face him, Beyle's face registered a moment's puzzlement, then recognition.

"Monsieur Chabot." Beyle made a slight bow—an ironic bow?—and introduced himself. "Henri Beyle, His Majesty's consul in Civitavecchia."

Amelia's desire to sink through the floor and vanish suddenly gave way to an impulse to laughter. Her voice was almost cheerful as she said, "Ah, you gentlemen know one another?"

Philippe glowered. His right hand was clenched in a fist. Was he going to strike Beyle? Amelia stepped quickly forward, to place herself between them. She tried to find an appropriate word. Offer them tea? Not at this hour in the morning, there wouldn't be any ready. Propose an outing? Leave herself?

Philippe opened his mouth. "You owe me an explanation, sir. Your card, so I may—"

Amelia reached up and covered his mouth. "No, I won't have any challenges. Beyle is not involved. I alone am at fault toward you, Philippe."

"Not involved?" Philippe's eyes darted venom. "How can you stand there and say such a thing?"

"Because it's true. Now go, and think upon it, and come back to see me when you are ready. If ever."

Now Beyle roused himself. "Monsieur, I have never refused a challenge. I can be found at home this evening." He fumbled in his waistcoat pocket, then passed a card to Chabot.

"No." Her own voice startled her by its loudness. "You are ridiculous, both of you. Can men understand nothing? Listen to me. Yes, I slept with Beyle. That was ill-advised, I know. But it's what I wanted at the time. In my own eyes, that makes no difference for my future as a woman and . . . even a wife, if that is in store for me. That's all there is to it. It's in fact quite simple."

She paused for breath. Neither Philippe nor Beyle looked as if they found it simple, though Beyle's eyes glowed with admiration. Whereas Philippe looked sick.

"If you can't understand it, that's not your fault, I know. But it's not my fault either. I was not put upon this earth to please you, or to be an open book to you. Now go away and think about it. Philippe, you go now. And I forbid you to wait for Beyle in the street. Begone."

Now she was speaking like a fury, but she had never felt herself more lucid in her life.

Philippe hesitated a moment, holding Beyle's card with his fingertips. He waved it in Beyle's face, his own face a portrait of exasperation. Then he turned on his heels and strode from the room. A moment later she heard the front door bang.

Beyle looked at her with a slight smile, his eyes quizzical.

"Yes," she said, "I told him everything. He came to propose marriage. I thought it only right that he should know."

Beyle reached out his hands. "My poor beloved Amelia! What have you done?" He moved toward her, reaching to take her into his embrace.

But she stepped back. "No," she said. "It was what I wanted, I'm glad it happened, but that is now part of the past. Of my past. Now it is your turn to leave."

"But Amelia. I love you, you know. And Chabot will never come back. I know his type. You are now mine, you—"

"No. I am mine. Now leave. Beyle, you have wit enough to know I mean it."

Beyle bowed. "I'll leave for now."

"For now, and you will please stay away until I tell you to come."

He bowed again, and turned to go. But he stopped in the door. "I myself will marry you in an instant, mind you."

"Enough!" she bellowed at him.

He nodded, and he was gone.

Amelia turned from the door, and burst into tears.

❧ 22 ❧

Consequences

H E STOOD — Guizot had not asked him to sit — looking across the large empty desk at the most powerful man in France, who had just finished explaining, point by point, the accusations against him. Tavernier's narrative — though whether direct from that vile worm or forwarded by Latour-Maubourg he could not tell.

Time had not been particularly kind to Guizot in the ten years since the two of them last met. His face was lined and dry, his severe expression was like that of an aging schoolmaster worn by the repetition of lessons and the meting out of punishments. With a rod, thought Beyle, which he now intends to apply to me. He checked his impulse to take it all as farce. Everything depended on appeasing the schoolmaster.

"Excellency, I take the point. It sounds as if I were masterminding a plot of *carbonari* intent upon toppling the crowned

246

heads of Europe—in Tuscany, in France—no doubt overthrowing His Holiness the Pope as well. This is all imaginary—due to the sinister imagination of one Lysimaque Tavernier, the chancellor in Civitavecchia, who is plotting to have me sacked so he can have my position. A vile intriguer and a most unstable fellow, this Tavernier . . ."

He gained confidence as he talked. He still had the power to unfold a story, in all its intricate details, with clarity and a certain panache. He could see that Guizot was annoyed at his volubility, which prevented the simple exercise of command. Keep on talking, and he will want this interview to end. He'll send you off with simply a reprimand. Sacking you would be more complicated for him.

"As for my visits to Canino, Excellency, it is just that I share with Prince Lucien a love of Etruscan antiquities. I think if you were to refer to the report of the spy Daponte to Tavernier, you'd find that my last visit there, in the autumn, was rewarded by the excavation of a most delicate Etruscan bronze hand. We never talk politics. And you must know that my judgment on the Bonapartes is every bit as severe as yours. Why, I've written—"

Guizot cut him short. "I'd prefer, at this delicate political juncture, not to make any changes in the diplomatic corps. So consider yourself saved by the circumstances. But only if you return to your consulate at once. Discipline this Tavernier—do you need to keep the man on? Deal with the Monsignore. Make your peace with the Ambassador. I will ask for his formal report a month from now. If everything is not in the clear by then, I shall have to let you go."

"Yes, Excellency. Thank you. I can assure you—"

"And one more thing. You will be expected to remain at your post. Leave canceled."

Beyle nodded. Guizot dismissed him with a wave of the hand.

BERTHE HAD laid everything out on the bed in piles, for Amelia's inspection before it all went into the trunk. But Amelia found it hard to concentrate on the linen and the dresses and the hats and the gloves. Anyway, Angelica and her mother would supply anything that was missing. The important thing was simply to leave. The announcement of Angelica's engagement to the Marchesino d'Albano meant the Cinis wouldn't be coming to Paris, and it gave her an excuse to return to Rome. More than an excuse, it would be negligent of her not to be there for the series of festivities planned.

Festivities wouldn't be easy, though. She had managed to create losses everywhere. That wasn't what she wanted, but the only way she could handle life at the moment was to extricate herself. As for Philippe and Beyle, so long as they obeyed her on the duel, they could look after themselves.

Lord knows she had never wanted to be a troublemaker. She didn't like the idea of causing pain to anyone, least of all Philippe, who was a decent, fine person whom she had wounded, probably irreparably. Least of all Beyle, whom she admired and liked, for whom she felt nothing but gratitude and tenderness. She could have summoned Beyle again, and there would be comfort in trusting herself to his arms again. And yes, it was flattering how he wanted her. She hadn't quite said yes or no to Beyle on what might come. It wasn't a good idea, of course, but more than that, it didn't solve any problems. It was a diversion from facing the future—Beyle knew that as well as she. She was on her own now.

Philippe had not reappeared, mostly to her relief. Only a three-line note, saying that he had gone to his sister and brother-in-law's château in the Île-de-France to think things over. Well, if he needed so much thought, it probably meant he would not be back. She didn't want to marry someone who would sit in judgment on her for the rest of her life.

His reactions were excusable, even if not what she'd have hoped for, in her romantic moods. What she couldn't understand, at this point, wasn't so much Philippe as herself. He had been readying a proposal of marriage, she was sure of that. Then she had cut him off, interrupted to make her statement about Beyle. Where was the sense in that?

She stood still before the cheval glass and looked intently at herself. Reflected in the background she could see the canapé on which she and Beyle had made love. In her face she saw anguish, yet the comfort of a partial resolve. No, she would not regret Philippe. That way lay suffocation, bending her will to another's, sinking into convention. She could never really have been herself with Philippe.

A future of freedom stretched before her. But what good was that, for a woman? Continue behaving like this, and you will ruin your reputation. Taking Beyle as a lover was bad enough, continuing in that line of behavior would be disastrous. Of course, she could become his faithful companion. Time sometimes consecrated those irregular situations, brought a measure of redemption and even social acceptability, up to a point. If she let him, he'd again suggest marriage. Madame Beyle, what an odd thought—everyone assumed there was never to be a Madame Henri Beyle. She thought on Beyle with tenderness and pleasure, but as a husband he was unimaginable. That's not what she had wanted him for.

A deep sigh, becoming more of a sob, shook her whole frame. She would have to start over, to flirt gravely with the young men in the Palazzo Cini, to keep silent about her experience with Beyle. To learn to be a woman, in the proper sense. Or maybe, become an improper woman, like George Sand. Write novels— a novel about Henri Beyle, for instance. She could feel a smile moving at the corners of her mouth. That idea gave her the first glimmer of happiness in some days. Yes, now she knew enough to write about love.

———————

Two days was all that Philippe found he could bear with Olivia and Jules, who insisted upon treating him as a conquering hero returned in triumph. He felt anything but triumphant. He was wounded, unhappy, and still tortured as to what to do. So he rose early on Sunday morning and scribbled a note to his sister telling her that he must cut short his stay to go do Guizot's bidding in Paris. This didn't make much sense, since he had announced a two-week grant of leave from Guizot, but it would have to do. The coaching station was only a half hour's walk on a morning when winter seemed to have momentarily released its grip. The sun was warm, the ruts of the road softening under his feet. He carried no baggage—that would follow on later; he'd spoken to old Claude about that. The ocher stone walls of the village, laced over with wisteria vines, made him happy, reminded him of the real France lying so close to Paris.

Striding past the shuttered houses, he summoned up the image of himself as a fortunate young man who had just carried off a major diplomatic mission, without flaw. He had entered the history book of France, on an expedition that after all was not lacking in glory. He had been given an extraordinary promotion for someone his age. Guizot was in power, and so long as he stayed there his career was secure. More than secure, brilliant. Ambassador to the Court of Saint James at age twenty-seven or twenty-eight. Unheard of, really.

He saw himself master of Hartford House, the center of receptions at Whitehall, in attendance on the Queen at Buckingham Palace. He would be powerful, the representative of the French nation, the man destined to forge the alliances of the future. Assuring the peace of Europe would surely be the work of France and Britain together.

He became aware that in these future pictures of himself as a man of power he was alone. Shouldn't there be some woman at his side, some beautiful, imposing, aristocratic woman? Amelia? It was as if a cloud passed over the sun. His mood passed abruptly from joy to a constriction in his throat. It had begun to seem almost as if the loss of Amelia was an inevitable consequence of his mission to Saint Helena. It was part of a logic of loss. The Emperor's body hadn't ruined his career, far from it. It had merely ruined his life. If he had been there to make his claim, to assert his right to her, then she never would have given herself to that bohemian, that scribbler, someone a Chabot shouldn't even take on in a duel. He deserved a whipping instead.

Not the point. It was a moment to be clear and honest with himself. Amelia lost? No, he could repair that. But the logic of loss might be proof that Amelia never was right for him. Yet she wasn't dishonest, on the contrary, she had told him everything when she didn't really have to. The problem was trying to get inside her mind. He couldn't imagine life with such an enigma at his side.

He had half an hour to wait for the stagecoach. No one came from the château to try to persuade him to stay on, fortunately. The journey itself brought no resolution or calm. Really, he decided, forgiving or not forgiving Amelia was not the main point. Something in the way their fates had worked out showed that she was simply not what his future required. He needed an ambassador's wife, someone who could take her place proudly at his side in the great world. Amelia was too—was unconventional the word? Was he then himself a prisoner of convention? He didn't want to lack the courage to face her intensity—that excited him. But it was her damnable resistance to behaving the way a woman should. Give her up. There will be no lack of other possibilities.

He reached Paris early in the afternoon, and shut himself in his room at his parents' house, alleging the need to write a report to the ministry. He dined alone in his room, and planned on an early bedtime. He was exhausted, and still bothered by his congested head. But he was restless too.

At ten o'clock, realizing he would not be able to sleep, he slipped through the quiet rooms—his parents had already retired—and down the stairs, out into the Paris night. The milder temperature had brought nighttime Paris alive again. Cabs moved through the streets, the cafés on the Boulevard des Italiens were full, a ruddy glow hung over the city. Paris had resumed its life of pleasure.

He turned into the rue de Richelieu, headed vaguely toward the Louvre and the Seine. But after passing the Théâtre-Français, he swerved to his left, toward the bright lights of the Palais-Royal. Music in the air, from one of the dance halls, and the usual crowd moving in and out of Frascati's gambling parlor. And as he moved through the arcades into the garden, the usual women of the night made their apparition. Their costumes were audacious, provocative. Mostly they wore mantles against the winter night, but opened them repeatedly, to show expanses of bare shoulder and bosom. Philippe found it all shocking, fascinating, too. So many women offered to him, just like that. The way Amelia offered herself to that writer? How could she?

As for himself, he owed himself further knowledge of women. Maybe that was the only way to understand what Amelia had done, and what he, too, wanted. All he had to do was call upon Joinville, let it be known that he wanted to be signed on for Paris pleasures. Joinville understood those. He'd pay him a visit tomorrow. That would be better than endless worrying debate in his sister's château.

Meanwhile, there was this. He turned from the garden back under the arcade, his eye arrested by a tall, haughty-looking young woman mantled in her cloak, leaning against a pillar. As he gazed at her, she turned to catch his eye. Slowly, almost majestically, she reached to untie the cloak, and pulled it open. She looked young and proud, elegant even, in her low-cut dress. Philippe's heart was suddenly pounding. Why not? he said to himself. No you can't, this is beneath you. Wait until the Prince finds you someone more suitable.

The woman moved toward him with a sauntering step, her face smiling.

———

THE DECEMBER night had fallen by the time Beyle left the ministry and made his way down the quay toward the Invalides. The dome rose before him as he walked, black against the deep violet of the sky. Now it contained the Emperor's body, the mortal remains, as the phrase went. Which is to say, nothing. And you too, Henri Beyle, alias Stendhal. For all your refusal to be old, death is not far. Amelia, she may be your last adventure. No, your last love. And she . . . she may refuse ever to see you again. Will Chabot get over his outrage and come back to marry her? Beyle tried to estimate the chances. The old mathematician in him stirred, calculating the variables in the equation. Pride. Convention. Love. Career. Forgiveness. But he didn't really know the man well enough to say what he was capable of—or rather, what he wasn't. Still, given his type, Beyle didn't think the chances were good. Say, ten to fifteen percent. No more. It would take a man of great maturity, even subtlety, to understand what Amelia had done, and he didn't think he'd detected that in Chabot.

The massive front doors of the Invalides were shut, of course, but it was possible those in the rear were open—the wake for the Emperor's body seemed to go on forever. He made his way around to the rear, giving access to the chapel. When he tried the swinging door to the side of the main entry, it gave way.

Inside, the gloom was suffused with a vague pink glow from the votive candles that surrounded the sarcophagus. A few scattered figures kneeling in prayer. He stared at the draped coffin. Those symbols he remembered so well: the garlanded *N,* the golden bees. Here a world ended. His world. It was too late to make himself another. He'd lived on, not exactly to thrive in the world after Waterloo, but to live his life, to write his novels. Would anyone read them decades hence—when they would still be coming to view the Emperor's tomb? He thought it unlikely.

What was this tomb going to mean in the future? The place of reconciliation for his quarrelsome compatriots? No, the Emperor's legacy, for all the man's dreams of a united Europe beyond conflict, was a legacy of war, strife, the clash of arms. If this became a shrine, it would be a shrine to Mars. It would become the rallying point of the discontents, of all those the present order pushed to the margins. If ever another self-proclaimed Man of Destiny emerged from the crowd, he would start from here, stand by this tomb to begin his conquests. And Beyle thought again of how his countrymen could never rid themselves of this shade, all the more palpable now that you knew the body itself lay uniformed in the coffin at the center of the rotunda. Not a shade to be so easily exorcised, whatever that foolish Chabot and the politicians he served might believe.

At the head of the coffin someone had placed a kind of medallion, wreathed in flowers, on which he made out the gilt lettering: *Je désire que mes cendres reposent sur les bords de la Seine, au milieu de ce peuple français que j'ai tant aimé.* Those words of the Emperor's last testament again—the words that would now be engraved in stone above the colonnade surrounding the marble sarcophagus Visconti was executing. Commanding to the last, demanding that his remains lie on the banks of the Seine, in the midst of the French people. From beyond the tomb the words had taken effect. But that love of the French must be measured in the hundreds of thousands of Frenchmen lying dead in mass graves on foreign battlefields, or in the mound of the dead on the plain of Waterloo. And the legacy was this petty excuse for a monarchy that he himself now served. If that could be called love, it made love no different from strife, from the will to power, from death itself.

The chapel was quiet, but vague forms and shadows moved around its edges. The candles guttered and flared, throwing out from time to time an immense and grotesque figure. This was a place of entrancement, of black magic. No other ruler of France had ever had so immense a resting place to himself alone. It proved that his countrymen were fixated on this particular ghost. And now they could remain so. Now Beyle was certain. For all his nostalgia for his youth and the heroic days of the epic, he knew Louis-Philippe had made a mistake. He had given form and lineament to that dream of conquest and glory that appealed to what was most childish in the French, most discontent with reality. They were not going to remain content with the dead body now that it was in their midst. It would become a relic demanding a new crusade, a new Bonaparte, more strife, empire, domination. It was incredible, really. They had gone on purpose to dig up a body that . . . would dig their own graves. It was as if the King and his ministers were acting, all unwittingly, within the ambit of Napoleon's posthumous will. Doing his bidding. They did not know it—and he himself might not live to see it—but the dead body now at the center of Paris would work its will. The stillness of that corpse was an illusion. It was going to send men into battle again.

Beyle sank on a chair. The interview with Guizot had been humiliating, but it had gone as well as could be expected. Probably Mareste had spoken for him, too, and his letter to Latour-Maubourg would produce a show of support in that quarter. He still had friends willing to vouch for the slightly disreputable but very clever Monsieur Beyle. So, back to Civitavecchia. Amelia would just become another might-have-been. But that had never been a real possibility anyway. A quiet union with a beautiful young woman was not to be his destiny. He must write to Giulia.

He felt his self dissolving, in an immense weariness, and a kind of deep but sweet lack of concern. So be it. He had pursued happiness. He had found some. Now let be. The future was not his affair.

❧ 23 ❧

In 1851

APHRASE THAT Beyle uttered long ago, at Castelgandolfo, came to my mind. "The true vocation of the
human animal is to write novels in an attic." How right
he was, though, as he knew as well as anyone, it is a lonely vocation, with no one to count on but yourself. Day by day finding
in yourself the words you need, the characters pressing to find
the right expression on paper, the incidents you need to make
their affairs move forward. Beyle had understood, of course he
had. And died with so much unfinished, including the novel
he claimed would make him money, about the voyage to dig up
Napoleon's body—but I never had the impression he was serious about that one—and the one about a young woman named
Lamiel who was determined to live with the freedom of a man.
I never had the chance to quiz him on that name, Lamiel: clearly
an anagram of Amelia. Unless it was that Amelia was the anagram of Lamiel. He claimed to have written most of that novel,

which somehow refused to get finished, before he met me. Which
would then make me a character who stepped out of the pages of
one of his novels? But I am not the figment of any man's imagination. I am the one who makes imaginary creations. How, then,
that strange name? There is some confusion here, some overlap-
ping of living and telling that I can't quite fathom. Who figures
in whose fiction? And without Beyle, it never will be clarified.

Dear Beyle. I miss you. I did the right thing, of course, in
not going off to Civitavecchia as his wife, or mistress. Even he
seemed to understand that. His letters were tender, regretful, but
always witty and wise, and full of pithy advice to the aspiring
novelist. We had planned to meet again, as friends—though who
knows, I might well have ended up making love with him. I did
enjoy that. He taught me . . . taught me I could do anything I
wanted. Made me a much more amiable lover for Paolo, when he
came along. I could have been much more fun for Beyle the second time. Now I know I've got a considerable capacity for love.
But just before the scheduled rendezvous, when after over a year
of uninterrupted service in Civitavecchia he had come to Paris on
leave—and I was making plans to travel in from Passy—he was
struck down by apoplexy, in the street, and he died.

From the small window to the right of the desk I can see
the apple orchard beyond the wall at the edge of the property,
the tree branches black and gnarled against the gray November
sky. I love this place. It was a great find after a long search. If
I write steadily, I can easily afford these three rooms over the
notary's—he has the first two floors, I the third. Papa left me a
modest amount, enough for a steady annuity, and writing now
makes up a sum I consider princely. I could really afford to move
to a larger place, into Paris itself if I wanted. But I would miss the
apple orchard if I did that. Those trees have been the companions
of so much thought, so much reaching into myself for ideas and
images, summoning forth creatures of my own invention from

wherever such things come from. It astonishes me, sometimes, the things I find and write, the things I didn't know I knew, that emerge while I am writing, that insist on getting said. Which is why I shall never be quite proper as a novelist. So much the better.

The manuscript on the table now forms a neat stack under the polished piece of Carrara marble—a gift from Angelica—that I use as a paperweight. It is done. At least I think it is. Time now to reread it, always the most painful part. But not today. One needs a break before rereading. But tomorrow certainly, since Buloz is pressing me. The first novel—written in the heat of what I like to call my time of torment, after the trip to the Cinis', after deciding that Philippe would never come back, after self-laceration and regret, and just as I was beginning the affair with Paolo Pallavicini—had been a success. Not a hugely profitable one, but a clear success anyway. The voice, some critics had said, of the new woman, destined to claim her right to happiness with the approach of the mid-century. I'd be more severe in my judgment of the thing. It was a bit posed, much of it. Maybe most of all the love scenes. They had created a scandal, of course. But I wanted to show that a woman knew, that a woman could be as cool and calculating as a man in finding her pleasure. That pleasure was itself an object of knowledge.

And that is of course what I am condemned to. I say that with good cheer now. I will never be any man's dupe. There's a loss there, of course; no more romance. But the role of the novelist is to understand—that's where the true pleasure lies. I was too knowing for poor Paolo. He lasted only a little over a year. He wanted me to fit some wild romantic imagining of his own. And his life as a revolutionary conspirator really had no place for a woman in it. To think that I met him through Lucien Bonaparte—that's a connection back to Beyle, in fact. Paolo had relations with the *carbonari,* and with certain French socialist conspirators—some of the many who were conspiring for the overthrow of Louis-Philippe and the making of a republic. He wanted me to be his inspiration and his reward. He disappeared for days on end, without explanation, and when he returned, I always had to be available, passionate, ready to spend the whole night in unrestrained lovemaking.

I always think of Paolo's passion with complete tenderness. It could be inspiring, even, when you were in the right mood. But he did tend to get in the way of the discipline I was trying to impose on my life. The book-writing animal has to be at her desk early in the morning, or nothing comes, the day is wasted. Paolo would lie abed for a while, then arise, looking adorably unkempt and hairy, and come up behind my writing table and put his arms around me, caress me, want to begin again. I rarely had the heart to say no. It was lovely, though I did more and more find myself absorbed in the life I was creating, reluctant to let that go. I must often have appeared distracted, I know I did. He would look at me with big melancholy eyes. But writing—Beyle knew this, though he always treated it with irony—writing is work, there is a job waiting to be done every day.

Then Paolo went underground, saying that the moment was ripe. *La poire est mûre,* he'd written in his last note. "The pear" of course meant Louis-Philippe, and indeed he had fallen, like ripe fruit ready for the harvesting. And so in 1848 there was another revolution. And then, and then—a republic which now seems to be on its deathbed. A president who is a Bonaparte, that old troublemaker Louis-Napoléon, now become respectable. But no republican. Hardly what Paolo and his friends had wanted. They have doubtless gone underground again. I don't like what's happening to France, either. But politics will scarcely change my own life, I suspect. I'm like a member of some monastic order, dedicated to the struggle to create.

I've been alone since Paolo left, but it doesn't bother me. The real vocation is here, I like that neatly stacked manuscript to which I've given birth. Another novel, more audacious than the first. I know also that I need to think about real life soon, before it's too late.

Sometimes I find myself slipping into a reverie about those events, some eleven years ago, when the Emperor's body came back, from that expedition led by Philippe Chabot. He wanted to marry me. Then I gave myself to Beyle, and Philippe changed his mind. Of course that made him change his mind. It would have been so suitable, too suitable. He's been a success as diplomat, back in London, and I heard he was even named ambassador. He must have survived the change of regime, but I have no details. Louise would know of course, but whenever we meet, we avoid the subject of Philippe—studiously avoid it, I suppose one would say. I should really tell her it's all right, that I'm not in mourning for him, that my kind of life suits me—not that she would ever quite believe it. In the meantime, that winter when the body came home is worth thinking more about. There is a story there. Not the one Beyle proposed to write, but my own story. It wants my telling it. That's my new project.

THE CAB he hailed outside the railway station traveled only a few blocks before the crowd became too dense for it to move. Philippe stepped out in vexation—he would walk the rest of the way to the rue Miromesnil, if it weren't for the heavy valise he had brought from London. The crowd was milling, and silent. Down the rue de la Paix he could see the boulevard. Empty. Then a shout and a clatter of hoofs, as a mounted troop raced down the Boulevard des Capucines. Their sabers were drawn. The plumes of their helmets whipped in the cold air. The crowd watched, silent, aghast. What was this?

He told the cabby to wait—there was no possibility of his

moving anyway—and began elbowing his way toward the boulevard. There, along the sidewalk, two bodies, workmen in their blue overalls. Blood trickled from the mouth of one of them, facedown, into the gutter. He scanned the mute, closed faces around him. What was happening?

The mounted troop was now down toward the Church of the Madeleine, but now he could see that gendarmes on foot lined most of the boulevard, bayonets fixed to their muskets. Then he came to a Morris column. Over the bright-colored posters announcing the current theater was pasted a huge yellowish bill, printed in large black characters. He scanned the message, his heart sinking. So here it was. The President of the Republic, Louis-Napoléon Bonaparte, declared the Assembly dissolved, the leaders of the opposition under arrest, and martial law established. All his worst fears realized. Now it had come to pass. The next step was evident: Louis-Napoléon proclaimed as Emperor.

His mind went tumbling back to the journey of the *Belle Poule,* the voyage out, the Valley of the Tomb, the voyage back, the steamship up the Seine, that cold and painful day at the Invalides eleven years ago. So this is what it had come to. And he bore some part in it. With Louis-Philippe fallen to revolution, Guizot too of course, and now the short-lived Republic as well, his own career in ruins, what was left? Back to England, he supposed, and his English wife, to make a life as a country gentleman. Not what he ever had wanted. Could it have been otherwise? What if he had married Amelia, instead of the placid Geraldine—in this moment of despair, all was gloom, and everything seemed a mistake. He never had loved Geraldine, never with passion anyway. His life unfolded before him as he stood dumbly before the proclamation of the coup d'état. He had avoided passion. He had lived for his career, for his public self, for the life a Chabot was supposed to live. Now it left a bitter taste in his mouth.

There was a groan from the crowd pressing round him. The

mounted soldiers were on their way back up the boulevard, flashing sabers, driving back anyone who had strayed off the sidewalk. Martial law. His country was under military dictatorship. All their dreams of a parliamentary regime gone. And all those who had spoken out in protest now taken prisoner, or fled into exile. Even Victor Hugo, he learned from another placard, gone to Brussels.

Tears started to his eyes as he moved back through the crowd, looking anxiously for his cab. He'd return to the station, get the next train back to the English Channel. Back to England, but no longer as a diplomat awaiting his next portfolio. As an exile.

APPENDIX

French Regimes, 1804–1848

NAPOLEON BONAPARTE, following his coup d'état in 1799, had himself crowned Emperor of the French in 1804, putting an end to the First Republic founded during the Revolution, in 1792. After the disastrous Russian campaign in 1812, Napoleon suffered a decisive defeat at the Battle of Leipzig in October 1813, abdicated in 1814, and was exiled to the Mediterranean island of Elba. The Bourbon monarchy was restored—though Napoleon escaped from Elba in February 1815 and rallied his troops for a final campaign of the Hundred Days that ended at Waterloo in July, after which the Restoration resumed.

With the Restoration, Louis XVIII—brother of Louis XVI, who died on the guillotine in 1793—became King of France, in a constitutional monarchy, in which he granted *la Charte,* a written constitution, to his subjects. He died in 1824, and was succeeded by his reactionary brother, Charles X, whose attempts to revive a more absolutist style of monarchy led to the July Revolution of 1830, which in three "glorious days" sent the last French Bourbon monarch into exile.

The July Revolution did not produce a republic but rather the "Citizen King" Louis-Philippe, from the Orléans family—the younger branch of the royal family. He took the title "King of the French," and ruled over a period of capitalist expansion and middle-class prosperity (and much working-class misery) until the Revolution of 1848. This created the Second Republic, with the poet Alphonse de Lamartine as President.

Late in that year, the first presidential election conducted with universal manhood suffrage brought to power Napoleon's nephew, Louis-Napoléon Bonaparte—who beat the other candidates in name recognition, and rode a tide of Bonapartist nostalgia. He dissolved the elected Assembly in his coup d'état of 2 December 1851—and a year later had himself crowned Emperor Napoleon III, inaugurating the Second Empire, which lasted until the French defeat in the Franco-Prussian War of 1870.

The events of *The Emperor's Body* unfold mainly in 1840, under the rule of Louis-Philippe. Henri Beyle (pen name Stendhal), Giulia Rinieri, Philippe de Rohan-Chabot, the Prince de Joinville, Emmanuel de Las Cases, and the others on the voyage to retrieve the first Napoleon's body are real. So is Clémentine Curial—but her daughter Amelia is the novelist's poetic license.

ACKNOWLEDGMENTS

THERE ARE a number of accounts of the voyage to Saint Helena, and of Napoleon's exile, by contemporary witnesses, including the memoirs written by Philippe de Rohan-Chabot, the Prince de Joinville, Abbé Coquereau, Emmanuel de Las Cases (both the father and the son), and General Gourgaud, all of which I consulted with profit. And the journals, memoirs, and correspondence of Henri Beyle (Stendhal) are rich in material. Among a number of works from our own time that study the expedition to retrieve Napoleon's body, deserving a special mention are: Jean Tulard, "Les Retour des cendres," in Pierre Nora, ed., *Les Lieux de Mémoire* (Paris, 1988); and the remarkable meditation on Napoleon's captivity by Jean-Paul Kauffmann, *La Chambre noire de Longwood,* published in French in 1997, and in English translation by Patricia Clancy (*The Black Room at Longwood*) in 1999.

ACKNOWLEDGMENTS

Let me thank a few readers who believed in this novel in various of its stages, and encouraged it on its way: David Shields, Marilyn Heller, my agent and friend Steve Wasserman. I discovered—like many before me—that Star Lawrence is a truly superb editor. He was ably assisted by Melody Conroy and Amy Robbins.